W9-CBQ-850

THE GOD WHO BEGAT A JACKAL

ALSO BY NEGA MEZLEKIA

Notes from the Hyena's Belly

THE GOD WHO BEGAT A JACKAL

A NOVEL

NEGA MEZLEKIA

picador usa
new york

www.picadorusa.com

ISBN 0-312-28701-1

First Edition: January 2002

10 9 8 7 6 5 4 3 2 1

To the Asters of the world

CONTENTS

BOOK FIVE: UPRISING

ACKNOWLEDGMENTS

I would like to thank Alicia Brooks, my editor at Picador USA; Cynthia Good, publisher and president of Penguin Books Canada; and Cheryl Cohen, a freelance editor living in Toronto, for their thorough editing and insightful feedback. My thanks are also owed to my literary agent, Jacqueline Kaiser of Westwood Creative Artists, Toronto, and the staff at Picador and Penguin, whose peerless efforts have made it possible for my works to reach a wide readership.

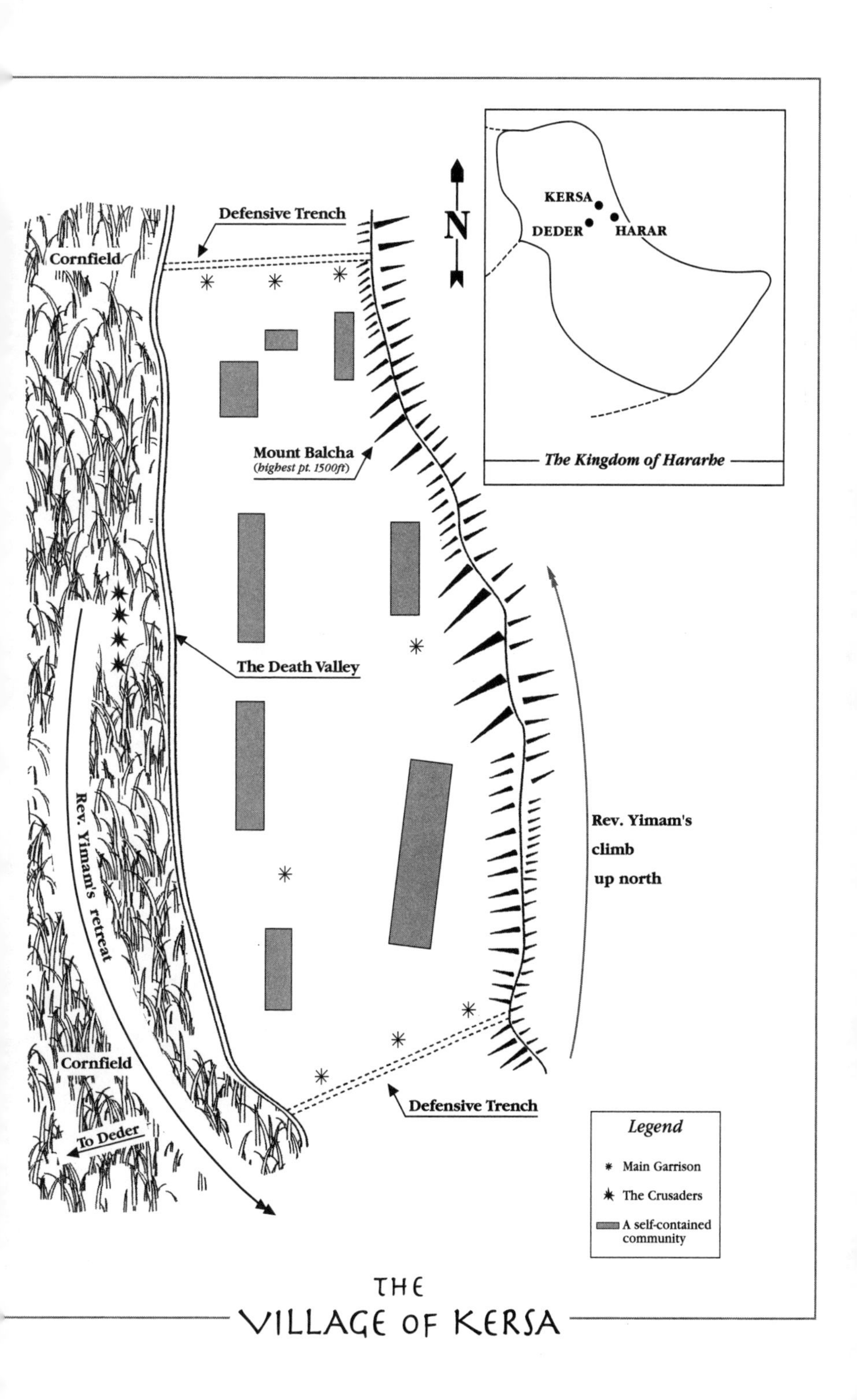
KERSA
DEDER
HARAR
The Kingdom of Hararhe
N
Defensive Trench
Cornfield
Mount Balcha
(highest pt. 1500ft)
The Death Valley
Rev. Yimam's retreat
Rev. Yimam's
climb
up north
Cornfield
To Deder
Defensive Trench
Legend
Main Garrison
The Crusaders
A self-contained community
THE
VILLAGE OF KERSA

THE GOD WHO BEGAT A JACKAL

BOOK ONE:

STARDUST

DEVIL IN THE WILDERNESS

Deep within the conquering blue sky, far beyond the feathered patrols and their scouts, lives the all-seeing Mawu-Lisa, God of my people. With two faces on one head, Mawu-Lisa is both man and woman. Mawu, the woman, is in charge of the night; Lisa, the male, directs the day.

Long before men organized their caves and went hunting for antelopes, warthogs, gazelles, and oryxes; even longer before there was any game to hunt, before there were any of the creatures that we would recognize today, a pair of twins roamed the African steppe: a male child named Da Zodji, and a female, Ananu. They were the first to be born to Mawu-Lisa and were sent to populate the earth.

Sagbata was the most disobedient of Ananu's children, and those of us who descended from him are considered a bad omen to the family. One cannot identify us at birth, but as we grow older our makeup becomes unmistakably clear to those around us. Persistent mischief, disobedience, and the accompanying misfortunes are some of the identifying traits. Often, a name change is enough to tame Sagbata's rebellious blood in us; occasionally exorcising may be required. I had been renamed twice, in vain, before a passing diviner read my signature in the stars and I became at last Teferi, "the feared one." I have since lost faith in the infallibility of the stars, for I have never in my life done anything menacing enough to earn the reward of such a fearsome tag.

The privileged in our midst are recognized as descendants of Legba, the ninth and last child to be born to Mawu-Lisa. Legba was the spoiled one. Delegated to oversee the realms ruled by his siblings and report his findings to Mawu-Lisa, Legba was never to see a day of hard work. His offspring expected the same degree of deference from us. I didn't realize this myself until, at the age of seven, I was called upon, as a rite of passage, to accompany Dad in his work, and I was thrust into the ever-widening reaches of Count Ashenafi's realm.

As an overseer of the count's estate, Dad made frequent trips far from home. As his only son, I was being groomed to follow in his footsteps, thus continuing the family tradition of elevating ourselves a notch above the lowly status and grinding life of a common vassal.

Our first journey together took us to the isolated village of Kersa, a three-day ride on a swift horse. No sooner had we left the familiar security of the mountains than my enthusiasm for the adventure waned. Ahead of us lay an endless steppe, punctuated at enormous distances by acacia trees. Sun-bleached bones of elephants, wildebeests, giraffes, and zebras carpeted the landscape. Near a dried-up water hole, we came across the remains of a large hippopotamus, whose insides had been carefully picked out by hyenas and vultures; the tough and dull hide stood oddly aslant like a hastily erected tent.

Nothing moved. Even the all-embracing sky, which is seldom without an itinerant or two, was ominously deserted. The sun glared at us with distilled anger, intent, it seemed to me, on sapping our souls. Not until we drifted into the middle of a dried-up riverbed did some sign of life stir from the ground: tiny columns of whirlwinds rose all around us. The budding twisters quickly linked arms, forming a huge pillar of dust that rose high into the heavens.

As we galloped to avoid falling prey to the dust devil, we came upon a pack of wild dogs. Dad's agitation grew, for a wild dog crossing the path of a pilgrim is ominous indeed. His concern was well-founded: within moments we were in the midst of another dust devil. And though Father was quick to stab the ground at the heart of the twister, wounding the devil stirring up the dirt, the damage was already done. We had lost our only horse along with its precious cargo: sleeping mats, *gabbi* cloth, food supplies, and water canteen. Walking away with our lives hardly felt like a blessing.

With no villages in sight and no human company on the horizon, the world suddenly seemed like a very solitary place. I began to cry, even more so when Dad told me our horse had been lost to an *ergum.* Wandering souls, suspended between the dead and the breathing, *ergums* are responsible for much of the danger that befalls pilgrims. Many a traveler has been lost without leaving a trace of his worldly existence, not even a trail of bones and skull, after being kidnapped by an *ergum.*

Ergums are more ominous than the most loathed spirits, for, unlike spirits that content themselves in their invisible world, *ergums* readily slip between the different realms. Often, they pose as pilgrims. Only a trained eye can catch one before it does a menacing deed. The remedy lies in the powers of *markesha,* a concoction that, when sprayed onto the face and eyes of a known *ergum,* will turn the creature into a pile of dust. Every family has its own brand of *markesha,* the ingredients of which are kept secret, passed from generation to generation under the strictest confidence. Not all *markesha* is effective, of course, which explains why some pilgrims remain lost.

Dad told me the secret ingredients of his *markesha*: gallstones taken from a striped giraffe, ground antelope horns, powdered cobra skin, droppings of a hyena, dried testicles of a lion, musk from the pouch of a spotted civet, and the ripened urine of a verifiable virgin—a boy or girl, it did not matter.

The dusk quickly settled in the wilderness. We scrambled to set up camp for the night. Gathering a small pile of wood, we started a fire sheltered between two giant baobabs—the only trees in the area. The dry tinder laughed and crackled, disseminating tiny sparkles all around. I wondered if that was how the stars in heaven came to be born, but Dad said it took a bit more effort than that. In his own words, Mawu-Lisa had often been depressed by the blank and gloomy sky, and in a surge of creation one night decided to adorn it. The Supreme God placed four cosmic signs in a flat disc, together with seeds of plants and crops, and set the disc revolving. As the disc gathered speed, it threw out water, which formed clouds and rain; the dry seed dispersed, becoming stars.

"What were the four cosmic signs?" I asked Dad, but before he could give me the answer an intruder startled us.

From the formless shadows emerged what looked like a lone giraffe. But, since our tallest neighbor was not known for seeking human company, we were on guard until the beast changed form, becoming a pilgrim on horseback. It was an old man with an overflowing beard, and eyes that had never been taught to see as one—one of them was trained on me while the other followed Dad. After unsaddling his horse, the monk walked toward me, with a sleeping mat rolled under one arm and a food basket hanging over the other, and demanded that I relinquish my seat. I asked him why, and he said it was because the spot I had chosen faced east. I moved only because Dad asked me to.

My eyes were trained on the food basket. I watched as the old man untied the leather straps and laid it open. The aroma of the sunbaked food stirred my stomach, and I felt something bitter well up in my throat. The stranger was in no hurry to feast. Pushing the basket aside, he fell into conversation with Dad, keeping one eye on me. I shuffled in my seat. A light breeze shifted, and I caught a conspiracy of the night.

"A stinkbug has its eyes on your food," I interrupted the holy man.

"Where is it?"

"I don't know."

"How did you see it?"

"I didn't."

"Maybe you are the bug," he mocked, and moved the basket closer to himself. But not soon enough. Before he could pick up the thread of his conversation, a large and resolute bug dived out of the darkness and landed in the food basket. Angrily, the monk snatched the insect and tossed it into the blazing fire. The excitement nudged his eyes into focus. For once, he stared at me with both pupils. Grumbling in a foreign tongue, he began to dip into the basket.

After eating his fill and drinking water from his canteen, the monk sealed the basket tightly and pushed it under the saddle next to him. Then he verified that we shared the true religion, Mawusa, before inviting us to join him in prayer. I was hungry and tearful and refused to pray, but Dad said that I must, so I knelt next to my father as the holy man delivered his petition:

Mawu-Lisa my father;
Mawu-Lisa my mother;
I killed two warthogs for you;
I killed a male wildebeest as well;
One day, I will catch twenty fish for you.
May I avoid hard things on my way;
May I come back safely.
Ohee!

And we followed after him: *Ohee!*

The monk removed a small pouch from his saddlebag and emptied strips of dried beef onto the end of his *gabbi* cloth. I could see that the meat had been dipped in red chili pepper before being hung to dry. The holy man picked a long strip and struggled with it, twisting it one way then the other. The meat was not completely cured, I said to myself, and it reminded me of the days when I used to pinch strips of beef from the drying line that Mam had strung. Suddenly, it seemed to me an eternity since I had last seen Mam, and I cried.

"What is wrong with the boy?" the monk asked.

"It is his first day out," Dad fumbled.

"Cheer up," the monk said to me. "You are becoming a man."

"I am hungry," I told him.

"That is one way of becoming a man," he concluded.

Dad resumed his lecture on astronomy. Pointing at four bright stars following three dimmer ones, he said they were called The Widows and were chasing The Three Old Men. Indicating a diffuse band of light overhead, he said it was the backbone of night, without which the darkness would come crushing down on us. He hesitated a moment longer as he puzzled over the identity of a row of blinking stars, uncertain if they were the harbinger of rain.

"Are those stars *gokwa*?" he grudgingly asked the monk.

"Sorry, I can't help you," the monk mumbled, while munching a mouthful of dried beef. "I am not from this part of the country."

Still gazing at the sky, Dad suddenly reached for the pouch at his waist, and with a swift movement of his hand he tossed handfuls of *markesha* at the monk, yelling: "Go and don't return!"

Bits of dried beef flew all over. Darkness engulfed the campground as the piece of cloth the monk had sat upon landed on the fire, extinguishing it. Dad and I retreated a good distance away. As our eyes grew accustomed to the dark, we saw the holy man rise to his full height and a bit more, sneeze, and buckle. He remained holding both hands on his eyes. Then, like a wounded warthog trapped in the open, he let out a loud and piercing howl before turning to us. The holy man heaped choice insults on Dad.

"You son of a blind mule, do you think I am an *ergum*? Is that what you think I am?" he cried.

Dad was crestfallen; his eyes rolled out of their sockets as he tried to weigh the inexplicable continued presence of the monk against the unmistakable traces of *markesha* on his palm. The holy man was unstoppable in his tirade. Spittle flew all over as he sprayed us with curses, words that I had never heard before. Lost in his own world, Dad was not in a position to respond to the abuse, so I raised my voice.

"Don't curse us!" I reproved the monk.

"Maybe *you* are the *ergum*," he snarled at me, focusing his anger. "I knew you were a strange boy the moment I laid eyes on you."

I yanked the pouch from Dad and readied to toss what little *markesha* I had at his mount—clearly a four-legged *ergum*—which would leave the monk stranded like us in the open, when Father intervened.

"Don't insult my son!" Dad snapped back as he came out of his daze and readied himself for any battle the monk might have in mind. The effect was immediate. The monk quieted, but he remained undecided as to whether to stay with us. Not until Dad told him of the incident that morning, how we had lost our horse and its cargo to an *ergum*, did he relax a little. "One can't be too careful these days," Dad emphasized sagely. The monk nodded his agreement. I was disappointed that Dad's *markesha* didn't always work.

Before the crack of dawn, the monk took his leave quietly, without bidding farewell. Had it not been for his foul scent, which lingered in the campsite, on my shirttails and hair, I would have thought that we had been visited by an angry ghost. There was, however, no time to dwell on what had happened, for the morning brought us new faces, merchants on a long journey east. Dad knew some of them, and after a drawn-out greeting that confirmed the health of the family, the cattle, and the crop, and the existence of unanswered prayers, we set out again on our travels. It would be another four days before the village of Kersa came into view. When the merchants proceeded to markets farther afield, Dad and I waited under the shade of a tree for the rising sun to lift the curtain that lay between us and the village. The Death Valley that ran the length of the settlement spewed toxic fumes, fumes originating from the volcanic mountains; the gas dissipated with a midday blast.

The village of Kersa and its listless inhabitants provided my first true glimpse of stark poverty. Many of the hovels leaned dangerously askew; where there was a door, it hung off its hinges. Children under the age of five ran around totally naked. Those old enough to have been awarded clothing were only half-dressed. Even the adults were in want of footwear. My patchless attire and matching sandals attracted the attention of two boys, who followed me around as though I was the most noble being to ever descend upon them.

Passing by a half-finished hut, I saw a woman delousing a child. She peered into the boy's hair as she gathered the lice, which she pressed between her thumbnails. Another boy sat on an upturned grindstone, his feet in a basin of water. At every other doorstep there seemed to be a figure or two observing the same ritual of soaking their feet in water. Years of walking barefoot had ravaged their feet; jigger-fleas gathered under the skin of their toes. Hot water laced with salt made it easier not only to remove the hatched jiggers, but also to drain the accumulated pus. The prolonged drought and the subsequent lack of chores to fill the downcast days had induced the villagers to bring out into the open a practice that had previously been observed only behind closed doors, before bedtime.

I thought Dad had picked the wrong time of year to make the trip, for there was no sign of any harvest that would enable him to collect the count's due. The emaciated shadows of the vassals and the bloated stomachs of their children betrayed that they had barely enough food to feed even their own families.

Dad saluted each passing shadow, but few of them answered his greetings. The tenants' hostility, their aversion to our visit, was clearly written on their faces. A meeting was hastily called, and, standing before a gathering of angry tenants, Dad made a fiery speech. He began with the vassal–feudal lord relationship, highlighting the fact that such a partnership was initiated when Mawu-Lisa delegated one of the First Children, Legba, to oversee the activities of his siblings. It was a divine wish, Dad maintained, that a mere 10 percent of the multitude, those who could trace their bloodline to Legba, should own all of the arable land in the kingdom, engaging the landless masses to toil from dawn till dusk for the rare privilege of going to bed with a full stomach; it was in the stars, he said, that the landless masses should be called upon to spill blood in a battlefield in order to defend this sacred partnership.

Dad cautioned that, in times of hardship such as the two-year drought that the tenants of Kersa had endured, it was easy to overlook such subtle realities. He urged the serfs to consider themselves fortunate for having a kind and considerate master in Count Ashenafi. He made further attempts to lay their minds at rest when he made it known that his current visit had nothing to do with collecting what was due.

"You can't claim a share of a harvest when there has been none," he joked.

I was surprised and disappointed that the feudal tenants should sit stone cold, regarding Dad with distilled hatred after he had traveled for five grueling days in the wilderness to deliver the good tidings. The clarity of his mind and the profundity of his message were completely lost on them.

Dad concluded the meeting by announcing his departure date and reminding the feudal tenants of the small gesture of goodwill that was expected of them. That turned out to be the finale they had all been waiting for. The shrine hall pulsated with the noise of angry vassals. Insults were heaped upon Dad. Fists shot up high in the air. And when I thought that Dad and I were doomed, that we would be trampled to death like a snake found defiling a temple, the high priest of Kersa stepped in.

The priest unveiled a rare and refined breeding in his person when he reminded the tenants that one should never send a visitor home empty-handed. Though the vassals had gone above and beyond their legal obligations to Count Ashenafi when they delivered four cows and a bull three months before, and a herd of sheep six months before that, the animals in question had all been destined for religious sacrifice. "Is there even one among you who would not stand to benefit from that selfless act?" the priest argued. The holy man made further references to the Scriptures, before passing his judgment.

Alas, the high priest blundered when he recommended that leftovers of salted beef and mutton stashed away by the farmers be sent to their lord. It might have been disrespectful to send a visitor home empty-handed, but, surely, this was an incitement to pack an ill-fitting gift. Many a battle had been waged and many a life spent after a reckless prince had deliberately insulted his peer by sending him the most inappropriate present. It took a bit of haggling before Dad wrested five handsome goats and three woolly sheep from the farmers. On our way home, Dad must have read the sympathy for the barefoot serfs that was written so clearly on my face, the anguish that I felt for the robbery visited on them, for he ruffled my hair playfully, saying: "Son, if there were no greedy people in our midst, even a poor dog would be warmly clothed."

STRANGE BUNDLE OF JOY

Count Ashenafi commanded power and influence that transcended the bounds of the visible world, but the extent of his sway became truly clear only with the singular birth of his daughter, Aster.

The count's wife was a young and blameless woman, a bundle of innocence, when she was burdened with the responsibility of childbearing. Her pregnancy remained unknown to friends and neighbors alike for many, many months. Her ample bosoms and generous girth were a testament to the wealth of her husband, but they made it difficult even for him to suspect that she was in a family way. When it became unmistakably clear that Countess Fikre was about to bear fruit, neighbors awaited twins. The countess set the record straight: there was only one child, and she had been nurturing it for ten long months. As no one had bothered to remind her that women give birth in nine months, Countess Fikre had slipped past the timeworn barrier unhindered. And now that she was accustomed to carrying her baby inside her, she was in no hurry to deliver it anytime soon.

Neighbors were alarmed at the precedent she was setting. Farmers were vocal in their protest, arguing that if other women were to follow her lead and wait ten full months before giving birth, all farming schedules would have to be shifted ahead by one whole month. Peasants depended on help from their children to plow the fields, sow, and harvest. A delay in the arrival of their offspring, even by one month, would create unimaginable chaos.

The alarm and concern in the valley of Deder intensified when a passing sage made it known that those born in ten months are single-humped camels; in eleven months, cape buffaloes. Countess Fikre seemed intent on giving birth to a young dromedary. And that would most certainly trigger unprecedented problems as women all around engaged in fierce competition with one another, delivering the unexpected: warthogs, wildebeests, hartebeests, suricates, and pin-striped zebras.

Soothsayers were consulted. They were undivided in their findings: Count Ashenafi must have fallen unknowingly under the spell of his wife's fetish or he would never have permitted her such unimpeded leeway in her pregnancy. A renowned diviner was more focused in his judgment: only a headless gecko buried under a man's seat would make him blind to his wife's unruliness, he pronounced. Six elders were dispatched to the Ashenafi mansion with the express mandate of establishing the state of the count's mind.

The elders took along a black rooster and three bottles of highland *arake*. At the entrance to the lord's home, they opened the first bottle and made libations while slaughtering the bird. Then, one by one, they stepped over the coursing blood. Inside, a second bottle of *arake* was opened and its contents sprayed on the walls, tile floor, windows, and doorframes. Count Ashenafi watched with mounting curiosity as the elders performed further rites: reading passages from the Good Book and singing choice hymns. He failed to fathom the object of their concern until the remaining bottle of liquor had trickled down their thirsty throats.

Count Ashenafi eased his neighbors' worries when he explained the reason why his wife hadn't given birth: his child had been waiting for escorts. In a land frequented by widow spirits—spirits of widowed and barren women—infants were easy prey if discovered alone. Like a herd of impala or besieged wildebeests, their safety could only be ensured through numbers.

True to the count's word, a few days later one of the girls in his servitude gave birth to twins; that evening, Countess Fikre unveiled her secret. Many more infants came to be born that night. Nine vassal homes celebrated a new addition to the family. The barns, too, stirred with life: a horse, two cows, a donkey, two goats, and a stray devil brought forth their young. The least-anticipated delivery of the day arrived close to midnight, when a fifteen-year-old slave named Enquan, whose pregnancy not even the count had suspected despite her slight frame and her proximity to him, gave birth to a healthy child. Count Ashenafi aptly named the baby boy Gudu, "the surprise."

The count ordered that his cherished daughter be sheltered from view for the first three days of her life. The lives of children are most uncertain at this age; as they vacillate between the various universes, the newborn are hunted by widow spirits, who lie in wait to capture them and make them their own. A fine *gabbi* cloth was all that was required to protect the count's firstborn; the cloth was draped over the infant's crib, hiding it from view. Seven times a day, the little girl was removed from this cocoon, in complete darkness, so that she could be washed, oiled, and nursed. Even the nursing mother was not permitted to spy the infant's bare skin, or, more important, the eyes.

On the fourth day, the baby was unmasked in the presence of curious neighbors, friends, and relations. A naming event was held. After a full day of deliberations, the elders could not agree on their interpretations of the stars and the whispers of the spirits; sixteen names were advanced. Count Ashenafi wanted to call his daughter Nigestae, "my queen," but this was unanimously overruled. With a name like that, the authorities argued, she would be a magnet for the evil eye. Twenty-six bottles of *arake* would be emptied and a pen of roosters would lose their lives before the elders reached an agreement: she would be called Aster—a name vague in its meaning, yet suggestive of divinity.

Aster was born to Count Ashenafi in the twilight of his years. He had been married and divorced twice before; the women were found lacking the seed to bear him fruit. In desperation, he had gone searching for his child out of wedlock, keeping many mistresses at a time (some said he had even slept with his bondswomen to test his fertility), but this had only heightened his agony. As the years progressed and his dreams became elusive, the mere sight of children started to pain him.

He felt insulted by a god who would think nothing of blessing a nameless slave or a barefoot peasant with a large brood, yet turned deaf ears to his pleas and prayers. He felt cheated by the Creator, who reaped from him a king's ransom in the form of sacrifices and offerings yet failed to deliver what was only right. Aster was born to him when he had all but given up hope; he felt vindicated.

Adding up the offerings and sacrifices he had made over the years, Count Ashenafi was dumbfounded at how steeply the price of a daughter had gone up. Aster had cost him eleven cows, six oxen, nine goats, a cape buffalo (wounded, and, therefore, counting only as half), and five sheep. Not a man easily deterred by adversity and precipitous odds, he doubled the size of the offering to his god and applied for a baby boy. He then waited patiently for the miracles to unfold.

The vast countryside changed its mood many times over. His little daughter, tired of the crawl of growth, began walking. But there was no sign of the baby boy he had dreamed of—not even another baby girl to acknowledge his immense outlay. It finally dawned on him that he was destined to become a one-child father. With a heavy heart, Count Ashenafi decided to hold dear what he already had.

The count committed himself to the day-to-day upbringing of his daughter. He monitored what she ate and how she spent her waking hours. Her playmates were carefully chosen for her; her playground was guarded. In the early days, Aster was permitted to mingle with neighborhood children. She built invisible houses and drank an even more invisible coffee with them. One day, the five-year-old daughter of a feudal tenant injured Aster bodily, shoving her off an earthen mound. In a fit of anger, Count Ashenafi evicted the girl's parents from his estate.

Neighbors began to forbid their children to associate with Aster. When they saw her running toward them, little girls and boys abandoned their play and disappeared behind doors. Aster cried and complained, but mothers were never short of excuses for their children's behavior. Often, it was merely because a sudden need had arisen for a child's help in the kitchen; other times, there might have been good reason to avoid the widow spirits, who were known to frequent playgrounds at shifting hours of each day. There were also mothers who were brazen enough to tell her to seek a deserving playmate elsewhere.

Aster became sullen and withdrawn. She ate little and grew thinner. Her days were spent talking to invisible friends in a language that no one else could understand. Wild animals became attracted to her. Thrushes landed on her tiny shoulders; lizards gave her the right of way. Absentmindedly, she wandered about asking the names of common, everyday items. One morning she winced at the sight of Countess Fikre's round and voluptuous figure in the garden; forgetting that the woman was her mother, she pronounced that unless that person cut back her meals, she would sprout two more legs and join the hippos in the wild. The countess's reaction to the remark was that Aster was finally losing her mind.

Count Ashenafi dismissed his daughter's oddities, believing that she was experiencing the tribulations of growth, until one evening when she got up from the dining table and walked right through a solid wall. The maids shrieked. Countess Fikre gasped. Count Ashenafi's eyes melted into a pool of incomprehension. When he finally came to, Count Ashenafi had his daughter shackled to a post, and sent for the family diviner.

A man of considerable learning and depth, the diviner excelled where all other experts had failed. Children were routinely brought to him with the most unclassifiable of afflictions; Aster's was the easiest diagnosis of all. After only a cursory examination, the diviner was able to pinpoint what was ailing her: the girl hadn't been immersed in the proper social conduct; no one had told her that whisking through a solid barrier, like chatting with songbirds, was not a human thing to do. Her tendency to talk to invisible friends did not strike the learned man as the work of widow spirits, as many had suspected, but as a mere hangover from the world beyond. In his own words: babies come down to earth burdened by many languages, hopes, and dreams. In their cribs, they laugh at the jokes of spirits, and cry at the waft of the Devil's noxious fart. Left to their own devices, the innocent would think nothing of debating with a pack of hyenas or singing in the tongue of a thrush. Child rearing is, for the most part, stamping out the budding languages from the baby's essence, giving room for only one to grow. It is a series of methodical and coordinated attacks on the baby's ability to perform a forbidden act—such as walking through a solid wall. Aster needed a qualified hand to help her unlearn some of the lessons of the world beyond, a job for which the diviner was uniquely qualified and, therefore, volunteered himself.

Aster spent the next six months in the company of the diviner, reacquainting herself with the small world around her and picking up a few tidings. Walking side by side, the two pondered the subtle workings of Mawu-Lisa. Often enough topics for discussion sprang up all around them, unsolicited. One morning, for instance, the sight of a bunch of boys swarming up a towering fig tree prompted the holy man to impress on the young lady that it was out of step with nature for women to climb trees. Aster had been running up and down trees since the age of four, with the ease of a nimble leopard. She attempted to prove the diviner wrong by scaling the fig tree, but was reminded of the new truth when she lost her grip and fell to the parched earth below, twisting an ankle.

Still another day, the diviner pointed to a soapberry shrub, and warned her that the seeds of that wild plant were poisonous to humans. Aster had eaten those very fruits just two days before. The only ill effect that she had experienced was the soapy taste, which lingered in her mouth for hours afterward. Ever inquisitive, she stole a few ripe seeds and slid them into her mouth. No sooner had she broken the skin than she collapsed on the ground, writhing in agony.

Aster had come to trust the diviner implicitly. The lessons had burned such an indelible mark in her memory that she could recount, with the utmost ease, all twenty-three creatures that had fallen from the grace of God, and the nine ethnic groups that the Almighty had meant to be slaves. She accepted that one shall not kill one's neighbor, unless it is to encourage others to do the same; one shall not steal, unless one can prove oneself lord-designate; and one shall show deference to an elder, unless it is decidedly evident that the elder is from one of the nine fallen ethnic groups.

On her sixth birthday, Aster was exposed to the art of calligraphy. From the comforts of her home, she was taught, by the same diviner, how to read and write, and compose poems. Traditionally, only boys were encouraged to pick up the skills of the pen. From the age of four, they traveled from village to village and across national borders in search of better learning. The boys relied on their ingenuity and unparalleled willpower throughout their quest. They mixed their ink from water, charcoal, and gum arabic; they cut quill pens and carved wooden tablets to write on. As each child had to support himself, the boys spent a large part of each day begging for food and clothing, and alms to pay their teachers. Only as a monk or a fortune-teller could one expect to harvest the rewards of learning. Aster was not cut out for such a humble calling; her lessons were meant to facilitate the opening of her Third Eye.

Many a monk aspires to be a master in the art of the Third Eye. The unprecedented monetary rewards and the elevated social status the profession lends have sent countless scholars to the brink of financial ruin and self-destruction when innumerable years of study failed to bring them closer to cultivating the necessary skills. Only a few ever acquire the distinction of attaining the status of sage. The one who achieves the highest rung of the profession becomes Sage of Sages and stands out from the rest by donning a white outfit and riding a milk white horse.

Aster was introduced to the Sage of Sages at the critical age of seven years, seven months, and seven days. The occasion was marked with festivities the likes of which had not been seen in the valley since the marriage of her parents nine years before. The serfs donated a herd of livestock for the event; the women came to lend a hand in the kitchen, while the men erected tents and waited on the visitors. Altogether, two thousand guests put in an appearance, not counting a family of jackals and two packs of warring hyenas that dropped in quite unexpectedly.

Countess Fikre hovered over the crowd, urging the guests to drain their cups, beckoning the attendants to top up the half-empty glasses. Count Ashenafi waited until the guests were happily drunk and, therefore, receptive to wit and wisdom, before inviting the Sage of Sages to deliver a fitting address. The audience quieted down at once; a mob of houseflies froze in midair in anticipation.

Standing high on top of a bamboo chair, his white outfit

shimmering under a flickering temple lamp, the Sage of Sages cut a remarkable figure, surpassing the expectations. For many of the guests it was a new experience to share a breath of air with such a learned mortal. Their awe was palpable; their reverence was written all over their faces. The Sage of Sages achieved instant immortality that day when he opened his speech by saying: "In the midst of life we are in death."

A rapturous applause greeted him. The din of breaking dinnerware echoed throughout the tent, as plates and glasses slipped out of excited fingers. Men whistled in approval; women shed tears of adulation. When the commotion finally subsided half an hour later, the guests turned toward their neighbors for an explanation of the bewildering pronouncement. Conflicting interpretations emerged. And the less they understood the meaning of the spoken words, the deeper their respect for the Sage of Sages became.

The glowing faces of the audience proved to Count Ashenafi the astuteness of his gamble on the wrinkled savant. Not a man to shy away from self-gratification, the count dazzled the guests with the extent of the sage's list of pupils, which included princesses and duchesses, and the sheer size of the fortune that he was willing to part with for the coveted training of the count's daughter. Indeed, Aster's sessions had begun at a mind-boggling rate of five *birr* a week—a sum that could easily support a family of five for seven days.

In the months that followed, Aster was fed wisdom by the line, twice each week. Present at her side, as a mute audience, were Count Ashenafi, the family diviner, and the cowed silhouette of Countess Fikre. Three cautious tappings on the wooden floor marked the beginning of each session, and the clapping of hands indicated the end.

"Fire that seems out oft sleeps beneath the ashes," the Sage of Sages touched off the first session, and waited patiently for Aster to struggle with her Third Eye.

Weighed down by the burden of paternal hopes and the lofty expectations of her teacher, Aster stumbled and staggered. She diminished in size. And, when it seemed that she was all but lost, the Sage of Sages stepped in to help, carefully nudging her toward the light. Rays of awareness broke through the shutters over her Third Eye, and she stabbed at an answer. It was not far off the mark, and the master applauded her effort. No sooner had he unveiled the true meaning of the mystery than he threw another piece of wisdom at her.

"Too low they build, who build beneath the stars," he yelled, and waited for her response.

Six months would go by before the master felt confident enough in his charge and upped the ante, feeding her whole paragraphs and chapters. Before the year was out, an entire scroll of wisdom was being laid at her feet. It was not long before Count Ashenafi could proudly invite his daughter to dazzle friends and neighbors with the brilliance of her Third Eye. And, as each visitor carried home memories of her singular refinement, Aster came to be viewed, by those who had yet to meet her, as a shooting star: achingly vivid, woefully elusive.

THE STUFF OF LEGEND

Aster's fame soared realms away from the valley of Deder when the fortune spent on her training quadrupled to twenty *birr* a week. The emperor's admirals were paid only half of what the old savant was quietly pocketing; for such weekly earnings, a judge could be persuaded to set a mass murderer free.

Count Ashenafi could have fought and conquered many kingdoms and still would not have commanded the respect that he gained by the simple act of doting on his daughter. Strangers crossed mountains and rivers to pay their homage. Counts and dukes who wouldn't otherwise set foot in the valley made express trips to catch sight of the girl who had captivated the entire nation of Hararghe. They brought Aster exotic souvenirs. Those who eyed the young woman for a future daughter-in-law brought her father gifts that startled him out of his normal reserve. A complete stranger gave Count Ashenafi a musket adorned with expensive stones; another noble unfurled before him the impaled head of a foreign god to mount alongside the horned creatures that adorned the walls of his study.

The ultimate homage arrived one sweltering afternoon from a place no one, except perhaps Count Ashenafi, had expected: two regal surreys pulled in, bearing the royal insignia, to deliver His Highness's commendations in a sealed envelope. The royal reins had changed hands only recently. The young emperor, whose ascent to power had been attended by strings of scandals, may well have viewed his small gesture toward the count as a means of muzzling the loudest of his critics—the hereditary peers.

His Highness would have been flattered, all the same, to overhear just how loud a buzz his surreys generated within the confines of the count's household. Not one to let a unique opportunity roll away, Count Ashenafi irrevocably altered his attitude toward his neighbors that very afternoon. Sheer possessiveness as well as haughtiness overcame him. To retain the aura of mystery that had sprung up around his daughter, he had a four-room bungalow built for her far from the main residence, in a glade hidden by giant fig trees. The prisonlike fortress was to be Aster's true home for many of her tender years. Two young maids would take the place of the mother that she hardly knew, a mother Aster was weaned from at the age of two by her doting father. Count Ashenafi was one of the few people ever allowed to set foot inside the hallowed edifice. In those rare moments when Aster stepped outside, to catch a breath of fresh air, neighbors were kept at least a stone's throw away. And that was not because anyone might dare hurl stones at her.

Despite Count Ashenafi's continued vigilance, however, the family serfs found ways to procure an audience with Aster. Word had already gone out that she could easily get her way with her dad; that a word from Aster could chain the wind to the wall, make a stork fly with a single wing. Pleas and petitions competed for her attention. Aster was often able to be of help by consulting with her father's councils, but when the occasion warranted she didn't shy away from confronting her dad.

Once, while walking in her garden under the terra-cotta of the dying sun, Aster was accosted by a disheveled woman. A skinny boy tugged at the woman's skirt, brushing his runny nose with the back of his hand; a toddler lay limp on her back, strapped in place with a piece of frayed rug. The woman was crying as she unburdened her grief. The eldest of her three sons was being prepared for his first day in school. Since purchasing a writing tablet was outside the family's meager resources, the father had decided to construct one himself. His master's words, that anyone caught harvesting timber from the estate risked immediate eviction, were ringing in his ears when the husband walked into the woods, but he reasoned that as long as he did not fell a healthy tree, and as long as the lumber did not end up in the family oven, little harm would be done to anyone. No sooner had the echoes of the ax stopped reverberating than a hateful neighbor brought the news to the attention of Count Ashenafi. The count fulfilled his promise.

Her eyes gleaming with unspent tears, Aster darted to the main house to confront her father.

"I must talk to you!" she cried.

"Can't it wait? As you can see, I am with visitors," the count pleaded.

"No, I must talk to you at once," she insisted.

No sooner had they stepped behind closed doors than Aster rattled off her accusations. Entire catalogues of indictments were thrown at Count Ashenafi's feet—wrongs that he had long relegated to the moldy recesses of his brain. A man accustomed not just to having his way but also to a company of men cheering his excesses, Count Ashenafi was dumbfounded; he was hurt that the one person he cared for more than anyone else alive should have such a low opinion of him. The count didn't attempt to defend himself; when he regained his tongue, he only begged for his daughter's forgiveness. And though Aster walked away the victor once more, this incident would prove to be the nail that sealed shut the last window of freedom she enjoyed. From that day on, she would be protected, round the clock, by two dedicated guards.

The Areru twins were chosen for the task. Born moments before their master's daughter, the twins held a mythical significance in the household. They were the only ones, among the family slaves and servants, to be invited to Aster's birthday parties; during the New Year holiday, they received a special gift from their owner. To Count Ashenafi, it was only fitting that the escorts chosen by the Almighty in his daughter's long descent from the heavens should protect her in this treacherous world as well.

Raised on a meager diet, the Areru twins were so emaciated that they cast no shadows, even on a sunny day. Their want of personal hygiene could be sensed by the stone blind. Dressed in tattered rags and accompanied by a battalion of houseflies, they were shunned by the Devil. But the most enduring reminder of their poverty was the fact that they shared the same given name: Areru. When the need arose to identify one boy from the other, people often looked for a memorable feature. Some might point out the differences in the boys' teeth, others the shape of their noses or some other defect. All that changed when Count Ashenafi singled the twins out for the prestigious task of guarding his daughter. They were issued crisp linen trousers with matching jackets, and were blessed with unmistakable signatures: they were now called Areru the Taller, and Areru the Shorter.

Count Ashenafi's interest in the twins' welfare earned him heightened admiration when it became known that the boys would share the food that came out of his own kitchen, and that they were exempt from any arduous task. When word reached the townspeople that the twins were about to be castrated, however, many wondered out loud why someone would visit such a hideous act on persons who were neither sick nor infirm. They received their answers from behind the pulpit: it was to help the boys remain alert and focused in their daily duties.

Locked behind a manned gate and deprived of the limited social contact she had enjoyed, Aster quickly became self-absorbed. Often she stood at her bedroom window, gazing at the distant mountains for interminable hours, registering little. When sitting quietly, she drifted in daydreams. One day, as she lingered at her dining table, her eyes fastened on a saltshaker, and she discovered a new dimension to her abilities: she could move objects without raising a finger. Soon, a mugful of coffee on the table started dancing with a bowl of sugar, pictures flew from the wall on mute command, and the fan spun itself.

Enthralled by her powers, Aster summoned her maids to witness the performance. One of the women fell into a dead faint; the other tore out of the room, screaming. Count Ashenafi was gone from the town that day. Countess Fikre didn't turn a hair when told about the incident; her celebrated reply was that Aster is irretrievably ill-behaved and that she had given up on her. Months would go by before word reached Count Ashenafi, but by then Aster had started communicating with departed spirits, and could foretell the onset of a disease before the patient showed outward symptoms.

Count Ashenafi, for once, was overjoyed by his daughter's afflictions; the moneymaking potential of her powers didn't escape his trained mind. Aster's residence, still manned by two dedicated guards, was thus transformed into a shrine where pilgrims might seek relief from the grinding problems of living. Mothers asked her to intervene on behalf of dying children; farmers wanted a reliable weather forecast; still others requested an audience with the spirits of departed relations. Count Ashenafi erected a small tent at the entrance to the compound, where, unbeknownst to his daughter, he collected fees based on the services sought and the particulars of the clients, most notably their personal value to himself. For ailments, he charged a cow for a baby, a bull for an elder, and a sheep or a goat for an adult who was distracted from work. When asked why he levied such a hefty fee, a cow, for a mere infant, Count Ashenafi retorted, "While a cow turns water into milk, a baby only turns milk into water."

Soon, Aster's day began with diagnosing the sick, followed by a quick weather forecast that included accurate predictions of the intensity of the dust devils. Her afternoons were spent communicating with departed spirits and attending to emergency cases. One balmy afternoon, a dying infant was brought to Aster on the back of its distraught mother. Taking only one quick glance at the baby's aura, she determined that the infant's passage was blocked, hampering its bowel movement. A young herbalist utilized the diagnosis and removed a crystallized substance from the infant's alimentary canal.

Still another day, Aster glanced at the aura of a young man who came escorting his ailing father, and pronounced that what worried her was not the old man on the stretcher, who could easily get up and walk away if he willed it, but the young man himself.

"But I never felt better," the young man protested.

"You may not have the symptoms yet, but you surely are far from feeling better," was Aster's reply; she went on to expound her diagnosis.

Aster's newfound knowledge was not entirely benign. The spirits, for instance, got her into more trouble than anyone could have foreseen. She was relaying a message between a young woman and her recently departed husband when the deceased man's spirit divulged the name of his murderer to Aster. Both victim and culprit were from a distant village, so no one could suspect that Aster had prior knowledge of either the incident or the identity of the individuals. Relatives of the accused came in droves demanding more proof. Not only was Aster able to spell out the location of the incident, but she could also identify the unusual weapon used by the culprit: a three-pronged pitchfork. This minor revelation led to a remarkable feud between the two families that resulted in the violent death of an additional six young men—three from each side.

On another occasion, Aster was asked to intervene on behalf of five orphans whose mother had just passed away. The people in the orphans' village knew that the deceased woman had inherited a large sum of money from her late husband, but none of it could be located with ease. If the money was not found soon, the children would be scattered and each would have to eke out a living as a beggar's hand. Aster was able not only to tell where part of the treasure lay, hidden under a mango tree in the backyard garden, but also to list the names of three renegade borrowers. Never having set foot in the village before, Aster, once again, had no prior knowledge of either the deceased or the accused; no one would say that she had a personal stake in the claim. Though the case was dismissed in a court of law, because of the unusual nature of the witness, Aster earned the undying enmity of the renegades. Years later, she would be accused of a trumped-up heresy by two of her enemies. Thanks to the fortune in the backyard, however, the children wouldn't be wanting.

Count Ashenafi was sorting out his daughter's most profitable insights from the dreadfully dangerous ones, shielding her from the repercussions, when she unveiled, yet again, another facet of her arsenal. During a rare visit to the family dining table, Aster looked up at her father and announced, rather casually, that he had been thinking of his young mistress. Count Ashenafi shot out of his seat. Bits of food flew in the air. Wine spilled on the floor, where the hundred-year-old decanter broke into a thousand pieces. Whether from rage or fear, Count Ashenafi stood trembling in his boots, his eyes riveted on the stranger whom he had called his own. When he finally found his voice, he barked at Aster for making irresponsible imputations.

"It is not imputation at all," she replied, smiling innocently. "Your mistress lives in Kersa, and you meant to visit her next week."

Countess Fikre grumbled her long-standing suspicion of her husband's infidelity, but he simply dismissed her. Father and daughter sat quietly, facing each other. An idea presented itself to the count, and he asked Aster to join him in his study; once again, the financial implications of his daughter's rare and startling gifts had not escaped him. No sooner had the two of them taken their separate seats than Count Ashenafi admitted to Aster his little indiscretions with other women. He wanted to know how she could read people's minds.

"It is not reading people's minds at all," she corrected, beaming.

"Well then, how can you tell what someone is thinking?"

"I share their thought."

"I don't understand."

"It is like smelling the air you exhale, except that I would have to be much closer to you to do that," she explained.

Count Ashenafi fell into a daze. Then a smile broke over his creased face as it dawned on him that the vast offerings he had made to his god hadn't been entirely squandered after all. Already, he had recouped the small fortune he had spent on Aster; soon, he would be able to recover the initial investment he had made on a baby boy that had yet to be delivered. In his grand machinations, the rewards of his daughter's latest flash of brilliance would not be measured by head counts of sheep and goats, much less the hollow gratitude of neighbors who had benefited from Aster's pronouncements, but by something more meaningful and enduring: a new title for himself. He thought of all those noblemen who had secured elevated status not through proven gallantry or direct descent from the First Children but by whispering small tidings in the emperor's insatiable ears. As a personal emissary, Aster could be of help to His Highness, Count Ashenafi believed, by uncovering unspoken plots.

So began the turn of events that would propel the young girl from the heights of innocence and virtue into the abyss of anguish, sorrow, misery, and heartache, and, finally, into the folds of history, not as a wronged person, but as a saint and legend.

UNATTENDED DAISY

His rise to the throne had been as underhanded as his pubescent reign. Few even suspected that the young prince had the drive to seize power, until it was too late. In the tumult of his father's untimely demise, he outwitted his siblings and took control overnight. He then dispatched his four brothers and only sister to a remote mountain enclave, where they would remain prisoners for life, while he consolidated his authority.

The kingdom of Hararghe began to take stock of its new ruler soon after. Where the young emperor's values and priorities lay became evident when he surrounded himself not with hereditary peers as his late father had done, but with self-made men and a bevy of women of easy virtue. Gossip cascaded over the wrought-iron gates of the palace about how the young emperor changed his partner with his bed linen.

The emperor's excesses became less of a laughing matter when secret agents began prowling the market stalls and social functions, looking for a captivating woman to sacrifice at his chamber. Even the shrine halls became unsafe for an attractive young woman; many were kidnapped from the altars to spend days drugged and disrobed. Soon it was not only innocence being lost, but lives as well. Indications of how bad things had become emerged when rumors circulated that the emperor had had one of his admirals murdered merely because the monarch coveted the man's young wife.

Count Ashenafi was not deterred by the proliferating scandals when he dispatched his daughter to serve the emperor. After all, those who fell prey to His Highness were all offshoots of common men; no person in his right mind would trifle with the jewel of a famed warrior.

The emperor welcomed Aster with open arms. Despite his excesses, the young ruler had kept the time-honored tradition of the monarchy by rewarding new ideas and uncommon talent, and he had flanked himself with fortune-tellers, rainmakers, spirit charmers, and devil tamers. In the case of Aster, though, he allowed a sense of mystery to develop, keeping the real reasons behind her visit secret to all but a handful of trusted courtiers—after all, the usefulness of a mind reader lay in the target's lack of suspicion.

Aster mingled with princes and princesses, dukes and duchesses, foreign diplomats and dignitaries. She charmed the entourage with the depth of her Third Eye, reeling off wisdom that most have yet to learn. She told riddles that only the unborn could unravel, poems that only the dead could compose. And, as the circle of her acquaintances widened and people felt at ease in her presence, she harvested a wealth of insight into the workings of their minds.

Aster uncovered plots and intrigues that startled the emperor out of his padded comfort. A visiting diplomat, on submitting a letter of intent from his government regarding a proposed cattle route to the port, found himself facing an irate emperor, who, after a secret consultation with Aster, picked apart the contents of the unopened pouch. The diplomat's colony, landlocked and in dire need of access to markets in the Mediterranean, had been secretly building up its army to slice a permanent route through the kingdom. The visit was meant to throw the monarchy off its guard. The attaché staggered out of court overwhelmed by the emperor's ability to read not only through a sheepskin wrapper but also one's unspoken thoughts. A palace diviner who stopped to couple with a farmer's wife found his sins in the open when he arrived for afternoon mass. His inopportune timing, more than the gravity of his indiscretion, had angered the emperor.

Aster saved the young emperor's life when she uncovered a plot hatched by his elder brother. In a mad attempt to reclaim the throne, the exiled sibling had arranged with a palace butler to assassinate the emperor. The butler had been promised a lofty position in the new kingdom. The emperor would not have survived the potent poison in his basket of dates had it not been for Aster's timely intervention. The emperor summoned the guilty servant and offered him a serving of the fruit. The butler declined the offer, feigning a stomachache, but the emperor proved to be a master at persuasion. Alas, the butler died of self-poisoning.

Aster's services were formally acknowledged when, on her thirteenth birthday, the emperor threw a grand party, replete with exotic foods and drinks. Dignitaries came from far and wide. Count Ashenafi and Countess Fikre arrived escorted by close friends and relations. Meals were sampled by all, and drinks flew without restraint. The guests were blissfully drunk when the emperor rose to his full height of four feet and a whisker and sounded a gong. The crowd quieted down at once. The emperor made a small speech, exalting Aster so far into the white clouds that, in the eyes of the guests, she began to assume the guise of a bashful saint. He bestowed on her the Order of the Virgin Moon—a much-coveted reward, seldom seen outside the aristocracy—and stamped her cheek with an ostentatious kiss (many would swear that he caressed her behind, as well). The audience's disappointment was palpable when the emperor failed to mention whose child she was and how she came to be in the palace. The last Aster remembered of the momentous evening was the standing ovation and smiling faces that greeted her when she got up to receive a golden necklace.

Peals rang out from the shrine bells urging parishioners to get out of bed and confess their after-dark sins. Aster struggled to open her eyes. She felt groggy because of the alcohol she had drunk the night before. Her head throbbed, her body ached. When her vision cleared, she was struck by the unfamiliarity of her surroundings. The mosquito net draped over the bedposts, the chandeliers dangling from the ceiling, the heavy dressers around her, and even the room she slept in were all out of the ordinary. She felt something wet and sticky under the bedcovers. Reaching down below, her fingers came out smeared in red.

Aster jumped out of bed, shaking. She tossed the bedsheet aside, revealing the depth of the mystery. When it finally dawned on her that she was in the emperor's bed, there was no stopping the tears. She cried, tearing tufts of hair from her head, rolling up and down the cold, waxed floor in her naked solitude. A maid who heard the commotion rushed inside, but her efforts to appease Aster fell on deaf ears. Aster didn't want to be touched by the maid; she didn't want to be patronized by someone who couldn't feel her anguish.

It took three stocky women to haul Aster into the shower, but getting her back out proved even more difficult. A tight knot of flesh on the shower floor, she refused to accept that the water in the tank had run out. The maids took turns dousing her with buckets of cold water. She shivered in her suffering. Her skin turned raw, and, where her hair had been torn out, parts of her skull showed. But no amount of water could make Aster feel clean. Guards had to be fetched to help restrain her.

Virginity is considered a yardstick of an unwed woman's upbringing, her values and social worthiness. A girl who has been deflowered while collecting firewood or water at the river, as is sometimes the case with peasant women, is reminded of her wantonness long after she has settled into her marriage. Many marriages do not survive the second day after the wedding, when the best man traditionally announces the bride's praiseworthiness to a crowd that has gathered outside the groom's door from the crack of dawn. A bloodstained handkerchief dangling high above the head of the best man is proof of a bride's chastity, while a clean piece of cloth reveals her most private sin.

Often enough, families of unchaste woman bear the brunt of her transgressions. They stand accused of deception and mockery by the groom, who might seek financial compensation. Some parents might buy their daughter respectability, and themselves face, through rigorous negotiations. A groom might be persuaded to substitute a rooster's blood for the missing essence. Such an arrangement might save the bride for the time being, but it rarely keeps the truth hidden for long.

* * *

Aster was taken to her bedroom, where a palace diviner and two herbalists awaited her. The holy men had treated other women who had fallen prey to the emperor's sudden urges. None of the victims had exhibited an agony such as the one facing them. The only remedy the trio could agree on was a potion originally intended for sufferers of unrequited love. The drink was concocted from five highland herbs, a scrub of hand stain from a doorjamb (in the case of unrequited love, this should come from the home of the jilting other), a touch of elephant dung, and water that was not of underground origin. A monk chanted prayers by her bedside throughout the afternoon; a spirit charmer was called in to contain her rattled spirit.

Two days later, Aster hadn't touched her food. Nor had she got out of bed. Many more experts came and went, prescribing medications as mystifying in their extract as the method of administering them. A balm of mixed herbs and butter was pressed on the crown of her head; a tightly sealed pouch was slipped around her neck; a foul-smelling blend was tossed over a hot burner, and she was forced to inhale the suffocating fumes; bags of fetish were mounted above her bed, doorways, and windows. Nothing seemed to work. On the fifth day, Aster was bundled into a carriage for the long journey back home.

As euphoric as her departure had been five months before, her homecoming was shrouded in complete secrecy. Aster arrived in the dead of the night, and stayed indoors in the days that followed. Negotiations ensued between Count Ashenafi and the emperor's courtiers regarding appropriate compensation. Elders came and went in droves. Priests kept vigil over the parties. Count Ashenafi appeared to be more and more determined to cross swords with the emperor for the sake of his family's honor—not a possibility to be ignored given the fact that the empire lacked a standing army, relying for its defenses on what the various warlords could rally. Finally, a settlement was reached whereby Count Ashenafi was granted dominion over the town of Harar.

Brought into the folds of the expanding empire a mere generation before, the enclave of Harar hadn't yet come to terms with life on the fringes of a large imperial drape. Its tenants had vented their frustrations, their longing for independence and self-rule, by slaying the governors appointed for them. Count Ashenafi had known two of the lynched officials personally. But the promise of riches was too tantalizing for him to be distracted by so minor an inconvenience as the mutiny of barefoot peasants. After all, the land involved in this new addition was twice the size of the territory of Kersa, though, unlike Kersa, Count Ashenafi fell short of owning the title deed. This simple change of hand would one day prove to be the undoing of the monarchy.

The undoing of his family wouldn't become fully apparent to Count Ashenafi until another week had passed. It was a fateful morning that would sear itself in the psyche of the valley, the day when a maid who had routinely gone to attend to Aster was confronted by a ghostly apparition in the patient's bed. The maid ran out of her lady's room screaming. Curious faces emerged from doorways and alleys to investigate, but the maid sprinted out of the compound and into the woods, her hands gesticulating wildly at an invisible pursuer, not once pausing to say what had frightened her.

A small crowd gathered at Aster's bedside. In rapt silence they stood gazing at the huddled figure, which had lost all human semblance. Aster's skin had been washed of its earthly colors, becoming transparent, revealing what no living soul had ever seen before in a breathing person: internal organs, the structural skeleton, blood rushing through veins, teeth visible through clenched mouth, eyes rolling in space. Overnight, Aster had turned into a living glass with unsightly content.

BOOK TWO:

MOONBEAMS

RIDDLES AND DECEPTION

In a rare spirit of camaraderie, the emperor decided to sail across the sea and take part in the crowning ceremony of a neighboring prince. He had never been on open water before, and didn't know how to swim. Barely had the ship left port than the vessel was rocked by the waves of an angry gale; it swayed from side to side and up and down. It seemed all but certain that the old bark was about to capsize when His Highness got down on his knees and made a vow to his god. "Lord," he said, "if I make it safely to dry land, I promise to weigh the first thing I see and give its weight in gold to the poor." As suddenly as it had appeared, the gale quieted; a peaceful wind prodded the vessel to a swept beach, and the emperor got to safety.

Looking around him for an object to weigh, all the emperor could see was an endless expanse of white sand. No stones, no fallen log, no plank from a capsized ship, no animal bones, nothing but a vast stretch of shimmering silt. The emperor gave orders to his escorts to dig up something from below the sand, and an assistant came up with a human skull. On the emperor's instructions, the skull was washed and scraped clean.

In his treasure chamber, the emperor proceeded to weigh the bleached skull, adding a handful of golden coins to a balance plate. The plate was full of gold, but not heavy enough. He added a large bag of bullion to the scale, but it was still too light. Puzzled and desperate, the emperor ordered the largest pair of scales to be brought from the customs yard—scales used for weighing crates and cases. Four men labored an entire afternoon, piling on the scale gold bars, ingots, bullion, cloths made of gold—in fact, half of the jewelry in His Majesty's treasury—but the skull was still heavier.

Fraught with despair, the emperor summoned his councillors, diviners, soothsayers, and devil tamers to a meeting. He wanted to know the meaning of this mystery, but no one would hazard a guess. He consulted a hundred-year-old hermit camping on top of a eucalyptus tree, and was referred to a Hermit of Hermits who was said to reside in an abandoned hyena burrow in the open savanna.

The emperor spent four days and three nights looking for the Hermit of Hermits. Dens of hyenas and warthogs were raided as trackers spent interminable hours looking for traces of the recluse. Disciples of the holy man were sighted, but they were also looking for their master. On the fifth day, when the emperor had all but given up hope, the elusive scholar was located in a crevice high up a rocky mountain; he had been hiding from his trackers. It took a long while before the holy man was persuaded to come down from his refuge and give counsel to the emperor.

Barely had the emperor finished telling the story of the scale and skull, and his pledge to his god, than the Hermit of Hermits flew into a rage. The holy man was angered that anyone should seek him out for a problem so trivial that it fell within the limited scholastic domains of a goat-dresser. "Your case is very, very simple," the Hermit of Hermits pronounced, looking the emperor in the eye, "because what you owe is not measured by the balance of an empty skull but by the enormity of the sand on the beach."

"But that will bankrupt me," the emperor protested.

"If avarice be thy vice, make it not thy punishment," the learned man retorted, before setting out in search of a better refuge.

The anecdote was told by Gudu to a cheering audience in a tightly packed room. As a dedicated court entertainer, the young slave traveled far and wide gathering fables, anecdotes, poems, and riddles, which he then tested on his fellow servants, as he had done this evening, to ensure that a presentation was appropriate for the ears of his master, Count Ashenafi. As a devout prodigy of Gudu's, I never skipped such performances.

Gudu and I were separated in age by a full seven years. While growing up, I sought his friendship, not merely because of the play-things we shared but also because I found an elder brother in him that I hadn't been endowed with at birth. In fact, I was treated as a younger sibling not only by him but also by Aster, who, like myself and Gudu, was an anomaly in that she was an only child. As I grew older, Gudu's seditious nature and wry outlook on life in the valley appealed to my rebelliousness.

There were many boys Gudu's age in the valley of Deder, but he favored me whether as a playmate or as a confidant. In group sports, Gudu always chose me as a member of his team; the other boys protested that, because I was so young, I might cause them to lose the game, but he would not budge. I tagged along with him when he ran errands, discovering places in the cavernous valley of Deder long before I was old enough to roam the neighborhood by myself. Gudu enjoyed nothing more than tutoring me on the fine art of mischief and the even finer art of getting away with it.

Once, when I was barely six, he asked me to escort him on a mission in which he had to carry a massive satchel containing two exceptionally large bull horns and yards of rope. The two of us ambled down the expansive valley and toward the bush country where shepherd boys gathered, tending to a mixed herd of bulls, cows, sheep, and goats.

As the herd grazed, the boys played in the shade of a shrub. Every now and then, one of the boys would get up and raise a ruckus to scare away a beast of prey that had strayed too near the herd. Gudu and I slipped past the shepherd boys undetected. Choosing a bull with the smallest of horns, Gudu proceeded to crown the animal with the trophy in his bag, securing them in place with the rope he had brought for the occasion. (It was not uncommon to see an ox with rope wound round the base of its horns.)

As we made our way back home with the bull in tow, the shepherd boys abandoned their play to inspect our acquisition. They were familiar with Gudu's mischief and suspected something was awry, but the bull was far too conspicuous for them to have missed if it had belonged to their herd.

At sunset, shepherd boys collect their herd, counting, more than once, each sheep, goat, bull, and cow before heading for home. But that day the boys couldn't account for one of the bulls. A frantic search ensued. Only when the boy in charge began wailing did Gudu and I emerge from our hiding place to give him back his animal. For days that followed, the valley of Deder talked of nothing but Gudu's mischief. Fortunately, the shepherd boy was never disciplined for his laxity; from that day on, the boy had become vigilant in his duties.

Gudu's mischief was not always playful. There was a time, for instance, when he decided to prove, once and for all, just how deserving his master's diviner was of the respect accorded him. The diviner was held with the highest esteem throughout the valley of Deder; his ability to foresee events both in the temporal world and in the Great Beyond had never once been questioned. Gudu sought his proof from a simple earthen pot filled with fine wood ash.

The diviner's residence was tucked away at the periphery of the compound. As a single man, with no family rituals to share with a neighbor, his front yard was eerily deserted after sunset. He whiled away the evening at his master's court, locking up his doors and windows; two fearsome dogs, tied one to each side of the door, kept all uninvited visitors at bay. That evening Gudu and I slipped inside the diviner's home through a broken window and hung the crock from the rafters at the doorway, making sure that an unwary entrant would bump into it. Before midnight, the compound people learned that the diviner's insight had been unable to penetrate the darkness in his own home. Doused in ash, he had gone knocking on doors to find the culprit, but the villagers merely laughed at his ghostly appearance. Fortunately for Gudu and me, no one suspected us of the ruse.

Our pranks attracted the count's attention when Gudu and I tampered with a bag of Holy Ash belonging to a visiting monk. The monk was a hated man. Even the lord of the manor had few good things to say about him. Though reviled, the holy man was never denied the hospitality of the valley when he came to visit, twice a year. He was fed and sheltered by the count until he took his leave a week or so after arriving.

The monk was a slave-runner. He bought mostly children under the age of ten, to sell at the monasteries. Unlike the Arab slave traders, who saw no reason to apologize for their chosen trade, the monk never ceased to defend his enterprise. He told anyone who cared to hear that he was not in it for the money but as a means of salvation. What better way of expunging one's original sin than through service at a monastery, he argued.

But the facts didn't bear him out. Most of the runaway slaves came from the monk's turf. Noblemen refused to sell him their young chattels, preferring instead a reputable Arab merchant, a merchant who could find a decent home for a worthy slave. If no one had told the monk to stay away from the valley of Deder, it was only because such a gesture ran against the grain of a good upbringing. Gudu and I found a compromise.

We had noticed how the monk applied a generous dose of Holy Ash to his face after each prayer. The white powder stayed with him until it wore off with the rising sun. Gudu and I mixed a powder of lime in the monk's bag of treasure. No sooner had the holy man finished applying the dust to his sweaty face than he rolled on the ground tearing at his skin with maniacal fury. The acid had torn a gash in the monk's face, but the most enduring scar was his eyesight, which dimmed thereafter (it didn't deter him from his trips, though). Count Ashenafi only chuckled at our mischief when alerted by a suspicious clerk.

While growing up, Gudu and I shared many things. But while he was brought up on the fringes of social acceptance—chosen as the count's court entertainer, yet denied schooling—I was privileged enough to be taught the alphabet and the language of numbers. Count Ashenafi nurtured the hope that someday I would succeed not only my father as an overseer of the estate, but also the count's aging bookkeeper. Like my dad, Count Ashenafi little suspected that since my first visit to Kersa, at the age of seven, I had rejected the thought of ever walking in my father's footsteps.

In my young heart, I dreamed of becoming a poet and court

entertainer, though my ambitions were not confined to the valley of my birth. I had hoped to grace the court of the emperor, or, at the very least, the courts of the princes and princesses. Many a day I spent in the company of Gudu, peering into the larger world that I was not yet able to occupy comfortably. Gudu's account of the gilded life of noblemen inflated my ambitions, while his stories of the downtrodden slaves and vassals left me with slumped shoulders.

Gudu rarely regarded the role of court entertainer as a privileged position. Others didn't share his views. Fellow bondsmen envied him, while monks and scholars expressed anger that Count Ashenafi should appoint someone of servile origins for a task that the Good Book clearly allotted to the freeborn and the enlightened. But perhaps the most bitter opponent of all was the mother of the Areru twins, Beza.

Beza had never been known for her kindness toward her neighbors. Tart and morose, she inspired little goodwill in those who came to know her. "Her looks weren't so bad in her younger days," commented those who felt charitable toward her. The cynics readily replied, "That is because when she immigrated to the valley, the word 'ugly' had not been invented." Whatever her neighbors thought of her appearance and temperament, Beza's dedication to her master was exemplary.

Young Ashenafi had not always been the difficult master that he was now. His childhood friends told of bygone years when he used to shelter a bondsman in his expedition tent, and Beza loudly reminisced about the days when she used to share a dining table with her master. "Deep inside, he is still a humble man," she told neighbors when she felt obliged to justify her doglike loyalty to him. Whether it was such fond memories, or undying faith in her master's imminent resurrection in his old incarnation, Beza never wavered in her allegiance.

When Count Ashenafi was still struggling to emerge from under his father's towering shadows and make a name for himself, often at the risk of financial and personal ruin, Beza was there to share his burden. Five of her children were sold to pay up blood money that he owed; her brother lost his life while defending her master's honor.

Now that Count Ashenafi was assured of his position in society, Beza assumed that he would look kindly on her and her children. She felt betrayed when he chose Gudu over her twins. But, above all, she was confirmed in her suspicion that Enquan, Gudu's mother, had eclipsed her in her master's good graces.

Enquan was presented to Count Ashenafi by a thoughtful cousin on his acquisition of a title, and soon she was looking after the personal affairs of the lord of the manor whether he was at home or far afield. Joining his large entourage during expeditions, she cooked for him and attended to his sundry needs. Like most cultured men in the kingdom of Hararghe, Count Ashenafi was never without a lap maid whenever he was away from home on an extended trip. The lap maid catered to his sinful urges. And though Enquan was well formed and had charms that would tempt the most chaste of angels, no one who knew the aristocratic count would suspect him of taking his young slave for a lap maid. A bondswoman, however attractive, was untouchable for a self-respecting nobleman. But Beza was not like most people; she saw a threat in the way that the count looked at his shapely attendant, and she decided to quash the danger when she saw it escalate along with Gudu's status.

Beza didn't simmer in her anger for long; she set out to exact revenge, to right the wrongs done to her. Twice, she attempted to blot out Gudu's talent through the invisible powers of graveyard dirt, sprinkling the ominous muck under his prayer mat, underneath his bed, and along trails that only Gudu was known to frequent; she planted a lizard's tail in the hollows of his bamboo flute, in the hope that the curse might deprive him of his voice. More ominously, however, she hired a renowned curser to render him blind, if not outright dead. Beza received ten lashes for this last mischief when the plot was unveiled long before it was hatched.

Beza had been blinded by her own ferment. Had she made the effort to get to know Gudu, had she tried to find out how he felt not only about his own fortunes but also those of his fellow bondsmen and women, she would have felt differently about him. For nothing made Gudu question servitude, the plight of his people, more than the sight of half-witted men and women, dressed up in exotic attire, patronizing him. Each night after his court performance, he brought his unanswered queries to his mother, but Enquan, knowledgeable about the fate of bondsmen who exhibited freedom of spirit, did her best to repress his seditious thoughts.

The job of court entertainer was not without its rewards, though. As one amused the rich and the powerful, one could expect to earn a generous gratuity—which to a bondsman, who was seldom compensated for his labor, was double riches. But perhaps the most noteworthy consideration came in the form of security from a reckless death. A gifted court entertainer is too valuable to his master to relegate to a task—raids and campaigns, say—that would imperil his life. Count Ashenafi's servants quipped, rightly, that if Gudu were put up for sale, his worth would be measured not by handfuls of silver coins or blocks of salt, but by the boy's bulk in ivory.

Gudu was not trained for his job; he was born to it. At an early age, he had demonstrated an uncanny ability to mimic the creatures around him. He could cry like a wolf and laugh like a hyena. When he was barely five, Gudu caught Count Ashenafi's attention by imitating the traveling beggars, singing each troupe's unique ode in its even more unique rhythm. The boy was never schooled. He couldn't read or write; he relegated to memory every fable, poem, anecdote, and riddle, reciting it on command, months or even years later.

Gudu sometimes found his sounding board in the neighborhood's children. Although I needed no urging, Dad encouraged me to attend such performances, as I might learn something without further taxing our family's meager resources. One Sunday morning, the boy gathered us for a lengthy rehearsal of his imported poems and to test a few riddles on us. "Guess who, Teferi," he asked, singling me out. "People do not like *him* to laugh, as *his* laughter is a great evil. When *he* laughs people weep; trees and grass die; animals leave their homes, becoming refugees."

I racked my brains but could not come up with an answer.

"*He* is fire," Gudu said, smiling.

"What is the occasion?" I asked, suspecting that he might have been rehearsing for an upcoming event.

"Elders are coming to ask for Lady Aster's hand in marriage," he told me. Aster had just turned sixteen, and despite her afflictions, suitors had begun parading.

Shortly before noon, guests arrived in two carriages, each drawn by a team of four horses. Escorting them were men on horseback carrying sabers, spears, bows and arrows, and the occasional musket. Altogether, four men dismounted from each carriage. At the compound gate, a small party awaited the guests, headed by the lord and lady of the manor. After a customary greeting that stretched well into the afternoon, the visitors were led to the big mansion, and into the drawing room.

Maids in uniform served beverages while a butler, standing at the foot of a flight of stairs, choreographed the maids' movements by taking cues from his master. The visitors spoke little. Countess Fikre, huddled in the shadows of her husband, stole catnaps in spurts, shifting her legs with each turn of events in her dreams. The embarrassed silence weighed heavily on Count Ashenafi, who ordered the court entertainer to be brought in. No sooner had Gudu taken his place before the audience than the mood of the house brightened greatly. Gudu told choice fables and anecdotes, including the story of the skull and the scale. For his finale, he recited a love poem that filled every soul in the room with wonder.

Rapturous applause reverberated through the halls, as the fatigue lines that had creased the faces of the visitors gave way to a glowing enchantment. The dignitaries lavished compliments on Gudu befitting the Sage of Sages. They pressed silver coins in his palm; some gave him scented kerchiefs and bottled potions that they pulled out of large shoulder bags. Gudu accepted the gratuities with both hands, bowed until his head almost touched the floor, and kissed the hands and feet of his patrons. Some of the guests appeared to be overwhelmed by his humility and tried to hide their legs discreetly before he could buss their shoes. The guests were impressed not only by Gudu's staggering talent but also his refined manners. His already august status noticeably improved, Count Ashenafi's face lit up. He was elevated in the eyes of his assessors for, outside the royal courts, few had seen such an enlightened performer.

* * *

As though the light drama was the cue they had all been waiting for, the dignitaries opened up at once. As was the tradition, the groom didn't join the envoy. It fell upon the head elder to introduce him to the family, but neither Count Ashenafi nor the family diviner could place the young man. As the man was from a faraway province, no one was disappointed that his eminent name drew blank faces. The elders proceeded to paint a picture of the would-be groom, beginning with his battlefield exploits.

Aster's family learned that her suitor was of such a caliber that the likes of him seldom crossed their valley. Long before he could say "Ma" or "Pa," the young man could identify the armaments in his father's vast arsenal by name; he began walking using a pair of daggers as a brace; before the age of thirteen, he took part in six pitched battles and two lightning raids involving lowland tribes, helping to tuck a vast tract of arable land into the folds of the expanding empire. He celebrated his fourteenth birthday on horseback, riding ahead of a detail in a concerted effort to bring down cattle thieves—and succeeded. At the age of nineteen, he felled a decorated swordsman in a celebrated duel. The emperor had decorated the young warrior more times than anyone would care to count. In his treasure box were to be found, among other things, the much-coveted Order of the Black Lion, the country's highest honor, and the Special Grand Cordon of the White Sun, the highest decoration awarded to a civilian. A year ago, at the mere age of twenty-two, he had earned the title of duke.

If Count Ashenafi was impressed by the breathtaking achievements of the young man, he did not let on. Count Ashenafi was an illustrious fighter in his own right. As he hadn't secured his title before the age of forty, however, and as no one in the long line of his distinguished family had earned the coveted Order of the Black Lion, one can't assume that the presentation had fallen on deaf ears.

But, stoic as Count Ashenafi remained, Countess Fikre began to beam like a kindled temple lamp. She had to receive a lash from her husband's disciplined eyes before feigning indifference. This did not go unnoticed by the elders, but, however hard they tried, they could not get the master of the manor to give an inkling as to his innermost thinking. He was like a cape buffalo bordered by a pack of hungry lions and backed up against a tree, determined not to give way, knowing full well that the moment he faltered, the instant he revealed his weaknesses, he would be made to surrender his trophy. Afterward, he would be remembered as the man who had sold out in a mere afternoon, and, God forbid, if the marriage proved disagreeable to his daughter, he would be left without recourse; he couldn't blame the elders for twisting his arm.

The vulgar task of recounting the suitor's wealth was left for last; it was touched upon in passing, as though money were the last thing on anybody's mind. Nonetheless, the bride's family couldn't fail to appreciate that it was indeed possible to sit on resources befitting a small kingdom without crowning oneself. It was not the head count of cattle, or a multitude of sheep and goats, that impressed Count Ashenafi. For nothing is more fleeting than wealth measured in livestock; anthrax was known to have reduced a celebrated rancher into a pauper overnight. What dazzled the bride's father was the swath of arable land in the young man's possession. As land was seldom bought and sold, it said much about the status of the owner—much more, in fact, than a million words ever could.

Count Ashenafi was a man who understood the significance of arranged marriage. And, unlike most noblemen, who preach one set of values to others and keep a different set for themselves, he sometimes set an example. His engagement to Countess Fikre, for instance, was concluded long before he cast an eye on the young lady. Her eminent family name and peerless upbringing were credentials enough for the count to recommend that she carry his name. Indeed, the only regret the count had had since the marriage was the fact that Lady Fikre could bear him no more than a single fruit.

Countess Fikre was the sort of woman any cultured man would like to have at his side. She never opened her mouth before checking for her husband's approval, she sought sanction from her man before stepping outside the invisible boundary etched around her (even before attending the weekly mass at the local shrine), and she overlooked her husband's infidelities unless she was confronted by her rival. The countess had been raised by a man who was cited, among other excesses, for the lap maids he kept in each of the six districts he governed and for maintaining his women on a very tight leash. Each time her father had sensed rowdiness in his household, he rounded up his wife and four daughters and threw them in his private jail until tranquillity was restored.

Countess Fikre might have regrets about her marriage, but the only time it became apparent was when she thought out loud—though not in her husband's presence—that Aster should approve the selection of the man she would marry. Her uncharacteristic goodwill didn't win the countess many converts. The family diviner reminded her of the time-proven fact that love and courting are for poets and hornbills. The head priest counseled her to get the pagan thought out of her head.

It was not because anyone bothered to get Aster's consent that the family waited for two long weeks before summoning the elders to give them an answer. The somber reception stood in stark contrast to the joviality of the fortnight before, keeping the guests on edge. But none of them realized just how close they were to the edge of the precipice until they had taken their separate seats. There were no more servants in uniform to cater to the thirsty, no court entertainer to smooth over the rough edges when the host rained torrents of abuse on the guests.

Count Ashenafi lashed out at length, accusing the elders of deception and mockery. They had insulted him by courting his only daughter—in whose veins coursed generations of distilled blood—for an offshoot of a weaver and a peddler. The young man's mother had been born to a man who spent a lifetime bent over a homemade loom, churning out *gabbi* cloth for local nobles; her mother spent the better half of her years hawking incense and herbs from village to village. The groom's father might have come by a rare fame and fortune, and, thanks to the avarice of the monarchy, the man had bought himself a title, but that couldn't buy him respectability in the eyes of the well-bred. The young man might have made a name for himself on the battlefield, but that was no consolation or remedy for the weakness of his blood. The elders had committed a sacrilegious act that in bygone days would have called for a duel. As a modern and sensible man, Count Ashenafi would settle for apologies.

But no apologies were forthcoming. Whether out of sheer defiance or dazed astonishment, the elders sat regarding their irate host in mute silence. Slowly, one by one, they got up to take their leave, declining Countess Fikre's offer for them to spend the night sheltered in the family compound. The setting sun did not hide their thwarted expectations; they vacated the premises so fast that they left their shadows behind.

Unbeknownst to Aster, many more suitors had come asking for her hand in marriage, but closer inspection had always revealed a flaw in the suitor's character that the elders had taken pains to hide: one was born to the niece of a potter and feudal tenant; another had blacksmith blood from his father's line; a young suitor from a nearby village, whose noble origins many believed to be unassailable, was found to have merchant ancestors; the most promising of all, a middle-aged man who at one point in his life was expected to marry a princess from a neighboring kingdom, was found to have been born on the eleventh day of the eleventh month—a clear indication that he was destined to contract leprosy.

Perhaps nothing offended Count Ashenafi more than an attempt made to conceal the ethnic origins of one of the would-be grooms. In his mad anger, Count Ashenafi rounded up the irresponsible elders and threw them into his private dungeon. The upstart candidate had to raise indemnity in the form of cattle, grain, jars of butter, and blocks of salt before earning their release. This decisive act gave many a rash elder pause for thought, and the requests for Aster's hand trickled to a halt.

PATRON SAINT OF SALT MINERS

Puzzled as to why his highborn daughter had failed to attract her equals, her compromise at the emperor's court notwithstanding, Count Ashenafi consulted fortune-tellers and soothsayers. Working in complete isolation from one another, scholars came up with a stream of findings that proved to be mutually exclusive. One man diagnosed Aster's troubles as the work of widow spirits, while another was adamant that the spirits of Aster's ancestors were responsible. Widow spirits were known to stay clear of protective ancestors; both diagnoses were set aside. A scholar suggested that Aster might have wandered into a graveyard at noon, when the Devil was known to hold a congregation; another expert found that the Devil never entertained mundane issues during a high-sun conference. A highly regarded soothsayer urged that Aster's backyard be combed for clues of buried fetish. When five days of hard work by eleven laborers failed to unearth anything of note, it became all too evident that the only key to the mystery lay in the hands of a Hermit of Hermits.

A monk attains the status of hermit by trading the material world we live in for a straitened life lived in seclusion. Should he choose to enclose himself in a jail-like cell, he could end up staying there for anything from a few months to years, even a lifetime. While in the enclosure, he would cease to communicate with the outside world in any normal manner. He would be reachable only through a small opening in the roof or wall, through which food and other necessities could be delivered to him and through which he could send out messages and deliver spiritual counseling.

One celebrated hermit in the village of Kersa took his seclusion to higher ground after deciding that the three years he had spent in a dried-up water well were insufficient; he chose to spend the last thirty years of his life tied up like a dog, with a neck collar, on top of a column. All those years, he never sought shelter from the elements, and was dressed only to cover his private parts. He even managed to increase his discomfort by raising the column higher and higher; for the first seven years, he lived on top of a six-foot-high column, then he raised it to forty-five feet and, in the final years of his life, to sixty feet. The column was held as a shrine, and pilgrims came from distant regions to offer prayers, make sacrifices, and seek spiritual counseling. But the holy man never achieved the status of Hermit of Hermits, for he had remained within easy reach of humans and their influence. To attain the status of Hermit of Hermits one needs to curtail human contact severely, so that one cannot be spoiled by the handouts of sinners.

It is never easy to come across a Hermit of Hermits. Only after a week of intensive searching was Count Ashenafi able to locate one—at the periphery of a vast steppe. The holy man was camped in the hollowed trunk of a giant baobab tree. Having lost his bodily fluid to legions of visiting bats, his skin had turned pallid. His hair had become red. The whites of his eyes dominated his shrunken face. When he moved, his bones clattered. Two of Count Ashenafi's assistants helped the hermit climb down from his lair. Once outside the living cave, he staggered and buckled, weighed down by the thin air.

Sheltered under the scrawny shade of the baobab canopy, the holy man gathered all the information he needed about the young lady, beginning with the day on which wild animals first showed an interest in her—when birds started perching on her tiny shoulders and lizards gave her the right-of-way. He heard, with keen interest, how, when Aster was barely five, she defied earthly laws, walking through a solid wall. He was intrigued that she communicated with the spirits of the departed, that she shared the unspoken thoughts of her neighbors and read the auras of the diseased. Her painful experiences at the emperor's hand, and the unique afflictions that rendered her skin transparent, were revealed to him.

The Hermit of Hermits pulled out four cowrie shells from a pouch about his waist. He rubbed the shells in his closed fist, blowing sanctifying breath on them as he chanted prayers. Afterward, he tossed one shell each eastward, northward, westward, and in a southerly direction—in the proper sequence. Having the distance of each shell paced out from where he sat, he made a mental note of the variations in pitch. Finally, he ordered that two bleached bones of a hyena or wild dog be fetched (it didn't matter which animal). And, when the bones were gathered, after two hours of frantic searching, he buried the remains in the ground at his feet and began praying in earnest.

The wind whistled. Eagles carved a circle in the dome of the blue sky. Count Ashenafi and his escorts sat stock-still, studying the wrinkled savant. Eyes closed, his face twitching, tiny murmurs emanating from his sunken chest, the Hermit of Hermits prayed for half a generation. When it seemed that this learned man, like many others before him, was destined to go amiss, he opened up his eyes and pronounced his findings. Two of the three reasons for Aster's troubles were revealed to the Hermit of Hermits that day; before the third cause became apparent, rain would have to settle the dust.

Count Ashenafi learned with a heavy heart that one of the reasons for his endless troubles stemmed from the ground his home was built on—it was on the route of migrating spirits. Also, he learned that he was being targeted by the spirit of a monk he had unknowingly killed in the heat of combat. As both cases involved restless souls, the remedy was within easy reach: animal sacrifice would do the trick. And though only two of the three causes were addressed, Aster's recovery was not entirely unattainable. Count Ashenafi was cautioned, however, to expect a few false starts before his daughter got over the hurdles.

"Of course, the remedy could come much sooner if the rains kept their promise," the Hermit of Hermits concluded.

Before heading for home, Count Ashenafi deposited a large parcel at the root of the baobab tree, consisting of dried meat, roasted flour, bags of incense, a new sheet of *gabbi,* and a few silver coins. The offerings were meant for the spirits the holy man served.

Only Gudu seemed to have thrived despite the absent rains. Loaned to his master's friends and relations, he dazzled an ever-increasing audience. His name came to be recognized in places where he had yet to set foot, by people he had yet to entertain. Count Ashenafi was elevated in the eyes of friends he had yet to make; his legend grew, nurtured by the eloquence of his court performer.

Though Gudu had secured the admiration of many, he had also earned the enmity of a few. Ominous things began happening in the places he frequented. Once, while walking past a hay barn, he heard a cry for help. Gudu poked his head through a broken window to see who was in distress, but another man walked in through the door to help, stepped on poisoned spikes hidden under a bed of straw, and died of his injuries two days later. Yet another time, Gudu was trying to retrieve his childhood toy, dangling curiously from the branch of a tree when his dog, sauntering ahead, disappeared into a trap in the earth; the dog was gored to death by a bed of sharpened pegs.

Few doubted who the intended victim was, but Gudu refused to believe that anyone would conspire to do him harm. It was, perhaps, this trusting nature that failed to alert him when he detected a sour taste in his canteen of water. No sooner had he placed the container back on his saddle pommel than he collapsed on the ground, writhing in agony. A small crowd gathered round him, believing the entertainer had discovered a new dimension to his trade. Only when he started foaming at the mouth did they realize that this was not a performance at all.

Gudu's worth to his master became unmistakably clear when Count Ashenafi offered a reward of fifty *birr* for information leading to the apprehension of the culprit. An eerie mood overcame the townspeople. They formed knots under trees and in alehouses, talking about the reward money, which, to many of them, was a good year's earnings; they winnowed suspects from their midst. As word of the prize money got around, slave traders came in droves, mistaken in their belief that the markets of Deder had ripened exceptionally.

They offered two, three, even four able-bodied men for the said sum of fifty *birr*. But Count Ashenafi was not looking for a replacement. Days gave way to weeks, and when it seemed that the culprit would go unpunished, Beza's spiritual counselor secretly collected the reward money.

It was a chilly day that was dawning. Peals from the shrine bells rang out incessantly, alerting the townspeople to the immediacy of the occasion. Doors opened and men and women came out, clad in a blanket or *gabbi*, rubbing their bleary eyes with the end of their cloth or palm. They gauged the chilliness with the depth of air they exhaled. And, as they exchanged quick greetings over the throng, they couldn't help but wonder if it was a newborn they were celebrating or someone's loss they were sharing. They didn't find out until they had stepped inside the shrine compound. For, tied to the trunk of a tree, her back completely naked, cowering under the burning gaze of her master and his usual entourage, was Beza, mother of the Areru twins.

A burly man stood over her, a hamper of bamboo sticks by his side. Picking up a cane from the pile, he flexed it listlessly, only to put it back again. Once the courtyard was full of spectators, with no more room to blink an eye or think in peace, men and women scaled the few trees in the compound; they balanced themselves on the perimeter walls and just about any other object that could carry their weight. For, deprived of their morning sleep, they would not be denied the spectacle, however unpleasant. Few paid any attention to what Count Ashenafi had to say about the condemned and her crime. The ruckus died down only when he gave the cue for the whip-cracker to flex his muscles.

The whip-cracker raised the cane high above his head, let it linger a moment in midair, then lowered it on Beza's back, where it was received with a resounding protest. Birds took to the air. An army of cranes broke formation, swooping down to investigate. But Beza remained unflinching. She was flogged until the bundle of canes was entirely spent, until more trees had lost their limbs; elders, their walking sticks; the blind, their staffs; teachers, their rulers. It was not Beza who, in the end, collapsed from exhaustion, but the whip-cracker.

Beza surprised her neighbors yet again when she refused to take to bed. For days that followed she attended to her chores as though nothing terrible had happened to her. Each morning, she got up with the songbirds to milk the cows and goats, grind sacks of millet and sorghum, and bake stacks of *injera* and hoecake. She gathered manure from the barns and laid it outside to dry as firewood; she fetched water and did the laundry. At no time did she speak of the incident that had rendered her back mellow, nor express outward anger toward any person.

Gudu suffered from bouts of stomachache for weeks afterward, but that did not deter him from entertaining the occasional visitor or taking long trips in search of fresh poems and fables. Then one day, approximately two months after the poisoning episode, he failed to return home. Trackers were dispatched to scour the cosmic savanna, in vain. Vast amounts of reward money were promised, but no information was forthcoming. It was as though the slave had melted into thin air. A month after his disappearance, Gudu's death was officially mourned by family and neighbors; he had fallen victim to an *ergum*. Count Ashenafi surprised his neighbors, yet again, when he donned a black patch on his jacket in memory of the bondsman he had lost.

I have a vivid recollection of the day, the week—even the month—that Gudu disappeared. A chasm opened in my young life that no amount of anguish and tears could fill. Two months would elapse before my family realized that I couldn't get over the loss of the boy that I considered a brother until I knew how he had met his end. Dad dug up what little money we had in the backyard, and the two of us began looking for an *ergum* charmer.

It was never easy to find a reputable *ergum* charmer. We came across one only after six weeks of exhaustive searching. A caravan of camels escorted a donkey-drawn carriage that carried the expert. The convoy stopped at marketplaces and auction stalls, wherever a paying crowd had camped overnight for an audience with a lost relation.

The *ergum* charmer we visited was an albino, barely three feet tall, her red-dyed hair festooned with feathers and beads. Two smokestacks adorned her carriage, one on each side. A stream of noxious fumes rose above the chimneys and hung over her carriage like a fluid umbrella. Two young maids hunkered down at her feet, feverishly trimming her finger- and toenails. Her nails jettisoned at a pace of a foot a minute. A ten-year-old boy in a hand-loomed shirt (with one sleeve missing) scooped the tangled heap of nails and fed it to the burner attached to the vents.

It was her nails that captivated her audience. The *ergum* charmer must have relished the attention, for the only time she turned her head was when she spied someone trying to pilfer a piece of the harvest. She demanded payment for a measure of the nails in the form of a block of salt, roots of ginger, tins of honey, or *birr*.

Patrons knelt at the wheels of the carriage and cried out their pleas for everyone to hear. The *ergum* charmer pronounced her findings through the hollow, sun-bleached horn of a bull for the large audience. Our turn came, and Dad stammered his request. The crowd shuffled, whispering, in not-so-subdued voices, why an overseer who had never owned a slave would cough up a small fortune to locate someone else's chattel. The *ergum* charmer spoke for many when she posed the question out loud. Dad merely pointed at me, as I stood pouting, and mumbled the reasons.

In a rare display of frankness, the *ergum* charmer admitted her inability to locate the lost slave anywhere in the seven known *ergum* universes. She returned the money to Dad. But, as we were taking our leave dejectedly, she beckoned me and pressed a small pouch in my hand, telling me to bury the fetish outside my window and wait for the spirits to answer my prayers.

Days went by, and I forgot about the buried fetish. Then, one morning, my family awakened to the most unusual sight: the fetish had broken out of the ground and grown into a giant vine that wound itself around our hut, twice, before climbing over the spire and slithering down the back. Snaking toward a cactus bush some distance away, the plant had wrapped itself around a nomad jackal, killing the creature. The vine's mad dash halted only after it descended down a dried-up well, a league and a half from its roots, and reemerged in the cemetery at the far end of town.

A crowd gathered in front of our hut, vine-gazing. Some tore a limb of the plant and sniffed at the bruised stem to determine its species, while others chattered. Dad decided to tear down the vine, and got nine neighbors to help take axes and machetes to the limbs, but the men couldn't keep up with the growth rate. Unless they uprooted the plant, the men would have to work round the clock to check its growth. With the help of an additional eighteen laborers, they began digging under the vine tree.

Soon it became evident that our hut would crumble long before the tree fell. Our desperation grew when the men looked around and noticed that the heap of broken branches had simply evaporated into thin air. At sunset, the elders decided that the solution to the riddle lay in the hands of the responsible *ergum* charmer, and word was sent out to trace the woman and her transient entourage.

Close to dawn, I heard a knock on my window. I thought the vine had been scratching at the walls and was about to go back to sleep when I heard the unmistakable call of my name. Opening the window a crack, I beheld not the vine tree, which had mysteriously vanished, but the *ergum* charmer. She was wrapped in her own nails as she urged me to get up and go to the main house. Despite my family's repeated warnings not to open the door after sunset, much less walk into the night by myself, I slipped out of the hut and headed for the Ashenafi mansion.

The *ergum* charmer was nowhere to be seen. But I was not the only uninvited guest at the count's house. A small crowd had already gathered at the doorsteps, bearing witness to the ruckus emanating from inside. My surprise at the sight of the household members standing there in their pajamas was eclipsed only by the presence of fearsome strangers in the living room. I pushed through the crowd at the door, past the bearded strangers in turbans, and stood gazing at an apparition on a chair—the subject of the unusual disturbance. My eyes blinked faster and faster, and I shook my head vigorously to clear my mind, but there was no mistaking the person sitting in the armchair. Gudu had come back in flesh and soul, rescued from the jaws of death by the foul-smelling, turban-wearing, saber-dangling nomads in the room.

After being ambushed in a remote woodland, Gudu had been left to die a slow and painful death before he was discovered by salt merchants. The merchants took him with them on their long journey through deserts and alkaline plains, stopping the caravan every so often to care for him. Delirious, the patient mumbled gibberish. When he was able to put together a coherent sentence, he asked only for more drinking water. The nomads did not find out the stranger's identity until a full month had elapsed. Two more months would go by before Gudu was able to walk. He had survived five broken ribs, a torn ligament in one foot, a crushed skull, a twisted jaw, and a gaping hole in his abdomen.

Count Ashenafi offered money and trophies to the nomads, but they declined the payment, arguing that only the Almighty compensated the likes of them, and that they had, anyway, been rewarded for their lofty deed. Soon after Gudu was recovered from the desert floor, two virgin salt mines were revealed to the nomads. Many a stranger who came to share the warmth of a bonfire with the patient went on to discover salt deposits in places where no one would have thought to look. Gudu is now recognized as the Patron Saint of Salt Miners in six villages.

Gudu's assailant was brought to face the victim. In a rare display of calm and reason, Count Ashenafi allowed Areru the Shorter to confirm his guilt and explain what had driven him to commit such a dire act. But the accused denied having ever been in the bush that fateful day, much less ambushing Gudu. Areru the Shorter was placed behind bars, where guards took turns keeping vigil at his cell. Days passed, and while neighbors were still wondering what was in store for him, Areru the Shorter was brought in shackles to meet his new masters—passing slave merchants.

Beza wailed, begged for mercy. She offered for her son to be flogged, instead; or for his leg tendons to be clipped, thus limiting the range of his movements—anything to keep him from being put up for sale. Count Ashenafi, however, had already made up his mind. Beza was dragged away by a guard, and Areru the Shorter was led out of the compound, brandishing his new iron fetters. He took one last and puzzled glance at his childhood home before the gate was closed behind him.

Areru the Shorter was led to the end of a long line of half-dressed men—slaves bound on the same journey. Two sets of chains were fetched; one was fastened to his leg iron and the other strapped to his arm, hooking him up to the band. A small wooden pear was suspended from his neck by a leather strap; when the merchants proceeded to thrust the piece of wood into his mouth and hold it in place with the strap, Areru the Shorter made a violent start. Awakening from his initial shock, he thrashed about. Tears ran down his face, and he mumbled his mother's name, but the merchants were unmoved. The young slave was flogged until a semblance of order was restored. Then the wooden plug was savagely shoved into his mouth, where it drew a streak of blood.

"Is this absolutely necessary?" Count Ashenafi couldn't help but ask.

"My lord, only two people are leading them to the port. We can't take chances on mutiny," the merchants replied, adding that the wooden pear did allow the captive to breathe; it only stifled his cries.

The long line of sunburned men drifted down a dusty trail, with the clanking sounds of iron chains trailing behind them. Count Ashenafi went back inside, little suspecting that this small incident, sparked by two rival slave families, would one day kindle a raging fire in his backyard, smothering many innocent lives and reshaping the valley beyond recognition.

A LOWLY GOD

Seldom does a planned expedition arrest the attention of the entire community in the way that Dad's intended raid of Harar did. For three days now, all activities in our home had revolved around him and his intended journey. Strange men came and went with such regularity that Mam began treating them not as visitors, requiring preferential treatment, but as family members. The men lingered about, long after Mam and I had retired to bed, charting out plans under the dying glow of the kitchen fire.

They were going to Harar. Since the emperor had granted Count Ashenafi dominion over the walled town about two years ago, no form of homage had been forthcoming despite persistent reminders. It began to emerge that the tenants had been rebelling against the payment of taxes and tributes long before Count Ashenafi was granted fiefdom—in fact, for six years. He had celebrated his acquisition too early; he could hardly go complaining to the emperor without the risk of becoming a laughingstock. Whatever he did, he would have to prove to everyone, but, above all, the rebellious peasants, that he could control his own territory.

A grand total of fifty men set out on the journey, including Areru the Taller. Harar was a weeklong ride from home. One would have to cross hostile terrain and territories inhabited by warring tribes, many of whom were unsympathetic to the central government and its far-reaching tentacles. Dad's entourage left home in the dead of night, to keep their intentions secret. Once behind the immediate mountain chain, they broke formation, traveling in twos and threes, keeping up the deception. Fate must have been smiling on them, for they closed in on Harar undetected.

Harar habitually closed its gates with the setting sun, when itinerant traders and less upright visitors were cleared out of town by dedicated guards. Sturdy wooden gates and high stone walls, topped with jagged spikes, made the enclave impregnable to anyone but airborne visitors. To the earthbound, the most opportune moment to raid the town was either early in the morning, when the cattle were in the barns and the humans at the breakfast table, or at sunset. Count Ashenafi's scouts opted for an early-morning visit.

With a precision that would warm the heart of a dead admiral, the expedition force swooped upon Harar from four different angles. Roaring men came riding through all four gates at once. Bewildered tenants emerged from doorways and windows to investigate, only to be rounded up and herded into an open yard. Barns were emptied of their livestock; the granaries, what little foodstuff they held; the shops, their merchandise; the blacksmiths, their iron; homes, their furniture; shrines, their bells. If the inhabitants of the ancient town had thought that they could bluff their new master, as they had been doing to the green emperor, they were proven wrong.

The raiders left town in triumph, their small efforts handsomely rewarded. Not only had they reclaimed the tributes due their master plus their own expenses, but they had extracted handsome forfeitures. A safe distance from the pillaged town, they set up camp for the night. Five goats were slaughtered, and the meat was roasted on a string of bonfires. The scent of sizzling flesh wafted through the woods, attracting uninvited guests: hyenas, jackals, wild dogs, and badgers. The soldiers were exceptionally generous, sharing the loot with their four-legged kin.

In the small hours of the morning, the raiders were awakened by the whine of excited horses and urgent hooves. Dust trails sprang up all around the camp. Patches of fireworks lit the shadowy jungle. Shots rang out. It was the raiders' turn to run about disoriented, searching for an enemy they couldn't see. When the dust finally settled, the waking sun laid bare the secrets of the night: half of the cattle remained unaccounted for and three of Count Ashenafi's men lay wounded. One of them was Areru the Taller, who had received a bloody gash to the head.

A further surprise awaited Count Ashenafi's men when they arrived back home. For camped in the alleys, streets, market stalls, and just about any open space in the expansive valley were old men, women, and children. Tenants of Harar had come to reclaim their livelihood; they were not plying their weapons, but using the powers of persuasion. Their children tugged at passersby, begging for alms, while their women knocked on doors, asking for a bowl of dough, a glass of water, medication for the dying, and burial cloths for their dead. Residents of the valley were appalled by the human misery visited on them. And, as the days gave way to weeks, and the weeks to months, it was the townspeople who decided to do something about the crisis and they who sent elders to Count Ashenafi.

Two months and eleven days after the human pests first descended upon the serene valley, Count Ashenafi was shamed into accepting mediation. For an additional year of grace and the return of stolen goods, he was promised not only the tribute he was owed but also what was due the monarchy—the six years of unpaid taxes. Only Count Ashenafi truly believed that he would receive the compensation.

Not long after the refugees took their leave, a monk came to visit us. He was a slight man with a pronounced hunchback, buckteeth, and eyes not trained to see as one. He wore a shiny silver cap on the tip of his nose, which I found quite mystifying. The monk was a menacing presence in our home. Taking one look at him, the family cat darted out of the room, screaming. Objects rattled when he stared at them. A framed picture came crashing down from the wall the moment he appraised it; a kettle on a dead-cold table whistled when he turned his gaze upon it. Mam took this to mean that the monk wanted a drink, and she freshened up the pot.

Mugs of steaming coffee-leaf brew were soon served, laced with salt and ginger. Mam apologized for not being able to provide milk for the drink, but the monk assured her that such excesses were sinful in hard times like the present. While Mam labored at the kitchen preparing our dinner, cooking stew on one side of the stove, and baking *injera* on another, the men sat talking away. Their chitchat revealed that my father and the monk had met before. As it dawned on me that this was the same monk who had shared a campfire with us in the wilderness some three years ago, my pity at the sight of his buckled frame gave way to glee at the divine retribution visited upon him.

Dinner was ready. With a mug of warm water in one hand and a washbasin in the other, I helped the men bathe their hands. A stack of *injera*, drenched in lentil stew and large enough, in fact, to feed a small army, was placed before the two. Mam sampled the food, as tradition required (easing the guest's mind that he was not being poisoned), before retreating to the corner. Mam and I sat beside the fire, sharing a small plate. From time to time, she rose to top up the men's mugs or sprinkle what little remained of the stew on their *injera.*

The hunchback monk didn't say what had brought him to our corner of the woods until dinner was over. Then he rolled himself a cigarette, snatched a long puff, squinted his eyes as he enjoyed the smoke, brushed away an invisible fleck of tobacco from his tongue, cleared his throat, and, when the house had settled into a state of palpable expectation, unloaded what had been weighing heavily on his mind.

"We are besieged by a hideous foe," he began, "but are unable to enlist warriors, because of the way the noblemen have been treating the peasants."

"What foe?" Dad asked.

"The Ammas are tightening the rope around our throats. If you push the peasants any further, we may as well surrender to the enemy."

"What is Amma?" I asked Dad, despite being told many times before not to squeak before visitors.

"It is the religion of the pagans," the monk spat.

"What is pagan?" I followed up.

"A pagan is an irreligious person."

"How come they are irreligious when Amma is their religion?" I asked, in all innocence.

The holy man sat up, his back completely straight, regarding me as though I had just slipped out of the thatched roof above. The room fell silent, until Dad took it upon himself to expound on the doctrines of the alien faith.

"Amma was a lowly god," father began, reiterating what he had heard while growing up, "for He assumed the shape of an everyday egg." Though the egg was believed to comprise four distinct compartments, each compartment represented one of the four elements that make up the world: fire, air, earth, and water. Amma's earth was a sad and barren place, and when He decided to populate it, Amma chose a direct method: He got down from the sky, under the blanket of darkness, and united Himself with the female earth, impregnating her with a jackal.

Amma soon found out His mistake, for the jackal was nothing but trouble to Him; it disobeyed His wishes, and proved mischievous. Vowing not to commit the same oversight again, Amma united himself with earth once again, but this time He fathered twins. The pair looked human above the waist; their bottom halves were snakelike. With eyes crimson like fire, tongues long like giraffes' but forked like snakes', arms sinuous and without joints, and bodies covered with short green hair that emitted light constantly, the twins must have been a sight to behold. Their name—Nummo—meant spirits, and they spent their formative years in heaven, studying the art of creation with their father. Upon returning to earth, the twins put to use their creative streak by producing, in quick succession, twins of humans, antelopes, warthogs, zebras, lions, buffaloes, hyenas . . .

Later in my life, I would come to understand that, ridiculed for their perceived simplemindedness, followers of Amma had never been considered a threat to the establishment until the day when their egalitarian culture and its influence on serfs and slaves could no longer be denied. Occasional skirmishes had led to irate slaveholders raiding the nomads' settlements to reclaim runaway slaves. The emperor had conducted two major campaigns in a single year to fight the poison of their perfidy. As these operations proved ineffective and much of the countryside fell under the influence of Ammas, the Supreme Pontiff of the Shrine of Mawu-Lisa had assumed the grave task of driving the heretics out with an avenging pitchfork.

The hunchback monk was an appointed legate of the Supreme Pontiff. He rode from village to village, raising money and enlisting warriors for an imminent crusade. He persuaded overlords to support the cause of the crusaders by refraining from antagonizing the peasants. He wanted Dad to impress upon Count Ashenafi the dangers of levying undue taxes and tributes on the tenants when the poor had nowhere to turn but the heretics and infidels. But Dad had his own ideas.

"Perhaps one should look for the solution to the problem in the way not the serfs, but the slaves, are being treated," my father said, braving a heresy.

Far from being offended by the unexpected impertinence, the holy man chose to expound on master-slave relationships, arguing that human bondage had been sanctioned in the Holy Scriptures and that to challenge that relationship was to impugn God's word.

"If slavery was sanctioned by God," Dad argued, "then how come monks and nuns on their deathbeds liberate faithful slaves as a pious act that might win them atonement for past sins?"

"Slavery is a remedy as well as a penalty for sin," the monk offered.

"But the Good Scripture teaches us that we cannot own an immortal soul," said Dad, to which the holy man responded by pointing out that a master-slave relationship was not unlike a father-son alliance; that when one buys and sells slaves, it is only their labor and service that one acquires for life, not their flesh and blood.

Dad felt encouraged enough by the monk's unparalleled receptiveness to fresh and thorny ideas that he proposed freeing some slaves—slaves fathered by freemen. He reasoned that since the Holy Scriptures teach us that a father provides the form and the mother the matter, and since the form weighs heavily on the soul of a creation, the son of a freeman and a bondswoman ought to be free.

The hunchback monk was quick to point out that the Good Book is replete with passages consisting of layers of meanings, which, to the untrained eye, can be not only misleading but also dangerously perversive. Dad had alluded to a passage that was best explained by the analogy of the promiscuous ass.

"As a mule born of a mare and an ass is more like a mare than one born of a she-ass and a horse," the monk reasoned, "so is a child born to a woman in bondage, regardless of its father."

Undeterred, Dad suggested that, perhaps, one should permit the most loyal slaves to marry from among their kind. But the holy man was strongly against such indiscretions because marriage acknowledges a contractual relationship of authority and obedience, rights and obligations within the family that violates a master's absolute ownership of a slave and, ultimately, the wishes of God.

I had been gazing at the monk in utter bafflement, wondering if he hadn't slipped out of the Devil's rucksack, when an idea presented itself. I rose to freshen up his jug of water. The family water tank, a large clay pot, was balanced on three large stones. With a slight movement of my heel, I removed one of the stones, replacing it with the monk's rolled bedding. The sight of his rucksack at my feet must have reminded the monk of something; he tugged at it from where he sat on the floor. The water tank toppled, emptying its entire contents on his bedding. His stomach might have been full, but I knew that the monk wouldn't go to bed that night. We were too poor to afford a spare bedsheet.

Hyenas howled as they descended upon the valley from the desolate mountains, their ominous cries piercing the still night with terror. Babies wailed, awakened from their sleep by the incessant barking of dogs. The drawn-out silence in our hovel weighed down heavily on Mam, who made a vain attempt to amuse our guest. She asked him if he would like another hot drink, or if he was ready for me to wash his feet before going to bed, but he only shook his head. The hunchback monk interrupted the silence suddenly to ask why an evening mass was not being held.

"We attend mass only twice a week," Dad told him.

"No wonder the heretics are running the country," the monk mourned, and he rushed out into the night to pay a call upon the parishioners.

Soon the shrine hall brimmed with disgruntled worshipers. The hunchback monk, as representative of the Supreme Pontiff, assigned himself the task of conducting the evening mass. Standing low behind the holy pulpit he delivered a passionate sermon, relating how the heretics and infidels had besieged the true faith. And while he preached how some among us had deserted the true religion, and in their folly wandered in the wilderness where there was no way for redemption, and how once the poison of faithlessness had infested the people it could no longer be easily dug out, I drifted into sleep resting on Mam's shoulder. The next morning, long after the visitor had taken his leave, I found out his name was Reverend Yimam, and, though no one had told me at the time, I knew it would not be the last that I would see of him.

Areru the Taller recovered from his head wound; the two others did not. The bullet that penetrated the back of his skull dislodged one of his eyes on its mad dash out, but the most talked-about scar of the celebrated ambush did not become visible until the boy was up and walking: a fire had been lit in his stomach that no amount of food would put out.

In the beginning people were sympathetic, even understanding. They believed that his affliction was temporary, that once the patient regained his full vigor and strength he would come to terms with the minor famine around him. But as the days gave way to weeks, and the weeks to months, it became horrifyingly clear that the young man would not stop eating until the entire town had passed through his stomach. Diviners and herbalists were of no help, for none had ever come across a man eating twenty-three breakfasts in one sitting. Concerned townspeople experimented with untested medication when they mixed cow dung and a scoop of fire ants into the patient's meal; they held vigil around him at mealtimes, chanting sacred words and sounding a gong to scare away the devil inside him, but the continued effort only heightened his hunger.

People closed their doors when they sat down for a meal. They hid under their beds what meager foodstuff they had, and placed guards at their doors. When a ground bale of sorghum was laid out to dry under the sun, boys were reminded to keep an eye not only on winged predators, but also on Areru the Taller. He would dash out from behind the houses and run away with a handful of the raw grain, munching it on the fly. Count Ashenafi compensated disgruntled neighbors for their loss, believing, like many did at one time, that the war veteran would recover from his affliction. But when the young man started chasing roosters, suckling pigs, and neighborhood cats with a roast in mind, even the lord of the manor couldn't feign indifference. Count Ashenafi gave word for the boy to be chained to a tree behind his mother's hut.

And so Areru the Taller spent his days tied up to a eucalyptus tree, moaning like a wounded warthog. He called out his mother's name until his voice turned hoarse. Beza brought him a human serving of food, twice a day; she kept a large pot of water at his side; and, at sunset, she untied her son and took him indoors. All hopes of a speedy recovery were dashed one windy afternoon, when the patient sank his teeth into his mother's arm, believing, in his hallucination, that he was chasing after a meal. From then on, a gag was placed in his mouth, not unlike the one used on his sold brother.

A CARING JACANA

With Areru the taller retired from active duty and his twin brother long out of picture, it fell upon Gudu to assume the task of watching over Aster's residence. Gudu had been chosen by the Almighty to be a rear guard to Aster on her long descent to earth. And so, when he was not gone from town in search of fables and poems, or entertaining the occasional visitor, Gudu could be seen sitting on a wicker chair outside Aster's door, rehearsing his store of learning. Twice a day he escorted his charge during her customary stroll, maintaining the required distance of three paces. He watched over her as she admired the bed of flowers in her garden and engaged in playful banter with neighborhood children. Gudu never initiated conversations with his mistress, and always answered her infrequent queries with absolute deference and rare vocabulary.

Aster was never a difficult person to attend to. In fact, doting on her attendants like a prayer child while asking little in return, she earned the adoration of those who came to serve her. Her two maids, considering her a friend, shared with her their wild fantasies and everyday gossip. Having seldom ventured outside the perimeter of her small place of refuge, Aster came to know the world outside through their eager eyes and ears; she looked forward to their morning visits. In the afternoons, when the maids left for their other chores, she felt lonely and dejected.

Loneliness had been a constant companion to Aster ever since she had moved into her own residence. Her life was depressingly predictable. Each morning, she got up early enough to witness the courting of the songbirds in her backyard; she lingered at her bedroom window until the trees were deserted and the sun began to gather fury. After a quick breakfast, she indulged in small talk with her maids, winnowing out what passed for news in the valley. Though she had long ago lost the power to move objects with her mind, Aster never tired of trying. She sat gazing at a saltshaker or a glass of water until exhaustion overcame her.

She would have welcomed the opportunity to try her hand at weaving or knitting, but Count Ashenafi frowned on such indulgences, though they carried little social stigma. Kitchen chores had always been the exclusive domain of servants. As the morning dragged and she tired of the small distractions around her, Aster put on her makeup—layers of body paint to hide her glassy features—and ventured out to the garden escorted by her guard. Children were always a welcome diversion to Aster; Count Ashenafi didn't mind as long as they were under ten. She laughed and frolicked with them, sometimes inviting three or four of them home.

The afternoon was the most dreaded half of Aster's day. Those few young women she once called friends had all been married off at the ripe age of thirteen and borne a multitude of offspring. None could afford the luxury of leaving home unless there was a death in the family or a marriage. Aster was encouraged to pay them a visit, but she avoided their company, for their busy lives only magnified the vacuum she lived in. She preferred her solitude, the company of her mirrors. She spent hours on end trying on her luxurious wardrobe and admiring her elusive reflections. Such episodes, however, left her even more depressed; she ended up curled up in bed, doors and windows closed.

It was on one such afternoon, not long after Gudu had taken up his station at her door, that Aster was nudged from her slumber by a hummed melody. Following trails of sound, she went outside—and stood facing the back of her young guard. Without betraying her presence, she savored the enchanting poem he next rehearsed; she marveled at his dreamlike intonations and theatrical movements. When he finished his performance, Aster greeted him with heartfelt applause. "Gudu, that was the most beautiful poem I have ever heard," she chimed, beaming. Though Aster was aware of Gudu's famed poetry, her knowledge of his skills and artistry had been limited to word of mouth. She wanted to know more about him, a lot more.

"Recite to me another poem," she eagerly asked.

Gudu fumbled as he weighed in his mind the appropriateness of each ode to the ears of a highborn lady. His awkward demeanor stood in stark contrast to the daring and confident poet that she had spied on a short while before. Aster put his mind at rest when she assured him that any of the poems he delivered in the presence of her mother would do. Gudu remembered "Plea of the Eunuch," one of the shortest poems in his repertoire:

Thirst has never been my foe,
Hunger, even less so.
Hardships I learned to endure,
Adversaries not to lure.
What I knew not how to staunch,
What no diviner could help me tame,
Was anger appropriating my name.
Without a land, without a home,
Without a friend of my choice,
With enemies not of my make,
I seem to live for someone's sake.
My heart asks my own end;
If the wish of God has been fulfilled.

A bright light went on in Aster's head. She saw an entire vista unfolding before her: the two of them would embark on a project documenting all poems, plays, riddles, and fables that Gudu carried in his head!

"But I can't write," he remonstrated, somewhat taken aback by her unexpected display of ignorance.

"That is the first thing we need to change," she pronounced, radiating a mischievous smile.

"Lady Aster, perhaps you should consult with your father," Gudu demurred.

"That won't be necessary," Aster said hurriedly. "Let this be our little secret."

Though she was inspired by the idea of committing to paper Gudu's treasure of oral knowledge, Aster soon set in motion plans to incorporate, in a book, her own catalogue of wisdom, wisdom long relegated to the deep recesses of her mind. She envisioned an army of monks in some distant monastery hunched over her manuscript, reproducing every word for mass consumption. And, as it dawned on her that she was pioneering the first book in the nation ever to be written not just by a female author but also by a man in bondage, Aster's determination sprouted formidable teeth and claws.

In many ways, Aster's plight was not unlike Gudu's. Her prison-like existence, for instance, was not a trapping of privilege, but penance for not being born in her father's image; her right to manage her personal affairs would not have been an issue if she had urinated standing up. Aster might have picked this master storyteller as her partner in a book project, but she had more than one reason for her choice.

The obstacles that lay ahead were never lost on Aster. She expected the first hurdle to arise the moment it became known that she was teaching a slave to read and write, but she hoped that would happen only after the young man had mastered the skills. Afterward, she might even invite those concerned to force him to unlearn.

And so Aster changed her life in mid-course. She became a crusader with a battle to wage, a mission to fulfill. Her past routine entirely forgotten, she now went to sleep when she could no longer keep her eyes open, and darted out of bed before the waking sun. She no longer dallied at her window or dresser. Her youthful confidence completely restored, she ceased wearing makeup or a veil to conceal her diseased skin. Not unlike a convict whose death sentence has been commuted at the eleventh hour, Aster adopted a carefree attitude toward life, unimpeded by the uncertainties of tomorrow.

No one was more surprised by her transformation than her father, Count Ashenafi, but whether out of fear of stirring up the hornets' nest or because of his undying faith in his god, he asked few questions. Whatever his daughter requested, he granted with pleasure. Crates of elegant paper arrived at her doorstep on the backs of mules and donkeys. Boxes of India ink and reed pens were imported from distant kingdoms. And with each passing day, Aster's appetite for supplies deepened, her original plan of one book giving way to two and finally three volumes. She envisioned a book on poetry, one on fables and anecdotes, and yet another on ancient wisdom.

Gudu might have taken a little while to feel at ease in the presence of his mistress, sharing a table with her, but he was no less passionate about the project. Indeed, he took to the books like a camel to a watering hole. In only six weeks, Gudu mastered the entire alphabet of two-hundred-odd letters; in another four weeks, he was able to put down his thoughts on paper. Before six months had elapsed, he had begun compiling the manuscript for all three volumes.

The two began their workday with a quick breakfast together, followed by a ceremonial coffee, for good luck. Fresh air drifted through open windows, filtered by the well-trimmed hedge that girded her bungalow, as they pored over stacks of ink-stained papers. The two had set themselves a minimum threshold they intended to reach by the end of each busy day. For Aster, this entailed some preparation as she had to retrieve wisdom that had long ago drifted into distant memory. Gudu often exceeded the two pages of poems, riddles, and fables that he promised to deliver by the end of the day. And though the job was divided according to their individual strength, each drew pleasure in reviewing the other's work.

As the afternoon lingered and the only distraction came from a solitary wasp that drifted through the open door, Gudu reached inside himself for an anecdote or humorous sketch that might put a smile on Aster's face.

"Let me tell you what I heard the other day," he offered one sweltering afternoon.

Aster sat up expectantly.

"Two men were walking to the alehouse," he began. "It was a cloudy day, and one of them carried a closed umbrella. All of a sudden, it began to pour.

" 'Hurry up and open the umbrella,' urged one of the men.

" 'No use,' squirmed his friend.

" 'What do you mean "No use"?'

" 'The umbrella is riddled with holes.'

" 'Then why bother to bring it along?'

" 'I didn't expect it to rain.' "

Aster burst out laughing, tears rolling down her cheeks. As she reached for her sash to dry her eyes, she pinched Gudu's arm playfully. That was the first time she had ever touched him, and a shock rippled down his spine. Aster's eyes lingered a moment longer as they traced the contours of Gudu's face. Of late, she had been wondering how he had come to be born to a bondswoman. It was in Aster's training to recognize the subtle facial differences in all nine ethnic groups the Almighty intended to be slaves. If she hadn't known that Gudu had been born to Enquan, Aster would have been mistaken for once.

Aster's growing comfort in the company of the poet was tested one memorable day when Count Ashenafi walked in unannounced. The sight of his highborn daughter sitting shoulder to shoulder with the family slave gave Count Ashenafi a visible shudder.

"What are you doing in here?" he barked at the disoriented guard. Gudu was too stunned to speak.

"Of course, he is helping me with my work," Aster answered for him.

"Don't you see how scandalous your behavior is?" Count Ashenafi redirected his anger at his daughter. "How dare you permit yourself to share a table with your servant?" His legendary temper flared with little provocation. Blood rushed to his face and temples; his eyes threatened to pop out of their sockets.

"You wait for me outside," he ordered the trembling poet. "I will deal with you later."

Father and daughter battled in a rare and impassioned war of words. Count Ashenafi felt betrayed on two fronts: his trust in Gudu had been misplaced, but, above all, his own flesh and blood had made light of him. Aster was old enough to recognize her position in society. She should have known that, however innocent her intentions, by sharing a breath of air with the family slave, she had compromised her integrity and the family's good name. Many a duel had been fought and much blood spilled because a member of the weak sex had discredited her family. Count Ashenafi wouldn't go down in history as someone who had lost his head because of his independent-minded women.

Had he known that Gudu was anything other than a court entertainer to his daughter, running errands at her command, Count Ashenafi would have vetoed the arrangement long ago. There were always scholars falling over themselves to be of service to him, and to his daughter. Why, Aster could have requested, and she would have been granted, the assistance of the kingdom's celebrated Sage of Sages.

Realizing this was one battle she couldn't easily win, Aster quickly relented. She assuaged her father's anger, admitting to him her mistakes; she beseeched him not to punish the poet for the fault that was hers. No matter how infuriated he might be, Count Ashenafi couldn't remain angered by his daughter for long—not when she pleaded with him, crying her eyes out. Forewarning himself as much as his daughter that this might be one decision he would live to regret, Count Ashenafi granted her wish.

"But," he quickly added, staring down Gudu, "there is no reason for you to stay inside once you discharge what she has asked of you."

Turning to his daughter, Count Ashenafi roared: "And you! You shouldn't be alone with him, if only to avoid gossip."

If he had died and come back kicking, Gudu wouldn't have felt more elated than he did when he was dismissed with a mere warning. He was happy, above all, for his mother, Enquan, who, since he first began frequenting Aster's bungalow, had never ceased to remind him of the dangers of feeling cozy with his master's daughter.

Enquan had known many a bondsman who had lost his manhood, and his life, because of a whiff of scandal involving his mistress. But she had more reasons for pleading with Gudu to stay out of Aster's range. These, however, were something she considered private. She told him the obvious: Gudu had the good looks and easy charm that could easily win him another sweetheart without risking his head.

Whether it was his mother's incessant pleas, or because he had seen danger breathing fire and steam, Gudu became his old reserved self following his close brush with his master. Addressing Aster with her formal title and cold deference, he proved unreachable. When escorting her during her daily strolls, he doubled the three paces of separation required of him; at times, he stood so far away that he seemed to be on a personal quest. Aster invited him in for coffee or a snack, but he insisted on taking it while standing at the door, preferably outside. When she tried to cajole him into reviewing her work, or resuming writing, he made up reasons why he could not do her bidding. Some days it might be his hurting eyes; other times, it was dizziness that overcame him when he glanced at letters.

But soon his passion for the project overcame his fears. He resumed work, at first taking bits of assignments home. After a month, he began spending extended moments with Aster. Still wary of danger, Gudu got up with a start whenever he heard a rattle at the door, or a shuffle at the hedge. One windy evening, when he seemed to be too restless to concentrate on his work, Aster asked him to tell her a story. Gudu sprang to life, for storytelling was something that he not only enjoyed, but also that his master sanctioned.

Once there lived a famous poet in the kingdom of Gojam," Gudu began. "His name was Getachew, and the emperor favored him. One morning when Getachew came to work, a palace gatekeeper denied him access unless the poet promised him a share of the day's earnings. Getachew agreed, and he signed a written contract, which the guard had already prepared.

"After an afternoon of dazzling performance, Getachew was rewarded with the sum of ten *birr*, and a new outfit.

" 'May I have a different form of compensation today?' The poet startled the emperor with his impertinent request.

" 'But of course,' the emperor assented, his eyes shifting from side to side. 'What do you have in mind?'

" 'May I have one hundred lashes, instead?'

" 'What a strange request,' the emperor said. 'Are you all right?'

" 'I am fine, Your Highness. And, if it is not too much trouble, I would like to have those hundred lashes today.'

"The emperor racked his brains for the kernel of the riddle; his eyes begged the counsel of his learned courtiers, in vain. When His Highness was about to pronounce that this was one riddle that only an *ergum* could crack, the palace diviner stepped in, assuring the emperor that it wasn't entirely uncommon for an aspiring scholar to draw his inspirations from the whip.

" 'Well, if it is the whip that he wants, so he must have it,' the emperor concluded, with a sigh of mixed relief. But, before the whip-cracker flexed his muscles, the emperor whispered in his ears to be easy on his favorite poet.

"Fifty soft lashes were administered before Getachew raised a hand to speak to the emperor once again.

" 'Yes, what is it now?' the emperor demanded.

" 'Your Highness, I have a contract to fulfill,' Getachew announced, producing a folded paper from his pocket.

"As he read the contract, the emperor's face turned from a tempered understanding to a fury of betrayal. He had the guilty doorkeeper summoned and visited by fifty severe strokes before banishing him to a distant monastery."

Aster got out of her seat, radiating a mischievous smile. Jabbing Gudu in the chest, she demanded to know if he was not the vengeful Getachew. "Out with it now!" she teased. "You don't have to think, you know. Out with it!" And, before Gudu could think of an answer to her jest, she gave him a heartfelt hug.

Gudu turned into a statue of clay. The two stood gazing at each other in total silence, caught up in a twirl of unspeakable thoughts. And though their hearts raced on the crest of the same wave, and their lungs labored at the heights of a shared dream, they remained separated by invisible, yet no less real, chasms: ancient taboos, inbred ignorance, cherished intolerance, and superstitions that transcended conflicting religious doctrines. Gudu eased his way out of the room a thoroughly bewildered man, without so much as bidding Aster good night.

Come the following morning, there was no sight of the poet; nor the day after, or for days afterward. When a week had passed without a word from her guard, Aster couldn't feign indifference any longer. She dispatched her maids to find out what had become of him. Enquan was vague about her son's whereabouts; others didn't seem to know, or care. As it was not uncommon for Gudu to take long trips in search of fresh fables, poems, and riddles, his absence didn't carry any weight unless it was noticed by his master.

Gathering her courage, Aster was about to approach her father when Count Ashenafi surprised her with the answer. Gudu had come to ask for his permission to spend some time at one of the monasteries, serving the monks and nuns, while at the same time honing his skills. As there was no better school for a man of Gudu's faculty than a good monastery, which would be home to the most sought-after scholars in the kingdom, and as his services were not urgently needed by the count, her father had seen no reason to deny the request.

"I thought the two of you had discussed the plan," he casually added.

In her quiet solitude, Aster racked her brains for all possible reasons behind Gudu's indefensible act—all the reasons, in fact, except the one she knew, in the heart of her heart, to be the actual cause. Overcome by a feeling that she couldn't place, she struggled through the day, and the nights were much worse. She spent many sleepless hours crying in her pillows. It seemed certain to her that she would lose her mind. "Over what?" she asked herself, in defiance. "A mere servant?" But no sooner had the words formed into thought than she had a thousand regrets for thinking of Gudu as a mere servant.

Her old habits returned. Aster spent interminable hours at her bedroom window, gazing at the sprawling woods, yet registering little. The songbirds didn't appeal to her senses anymore, and the lovebirds seemed to mock her sorrows by their conspicuous courtship. As in the past, she went to bed in the afternoon, closing the doors and windows, but sleep eluded her. If only there were a friend to share her anguish and sorrows, a parent who would understand her needs and desires, a spiritual counselor who could relay her pleas to the All-knowing above without losing their essence in interpretation, Aster would have felt better.

One exceptional evening, when her mind wouldn't stop racing and her feet refused to remain in place, Aster sought solace from the Holy Scriptures. Seldom did she look at the Good Book with anything but detached ritual, but this day each leaf screamed with characters that she could easily place, prophecies that had almost matured. She found fresh interpretations and hidden meanings in every line, every word. She had lost herself between the frayed sheets, oblivious to the gale that rattled the building, when, suddenly, she felt a presence in the room. Raising her head ever so tentatively, she froze at the sight of a bearded apparition. When his knocks at the door had remained unanswered, Gudu had quietly let himself in.

Aster tore out of her seat, scattering chairs and footrests. Loose pages flew in the air. Though she had promised herself never again to betray her emotions, not to commit the same oversight that had resulted in her sorrows, she couldn't control herself any more than a caring jacana at the sight of a stray chick. She abandoned herself in his arms. When she raised her head, Gudu's pleading eyes greeted hers. As in an enchanted dream—more aptly, perhaps, like a gull over a warm breath of sea—she drifted toward him, until her lips found his, and she was reborn in his love.

BOOK THREE:

INTRIGUES

A FORBIDDEN AFFAIR

Enchantment filled the air. Servants dashed up and down crowded aisles, serving vintage *arake* and *tella* to invited guests. Countess Fikre perched on a padded arm chair, fanning herself with a palm leaf. Every now and then she issued whispered commands that sent the maids scuttling around. Count Ashenafi stood gazing at the crowd with an uncharacteristic grin. Having let his guard down, he was seen pinching the rear end of his shapely attendant, Enquan, as she whisked by. The countess shook her head at her husband's indiscretion. But who could blame the count for feeling liberated.

And what an unjust imprisonment it must have seemed for a young woman like Aster: to have to spend her precious years locked up behind doors, afraid of being seen in public without a thick layer of makeup to disguise her otherworldly skin. But that was in receding memory. Now, she could rejoice in the simple pleasure of looking mundane; she could look at her reflection in the mirror without a sigh of heartache.

The miracle that transformed her life took shape in her dreams. On the night of Gudu's return from self-imposed exile, she had gone to bed with rosy thoughts. Early the next morning she walked into her washroom humming a half-forgotten tune, and was greeted by a stranger in the mirror. A character out of her dream had followed her into daylight; she darted out of the room screaming, dressed only in a nightgown. Birds took to the air in fright. Dogs barked, tailing her. Doors opened, and neighbors came out one by one, rubbing their bleary eyes, wondering what might have come over their uncrowned queen. As the reason behind her half-naked dance finally dawned on them, their scowling faces gave way to a shared bliss.

The celebration continued for a week and a day as friends and relations made the long journey to put in an appearance. Aster would look back on those eight days with a sigh of exasperation. Forced to spend her daytime hours entertaining the many guests, and the nights sharing her sleeping quarters with visitors, she was seldom able to snatch a private moment with Gudu. She saw him hovering over the streaming crowd, like a fish eagle shadowing a drifting trout. She searched for him with her longing eyes and assured him with her infectious smile, but the pain of separation remained as punishing to him as it had been to her. Only when the tent was folded and carted away and the guests had gone their separate ways could they look forward to each other's company.

The years past had been punishingly lonely to Aster. Her mornings were seldom busy, but she had dreaded the afternoons, when the only company she could count on was, often, wasps and horseflies. Count Ashenafi encouraged his daughter to venture out and mingle with a crowd of her peers, but Aster loathed meaningless social visits.

Though the partying was over and little had changed in the number and frequency of her regular visitors, her life seemed to Aster dreadfully crowded of late. She began noticing how difficult it was ever to have a truly private moment. The coming and going of servants seemed to occur at all times of the day; Gudu appeared to be summoned from his guard duty, to run an errand or entertain guests, with suspicious regularity. And, though no one had ever hinted, much less articulated, an intention of replacing her guard, she felt nauseated at the thought of his being forcibly removed from her life.

Aster manifested signs of diminishing health. She cried for no apparent reason; she ached and lamented. She made up reasons for staying behind locked doors. When she appeared at the family dinner table after some wheedling, she excused herself long before the after-meal grace, drawing curious glances. Count Ashenafi remained tolerant of his daughter's eccentricities until she mounted a bell outside her door and demanded that her visitors announce themselves, using a prearranged code, before making their entrance: three peals of the bell would identify her maids; five peals, her father; two peals, any new visitor; and a peal at long intervals, members of the clergy. Fearful that she might soon come down with a disease more dreadful than mere bleached skin, Count Ashenafi assigned his daughter imposing company, breathing life into her deep-seated fears.

The family diviner, who had looked after Aster during her formative years, shaping her thoughts and views of the world, became her intimate guardian once more. Camping in the corner of her living room, he watched her every move. He monitored the food she ate and the few visitors she entertained. The holy man spent many a grueling afternoon hunched over Aster's incomplete manuscript in a peerless effort to pin down where in the vast text of her life the Devil had made his first entrance. Though Aster resented this naked aggression more than mere words could communicate, she concealed her feelings lest her father felt justified in augmenting the diviner with the not-so-distant soothsayer and herbalists. She did, however, think of a plan that would enable her to indulge in her forbidden love while avoiding the prying eyes of the offensive monk.

At sundown, men gathered at one of the better homes for an evening toast, while their women left the steamy kitchens with tins of lukewarm water in hand and headed for the open fields. Outing is more than a ritual in the life of a married woman; it is, to many, the only affordable alternative to a shower or bath. As they splash warm water on their private parts, the women linger around, snatching yet another rare luxury: socializing with their peers. Outing is, indeed, the only time in a woman's daily routine that she can truly claim a free moment.

Though only young—seventeen—and unwed, Aster began observing Outing. She didn't join any of the other women, however, preferring instead her own little corner—an abandoned barn. The old barn held a mythical significance for Aster. While growing up, she had spent many mornings and late-afternoon hours gazing at the shafts of sunlight filtering through the aging walls. Unlike her experience of the sharp and defined rays of the everyday light, or the hazy and tentative glow of a cloudy sky, she felt a divine presence in what she saw in that old barn. Often, she said her heartfelt prayers kneeling before the light. Count Ashenafi, more than anyone else in the compound, appreciated her undying affection for the decrepit building. More than once, her strong protests had dissuaded him from removing the eyesore.

Aster hoped that her love affair would blossom where she had felt the god's presence. Each night, she left the confines of her quarters for the embrace of the old barn. As she retraced the beaten trail, she scanned her surroundings for signs of danger. Danger materialized out of thin air in the valley. One had to be constantly on the lookout, not only for four-legged prowlers but also two-legged beasts.

Aster weighed the texture of each shadow and the shift in the mood of the wind. A few steps short of the barn's belly, her stride quickened; the shuffles of her dress amplified; her heart raced upward. Conscious of Gudu's eyes behind the rusty gates, she blushed. Unable to carry herself past the last hurdle, she fell into his waiting arms.

In the oppressive darkness, her lips traced the contours of his mouth, and she melted in his warmth. The two lovers became one once more, sharing an intake of breath, skipping the same note of heartbeat. The forced separations, the heavy weight of the day were soon forgotten. What mattered most was the fleeting moment, and they latched on to it with the grasp of a sailor fast disappearing beneath the waves. Words did not convey what they felt for one another; a language has yet to be invented to paint the feelings they shared. The two lovers remained huddled in utter stillness until their legs could no longer support them.

A space behind a maze of broken wares became their preferred hideout as they whiled away the evening. The quietude was interrupted only by the shifting wind, which swayed and creaked the old building frame, and the occasional mice that darted across the dirt floor, attracting the attention of a barn owl. With each abrupt sound, they sat up alert, waiting for a more ominous foe to walk in through the door.

* * *

One exceptionally carefree evening, the two drifted into sleep as they sat in each other's embrace. The darkness deepened. Beasts reclaimed the night. Jackals howled as they marched toward the chicken coop; hyenas laughed at the vagaries of death as they fiddled with the cattle pen. The guard dogs raised a racket, alerting the owners to the raid. The old diviner was awakened from his sleep; he was startled to find the front door ajar. Darting out of bed, he secured the door once more. He called out Aster's name, but received no answer. Ever so cautiously, he walked into her bedroom, where he was greeted by an empty bed that had not been visited yet that night.

Overwhelmed with fear of his master's wrath, the old diviner threw the front door open and stumbled through the darkness toward the old barn. With each pace he took, his heart leapt to his mouth, blocking the passage of air. As he paused for a snatch of breath, he chanted prayers, pleas, and petitions. He promised his god that if he was shown mercy this time, if his sin was for once overlooked, he would never sleep a wink again. His fear deepened when Aster failed to answer to her name. Perspiration broke over his face. And, when he was about to drown in his own bile and pass out cold on the shifting ground, a whispered response greeted him from the deep recesses of the old building. His young charge came out rubbing her sleepy eyes.

Without much ado, the diviner grabbed Aster by the arm and dragged her along. Not a word passed between the two before they reached the safety of her home. Once behind closed doors, there was no stopping his tirade. He rattled like a crazed magistrate before a band of repeat offenders, swinging his arms wildly and pounding the table with a clenched fist. Smoke bellowed from his nose and ears. His eyes shifted markedly; his hair turned moss green. Having lost control of himself, he drifted upward, rising higher and higher, until he could go no farther because of the sturdy rafters. Only when Aster screamed in horror did he realize that he was hanging in midair.

His rage entirely spent, the diviner reached for an armchair and quickly shrank to his wrinkled self. His hands shook. Burning for water, he struggled to lift a pitcher from the table, but failed. Spilled water soaked his outfit. Moved with pity, Aster fetched a fresh jug and helped him wet his lips. She attempted to appease him, telling him an imagined reason for staying out so late. She mumbled how she had been engrossed in prayers when, overcome by a divine presence, she had passed out on the dirt floor. The ill-conceived defense served only to trigger a primitive suspicion in the tired monk. Eyes narrowed and focused, he continued regarding her. He had raised Aster from the crib; he could tell when she avoided telling the truth. Ordinarily, he would have winked at her lies, but today, under such mysterious circumstances, he did not know what to think, how to respond. With a sinking heart, he realized that a trust had been permanently severed between the two that no bonesetter could ever hope to heal.

Tossing and turning in bed, Aster reached for inner guidance to her plight. Not for the first time she compared her sequestered life with that of the young women she had grown up with, many of whom had long ago married and begun raising families of their own. Her maids and servants seemed to have an enviable life compared with her suffocating existence. For the hundredth time, she asked herself if she would ever have a say about her own life, if she would ever be allowed to choose her company. As a child, Aster had never known much of a carefree life; as an adult, her life seemed even more grim.

As she struggled in her solitude, sorting out her problems, dreams, and aspirations, an idea presented itself to Aster that almost knocked her out of bed. She sat up palpitating, mulling over a plan. The design was so dramatic, its inception so out of character for her that, at first, Aster thought the Devil had whispered the idea in her ears; she struggled to put it out of her head. But, the longer she thought it over and the harder she considered the alternative, the plot seemed to be the only course available to her. If Aster were to lead her life on her own terms, if she were to seize control of the rudder of her ship, she ought to get out of reach of her father's long arms. Aster must simply elope!

For days that followed Aster thought of nothing but realizing her dreams. Forming an escape plan was never easy, even when one had a better knowledge of the larger world than she did. The few places that Aster had visited were no different from her home—they all fostered the values and prejudices of her father. The few runaways she had known had been brought back home in shackles. Count Ashenafi had ridden ahead of a posse more times than Aster cared to remember, hunting down runaway slaves, even when one of those runaways was the property of a loathed neighbor. One could only imagine what he would do for his own daughter.

The only fugitives who seemed to have successfully eluded capture and gone on to live life on their own terms were bandits and murderers. Fables were replete with their adventures. Poems were composed for them. Women named their sons after the most celebrated outlaws in the hope that their bravery would rub off on their children. Some of these rebels returned home years later, following a royal pardon, and their fame and fortune blossomed as they entranced a paying audience with colorful accounts of their wild exploits. Invited to high office, they influenced policy-makers in their effort to curb banditry. A few went on to write guidebooks, advising frequent travelers on how to survive an encounter with the occasional outlaw or territorial beast.

Some of the reported escapades were, indeed, the stuff of legend. There was a man in Kersa, for instance, who tackled a pride of lions barehanded, killed the resident male with a swift movement of his arm, impregnated all his females, and waited in the open savanna for months on end to witness the safe delivery of eight cubs with eerie human features on the torso of a beast. The most remarkable feat of all time was, perhaps, that of a young man who had trained the two orphaned cheetah cubs he had rescued how to sing the Sixth Hymn before reintroducing them to the wild. The Supreme Pontiff of the Shrine of Mawu-Lisa considered this account blasphemous, and sentenced the egotist to fifty public lashes.

Confronted with the certainty of her own adventures in the wild, Aster spent many afternoons reviewing the documented cases. In four short weeks she read nine large tomes and six ancient scrolls; she spoke to visiting elders about the unwritten accounts of legendary fugitives. Upon being granted a rare audience with the Oral Historian of the province, she spent five days under the spell of his learning.

The Oral Historian, whose old age could only be approximated from the number of wars he had lived through, was a breathing archive, more versed in what went on in his domain than the library of a reputable monastery. His knowledge had been passed on to him through word of mouth and spanned fifty generations. It covered all battles concluded between nobles in the province, all slaves bought and sold, marriages ordained and annulled, prayers answered and celebrated, criminals sent to the gallows, and fugitives of justice. He knew of the infidelities of his subjects and the bastards they often left behind—the single most profitable and closely guarded piece of information in his archive. (Many a lord pays handsomely to keep his extramarital affairs secret from the prying eyes of a righteous monk.) And, like all oral historians before him, he kept his treasure out of print, passing it on to a chosen son in small installments.

Aster learned of the existence of underground kingdoms, tunneled by men who had run out of places to hide in the open; criminals who had mastered the art of changing their skins, and, therefore, lived out their lives without leaving their familiar surroundings. Accounts of the Oral Historian, like the faded documents she had read, gave little consolation to Aster. She realized with a heavy heart that life in the wilderness was, indeed, the stuff of legend. Besides the constant struggle to stay a step ahead of a stalking beast, such an existence was riddled with the uncertainties of a spring rain. If Aster were to elude the steel grip of her father and live life on her own terms, she needed to think of a place where no one knew her name. Aster was debating with herself in the company of her sorrows when the veil that shrouded her private life began to fall away.

A CHANGING DIVINER

Premonition might have been one reason. The need to vent his heartache was certainly another. Barely days after his close brush with the Ashenafi diviner in the old barn, Gudu decided to confide in me about his secret affair with Aster. Even at the age of ten, my instincts were sharp enough to figure out that this was not another of his common adventures.

I was no stranger to Gudu's liaisons with women. On many occasions I had accompanied him to his secret rendezvous with one girl or another, servants who had left home on the pretext of gathering firewood, doing the laundry at the stream, or collecting water. While the two capered, my job was to keep guard, watching for passersby who might walk in on them.

Only once before had Gudu experienced a dangerous escapade. The young woman concerned was the servant of an affluent merchant. Her master, who had moved to the valley of Deder only recently, had built himself the most extravagant mansion at the outskirts of town. High stone walls spiked with broken glass girded the residence. Little of what passed inside the compound trickled out. As the family kept out of all religious, social, and other communal affairs, even their spiritual bent was a topic for debate. I was, therefore, quite surprised to learn that Gudu had met and won the heart of one of the merchant's servants.

Soon I would join Gudu in his trysts with the young lady and partake of the bounty he unfailingly received from her. Gudu and I would approach the stone wall circling the mansion, passing an old blind lady who invariably sat just outside the manor gates enjoying the last of the sunshine. Though her eyes were unable to witness what occurred next, she could always hear Gudu whistling to the young maid in a treble code, which changed from week to week. Upon hearing the whistle, the young lady dropped a prepared package over the wall and into Gudu's hands. In the package were sweets and choice tidbits from the day's menu. The dishes were excellent, exotic, and very well prepared. Gudu and I would run past the blind woman with our bounty and find a hiding place where we could enjoy the gastronomic spoils of his adventure.

The blind woman was a relative of the lady of the manor. She described to the woman of the house the strange occurrence that seemed to take place so often. The old woman was confused by hearing a strange whistle, one that invariably caused a commotion in the kitchen, followed by the steps of someone running past her, package rustling in hand.

The next time Gudu came to the fence and whistled, the two of us were doused with a large bucketful of dirty dishwater and regaled with the colorful curses of the lady of the house. Curses no less choice or well prepared than her secret desserts had been. We didn't stay to hear the final pronouncement. We bolted, running for a full league before stopping short and laughing. The young maid in question, unfortunately, was relieved of her duties and had to move out of the valley for her part in the affair.

Gudu's affair with his master's daughter was unlikely to have such a humorous end. If there were someone who had sense enough to flee the valley now, I realized, it was not Aster. I saw the biggest danger in the Ashenafi diviner, who might at any moment pounce on the two lovers unawares. The old man was known to have accomplished feats beyond human powers. Once, a grain merchant who had stopped by to deliver two sacks of sorghum found himself detained by the diviner, who had detected tightly packed bales of hay hidden deep inside the bulk without having to open the securely woven sack. When the hay was removed, only three-quarters of the sack was found to contain grain. The merchant stammered his innocence, arguing that someone had tampered with his merchandise while he had left it unattended, but the diviner was unconvinced. Count Ashenafi ordered the deceptive merchant a punishment of ten lashes and had his merchandise confiscated.

Another trader—an Arab man who brought his trinkets of looking glasses, boxes of matches, pans, and pails to the valley to exchange for ivory, coffee, the skins of lions, leopards, or zebra, and the occasional slave—found himself grilled for a crime that he thought he had managed to get away with. The Arab had killed his partner in the wilderness and stolen his merchandise and mount. The old diviner exposed the offense by whispering to the deceased man's horse. The guilty merchant lost not only his merchandise to Count Ashenafi—who felt legally bound to confiscate the properties of criminal itinerants—but also his freedom. A judge sentenced him to life in a dugout.

Count Ashenafi's diviner's type is known to change skin at will, turning into a perceivable other self or, sometimes, an invisible presence. Famed diviners might assume, for instance, the form of a straw-tailed whydah, a pied crow, a golden-breasted starling, or a white-tailed mongoose.

Neither Gudu nor anyone else in the valley of Deder could say for certain which one of the sacred little creatures the Ashenafi diviner could become. But a fortuitous event brought to the valley the *ergum* charmer who had been responsible for Gudu's safe return home. An *ergum* charmer was hardly the person to consult in matters pertaining to the identities of a skin-changer, or for advice on the course of a love affair. But both Gudu and I felt that since this particular expert was unlike any mortal we had seen, or heard of, her knowledge would know no bounds.

The *ergum* charmer had changed markedly during the past month: she had lost almost a foot of her diminutive height. But the most significant symptom of her decline was her pale skin, which showed signs of turning green, and the extremities of her fingers and toes, which she had wrapped in white bandages, confirming sceptics' predictions that her nails would soon run out. All her assistants had donned black cloth, validating the rumor that she was fading quickly. The *ergum* charmer no longer blared her pronouncements through a horn. Instead, she whispered her findings to one of her aides, who in turn announced it out loud to the crowd. She tired easily. There was still a large crowd waiting when she decided to retire for the day.

Gudu and I sneaked into her tent via an unattended side flap. If our unexpected appearance at her bedside surprised her, she didn't show it. The *ergum* charmer was in no condition to speculate on the secret identities of the diviner without the old man's clean underwear and brush twig to analyze, but she did agree to help Gudu with his amorous entanglements and asked him to extend his palm. She read his inner secrets as written on the crisscrossed lines of his lighter skin, turning from page to page—from left palm to right. Unsatisfied, she asked him to get closer and peered into the valleys of his eyes, moving her temple lamp from side to side for better inspection. The *ergum* charmer sighed a sigh of frustration and dropped her head on her pillow.

Gudu was mystified to learn that there was a silver string, an endless chain, that bound him, his mother Enquan, Aster, and the count firmly together, which the *ergum* charmer was unable to unravel in what little time she had on earth. What lay ahead for him was no clearer to her than his beginnings had been. She gave him, however, a small pouch that she pulled out from under her pillow, as a temporary remedy. In the pouch was an ashlike substance that Gudu mixed in the diviner's snuffbox as instructed. No one was more surprised by the effects of the concoction than Gudu himself.

Soon after the diviner took a pinch of the special snuff, he turned into a zombie, not dead but not entirely conscious either. At first Aster was cautious, believing that the old man was playing a trick. She threw scoops of gruel at the walls, knowing that such wastefulness would upset the diviner more than the loss of an arm; she even cracked unseemly jokes to see if his eyes would betray a twitch. But the diviner was as good as dead until the effects of the potion wore off with the first croak of a rooster at dawn.

And so the two lovers resumed their affectionate embrace in the safety and comfort of a lit room and under the nose of their enemy.

Not that they indulged in any immoral act, mind you. For nothing that would cause an angel to blush passed in those nights. It was the mere act of sharing a breath of air, holding hands, or gazing into each other's eyes in mute silence that comforted them.

Outward expression of love and affection has never been part of our culture. At the time of those early meetings between Gudu and Aster, holding hands in public, much less caressing each other, was considered ostentatious. To admit that one was in love was bad form; besides revealing one's vulnerabilities, such an admission was considered unmanly. Lovers never display their innermost feelings to each other, unless it is when attending a partner at his or her deathbed and it is clear that one will never be asked to repeat the words that escape one's lips there.

Gudu and Aster have been, and will always remain, the epitome of love to me, the true subjects of romantic poetry. I can still picture the two arm in arm, foreheads pressed against each other, the tips of their noses rubbing. I vividly recall those enchanted moments when the only noise that punctuated the still night came from the snore of the diviner in the corner.

Like babies chuckling at the sounds of a key chain, they were amused by my most outlandish pranks. I found my favorite jest in toying with the old diviner quietly lying in the corner. I painted his face with ash and soot and planted feathers in his hairs. I mimicked his shrill voice and habit of twitching his mouth. As I gazed at his prostrate form while trying to think of the next prank, I felt that he had stopped breathing. Unlike the days before when his face twitched or he groaned, no sound emanated from him. I was about to hold his nose, forcing him to cough, when he suddenly came to. "So, this is what you two have been doing!" he suddenly barked at Gudu and Aster, still locked in each other's arms.

Aster screamed in horror. Gudu flew from his seat. I darted under the giant dinner table and hid my face behind a forest of chair legs. "So, this is what you two have been cooking up," the old man repeated, rising to his full height. He barely noticed me at his feet. His attention shifted from Gudu to Aster. Aster stood with her back pressed to the wall, her hands on her mouth, tears rolling down her face.

"You should leave now," the diviner instructed Gudu, in a much calmer voice. "And you, too," he added, without looking my way.

The diviner had been troubled by the time he couldn't account for—the better half of most days. For weeks, he couldn't remember where and how he spent his after-dinner hours. When he noticed that his snuffbox, which usually emptied in three to four days, had remained half-full after three weeks, he realized that something was amiss. That fateful night he had quietly replaced the contents of his snuffbox. Sticking to his old habit, he had sniffed a couple of pinches of the tobacco in full view of Aster, the only other person he expected to see in the room, and he had pretended to pass out, only to witness what occurred next.

I might have been the only one of the three who slept that night. Gudu didn't even go to bed. Despite his mother's baffled pleas, he passed the night sitting outside his home, under the thatched roof, gazing at Aster's residence from afar. It came as little surprise to me, or Gudu, that Aster spent her night being grilled by the diviner for compromising herself with, of all living things, her father's chattel.

If Gudu had expected to face his master's wrath the next morning and follow the route of Areru the Shorter to markets afar, he was pleasantly surprised when nothing more than simple restrictions were imposed on him by the diviner, who told him never to set foot near Aster again. It was as though the old diviner had reached deep inside himself for unexpected kindness. Only days later would the true reason for his seeming goodwill became clear: the diviner had decided to take the place of Gudu in Aster's heart!

The night after he worked out what had been going on, the diviner went to Aster's residence uncharacteristically drunk. His eyes wandered nervously. His mouth twitched so badly that he could barely finish a sentence. Unable to rest in one place, he paced up and down, circling her chair, like a jackal wearing out a formidable prey. He touched Aster's back and fondled her hair. Aster didn't think anything of his moves until she felt his hand sliding down her chest.

She shot out of her seat in disgust. "You must leave now," she ordered, as though her fate were in her hands. Her adversary gave a wry smile, and reminded her that the young slave was still alive.

"I am going to scream," she continued.

"No, you won't."

"What has come over you? You are like a father to me," she attempted to reason with him.

"But I am not!" He sounded as though he was about to cry. "I am a man! More of a man than that slave who has been fondling you!"

Aster darted to her bedroom, latched the door, and fortified it with chairs and boxes. In the days that followed, it became routine for the diviner to come home drunk and attempt to force himself on her, and for Aster to fortify her hideout. She suffered in her solitude. Whom was she to confide in? Whom should she ask for help? Little wonder that when her father declared war on the tenants of Harar and saddled his horse for an uncertain outcome, Aster was the only one in the valley who applauded the scheme. Count Ashenafi never left on an expedition without his diviner by his side.

PESKY PEASANTS

A year had already passed since Count Ashenafi had made a small concession to a throng of peasants camped at his doorstep: the postponement of the deadline for payment of all taxes and tributes owed to him for another twelve months and the return of the livestock and sacks of grains that his soldiers had carried off. He had even dipped into his dwindling granary and handed them bags of seed for the coming harvest. Now that the year was up, he had yet to hear good tidings from them.

He had heard something from them, though. Not long after they arrived home the peasants sent emissaries, advising him of their displeasure with the terms imposed on them. It seemed unjust to them that Count Ashenafi should lay claim to tributes for the period before he had been granted jurisdiction over Harar. The unpaid dues for those years should have gone to the emperor, but His Highness hadn't dispatched his cavaliers to balance the account, as in past years when he had suspected a tax revolt. The tenants of Harar had taken his lack of response to mean tax exemption. Now, more than ever before, they hung on to their convictions.

Count Ashenafi hadn't sorted out their differences in interpretation of the royal edict when he encountered further dissent: the peasants refused to pay up even the moneys that they admitted owing him. The drought had not let up. The farmers' gamble with the rains had cost them bags of seed that would have saved their families from a certain famine. Disease had run rampant, claiming much of their herd. What little remained of their livestock had fallen prey to wild beasts, which had grown bolder and more daring with the lengthening drought.

One hazy afternoon, the peasants vented their frustrations on two messengers dispatched by their master, roughing them up and leaving them for dead in an open ditch. Count Ashenafi could not possibly ignore this act of provocation without appearing an imbecile in the eyes of his peers. He called for a passage of arms.

Some two hundred men showed up to lend Count Ashenafi a hand. More than half were friends and relations, the rest, chanting foot soldiers. Count Ashenafi had never asked for any help other than that of his usual army of bondsmen, feudal tenants, and the overseer. As a man who bore arms long before he could lace up his boots, he recognized the strength and weakness of his opponents. He knew, for instance, that when it came to a pitched battle, peasants were not worth their salt, that they might fire the first bullet, but they would also fall victim to the ricochet. He was even less charitable toward the tenants of Harar, who, he believed, could easily be subdued by a choir of nuns armed only with crooked firewood. Asking for reinforcements was giving the enemy undue credit, he declared, and urged his kinfolk to disband.

But his kinfolk had clear enough heads on their shoulders to realize that peasants never sow before readying the seedbed. A covert hand was at work. Examples abounded of how Amma warriors had joined the ranks of beleaguered villagers in disguise and fought off superior armies. Only the year before, a celebrated feudal lord had been pitifully defeated by an army of feudal tenants. Held captive, the man languished in a dugout cell for twenty-five days while his family raised the indemnity imposed. The same year, a lord in hot pursuit of two runaway slaves was ambushed by high-minded Ammas who left their signature—nipping off his ears—before letting him loose.

Count Ashenafi was finally persuaded to retain the reinforcements, but he wouldn't be reined in until the war preparations were complete. Confident that the battle wouldn't last more than a day, he did not even enlist the company of priests when he rode ahead of the militia in the rosy glow of the waking sun. Women ululated behind the army. Troupes sang war songs, and the shrine bells chimed until the trail of dust that sprang up with the marching men died down two hours after their passage.

The excitement propelling the musketeers subsided with the pitch of the rising sun until, at high noon, quiet reigned. Eagles curved in circles in the vault of the blue sky. A lone starling, perched atop an acacia tree, sang songs of solitude. Every now and then, a meerkat emerged from its underground burrow to review the advancing army from the safety of a molehill or a fallen tree.

The journey that would normally have taken three to four days stretched into an arduous week as the foot soldiers and coolies struggled to negotiate the scorched earth barefoot. Some of the men took sick in the open savanna, struck down by the sudden appearance of the moon and the glare of a passing wild dog. They had to be left behind to find their way home. Many more men succumbed to hunger and sunstroke as the food supply diminished barely four days into the journey. There were no villages to raid for food, no wild game the Good Book permitted to be consumed. On the seventh day, when the campaigners had all but surrendered before reaching the battlefield, they arrived in Harar, but the element of surprise had been lost on the way.

Armored in a thin crust of dust and grime, the musketeers stood gawking at the closed gates of the ancient town. To most of the warriors it was a new experience to come across a walled community. None had ever gone to war with an enemy they couldn't see. In his long list of battlefield achievements, Count Ashenafi couldn't cite a single instance where he had had to scale a curtaining wall to ply his weapons.

The campaign that had begun with unpaid tributes quickly turned into a battle of wills as the musketeers, like the besieged villagers, refused to consider a middle course. Count Ashenafi wouldn't compromise, because to do so meant, in his eyes, admitting defeat. The villagers wouldn't give in for fear of being levied retributions beyond the means of an affluent prince.

Seething in their pent-up anxiety, the soldiers set camp for the night. Bonfires were lit, and the din of angry musketeers reverberated through the still shadows, as invasion plans were drafted, debated, and revised. Horses whinnied; they pounded on the dirt floor and farted. Pairs of twinkling eyes emerged from the deep recesses of the darkness, stirring up a shuffle in the herd; alert guards chased away the stalking beasts before they could claim a feast.

In the small hours of the morning, the soldiers were awakened by a tide of urgent hooves. Their horses were galloping on a cloud of rising dirt, bucking invisible riders as they wove in and out of the woods with maniacal fury. Some among the men attempted to rein in the excited beasts, only to be caught up in a deadly stampede. Others took up positions, guns drawn, for a wave of raiders that did not arrive. Instead, a draft of winged enemies visited them. With a sense of dread they realized that someone had sneaked into the camp under cover of darkness and unleashed a hive of bees on the horses. When the damage was assessed at dawn, two-thirds of the horses had gone missing, but the most mystifying loss to Count Ashenafi was the old diviner, who lay dead in his blood-soaked *gabbi*; his throat had been slit from ear to ear.

Deprived of their mounts and short on all provisions, the musketeers were pressed into seeking an early conclusion to the standoff. Trees were felled and ladders hastily constructed. Two men volunteered to brave the unknown in order to unlock the fortified gates, but no sooner had they poked their heads above the spiked stone walls than they fell back to the parched earth below, caught in a hail of whizzing arrows. The besiegers had just been given their first lesson in the art of siege warfare.

Not a man given to easy capitulation, Count Ashenafi rallied his men yet again for another engagement. He set his eyes on the weakest link of the fortification—the wooden gates. Trees were felled once more, and the largest of the trunks was fashioned into a battering ram. Forty strong men were chosen for the task. A crowd of hungry musketeers cheered the assault team as it rammed the wooden gate with diabolical ferocity. Echoes of the shivering walls reverberated through the mountains and the valleys. Weaverbirds took to the air, abandoning their nesting trees in fright; an army of wattled cranes made a swooping detour over the wrinkling sky to inspect the racket.

The sun ran out of fuel and vanished. Pressure built up on the crusaders to come up with something drastic if they were to avoid spending another night in the cold and with empty stomachs. A ray of hope flashed when frantic calls were heard emanating from behind the walls, followed by the unmistakable sight of a wooden platform being dragged toward the entrance. The besiegers knew that it was a desperate attempt to try to reinforce a battered gate with a wooden platform. And while they were musing over the folly of the enemy, a few heads popped up from the towering structure to spy on the assault team. Without warning, a shower of oven-baked sand was thrown over the gate, dousing the besiegers.

Tortured cries shattered the closing day as the singed soldiers rolled in the dirt, tearing at their hair and clothes with wild abandon to dislodge the tiny grains of red-hot sand that clung to their skin. There was no water in the area to soothe their searing hides, no leafy plants to wrap around themselves. Hours after calm was finally restored, the pouting men were still huddled at the remote end of the camp, naked, with the resigned look of baboons that have been banished from their ancestral colony.

Another day dawned, and a different team was organized with the benefit of the recent experience. The men wrapped themselves with borrowed layers of cloth and dappled hide, leaving no patch of skin exposed. Their mummified figures might have afforded them needless anonymity, but the cloth was no protection from the enterprising enemy, for buckets of scalding water were tossed at them. As they struggled to remove the soaking layers of cloth, showers of quicklime were visited on them. The acid blinded some of the men; the rest escaped with searing skin.

Despair gave way to panic. The campaign that had been so hastily organized and launched had just remade itself, becoming a monster with a life of its own, intent on consuming the author who had breathed life into it. Count Ashenafi was no more in control of events than an aimless wildebeest riding a high tide at dusk. Many of his soldiers stole away under cover of darkness, thinning the ranks of the able-bodied men. Those who stayed behind attempted to prevail upon their master, urging him to abandon his senseless effort. But Count Ashenafi, a man of aggressive mien and acquisitive habits, could not easily be deterred.

Many a potentate had made an attempt to bring Harar to its knees. Tenants of the walled town arched their backs, knowing that a siege-maker was unlikely to achieve a quick victory unless he had a ten-to-one superiority in strength and a deep pocket afforded only by a prince or a king. If only Count Ashenafi had bothered to consult the history books, he would have read of warlords who had lost their shirts and saddlebags on a siege that lasted longer than their meager resources could support. Harar was brought into the folds of the expanding empire only because the emperor had acquired a cannon—a weapon beyond the means of a common war-maker.

Count Ashenafi committed himself to personal and financial ruin when he decided to stay the course. The ball that had slipped out of his fingers would soon roll far beyond the small perimeters drawn, luring all eyes and ears to this remote enclave. Storytellers, poets, chroniclers, and admirals crossed mountains and valleys to witness the outcome of the siege. Bookmakers raised a chorus, congregating under shifting shadows, as they took bets on the casualties of the day and the outcome of each engagement. Spell-casters strove to influence the outcome of each encounter through the powers of their concoctions, sprinkling ominous muck on the route of unsuspecting besiegers one day and tossing a mysterious fetish over the wall the next.

Through it all, Gudu secluded himself in a remote corner of the army's camp, brooding over the wantonness of justice. Gudu had not been asked to draw his sword on the renegade tenants. He was only required to entertain the soldiers and keep watch over the encampment for possible infiltrators. But the experience was no less painful to him. The Siege of Harar had revealed to Gudu a dark side of people that he had not known about before. He was disturbed how the most reasonable of persons—my father, to name one—could easily turn into an unseemly beast, viewing the men and women behind the walls as though they were a plague of mosquitoes.

Dad had proposed shooting arrows at random over the walls. He argued that with the absence of information on the enemy movement, the only clue to the whereabouts of the defenders lay in the wails of the shot victims. Wherever the pitch of the racket was the highest, he offered, the besiegers ought to concentrate the assault. Count Ashenafi ruled against the initiative on the ground of limited supplies of arrows.

All his life Gudu had seen mothers snatch food from their children's mouths to sate the ever-burgeoning appetite of the master of the manor; fathers, forced to spill the blood of a cousin, not because of personal animosity but because the two belonged to feuding lords. However repulsive these practices might have been, he reasoned that they were the human miseries that stitched together the fraying rags of the imperial drape.

What Gudu couldn't comprehend, what no one could explain to him, was, however, why anyone would even begin to contemplate showering a village full of children, women, and elders with blind arrows, when their only crime was boycotting the payment of tributes. He was repulsed by the men of God—priests, deacons, and monks—who applauded the excesses of the murderers, looters, and war-crazed; these men of God hadn't paused for a moment to reflect on the plight of those at the receiving end of Count Ashenafi's wrath. It was, perhaps, this particular episode more than anything else that cultivated Gudu's rebelliousness.

The battle had reached a stalemate. Only outside help seemed to hold the key for an end to the deadlock. A spell-caster was the obvious choice; shadowy men always swarm battlefields with the promise of a favorable outcome for the price of half the loot. Count Ashenafi had never been the type who would pay a spell-caster to bail him out of a war that he had taken upon himself; nor would he accept reinforcements offered by complete strangers—warlords who had made a common cause with him. Self-reliant as ever, he struck upon an idea, during the third week of the siege, that promised a turning point to the drawn-out battle: he decided to dig his way into the fortification.

Success or failure of the plan hinged on complete secrecy. It was necessary to keep not only the besieged in the dark, but also the ever-increasing number of spectators and speculators. Though victory meant a record bounty to the besiegers, miscarriage of the scheme would amount to suicide for Count Ashenafi, who, having lost over half of his men to desertion and mishaps, barely held his own.

Provisions were urgently needed. It takes well-fed men to mine fields of rocks and taproots; spades and shovels were in short supply, and concealing the tunnel mouth from prying eyes meant erecting a tent camp. Four men were dispatched to Deder to raise the supplies required. It would be the first opportunity for family members left behind to learn about the fate of their loved ones at the warfront.

GREEN AND ALIVE

Her father's excesses were more punishing to his own flesh and blood than to anyone else, it seemed to Aster. She spent her morning hours at the shrine doorsteps, praying. She burned incense and *ood*, and drifted in the world of aromatic plumes, reassessing her fate and the plight of her young love. She visited a seer who had taken up residence in one of the burial chambers. She listened with rapt attention as he communicated to her the intelligence he had received from the warfront, care of his spirit messengers. The tidings were always given to Aster in riddles, so she spent many wakeful hours attempting to interpret their meaning. "A two-headed hawk has darkened the horizon," the seer began, one fine morning. "The dove of peace is in danger, but one shouldn't lose hope, for the fig of righteousness is still green and alive."

Before the morning was out, Aster called upon her former guard, Areru the Taller, who was still chained to a tree. From her kitchen, she brought him a basket filled with choice food, the sheer quantity of which did not betray the fact that a minor famine was spreading throughout the country. Aster sat at the foot of the tree, watching her beneficiary devour the delicacies with pathetic haste; she entreated him, in her soft-spoken manner, not to choke himself since no one was about to snatch so much as one morsel from him. After the meal, she lingered about, comforting him.

Neighbors cast curious glances at her, congregating at doorsteps and kitchen windows, wondering whether her mind had gone. Aster's affection for her father was never in doubt. Her father's passion for war was not new, either. In fact, the battlefield was to Count Ashenafi what a monastery is to a dedicated monk. He had always spent many of his idle moments preparing for a nonimminent conflict; conducting a war game with friends and visitors; analyzing a long-concluded battle, or wagering on the outcome of an ongoing one. Count Ashenafi had saddled his horse for a battlefield more often than his spiritual counselor could count.

The mystery surrounding Aster's afflictions deepened after the arrival of the envoy from Harar. Seldom was she seen outside again; she spent most of her waking hours bent over her dining-room table, drafting letters. She copied page after page of hymns and prayers for Gudu. Realizing that her correspondence with her guard would be thoroughly scrutinized, she left out all personal references. Instead, Aster communicated her most private and intimate affairs in invisible ink.

A fortuitous event that had taken place months before came to Aster's rescue. In an idle moment she had dipped her quill pen into a half-eaten orange and scribbled a note on a piece of paper. Holding the paper up to the candlelight, she discovered that the letters, initially invisible, sprang up to life when heated. Both Aster and Gudu marveled at the discovery, and whiled away many a lazy evening sending each other invisible notes; neither had foreseen that this minor breakthrough would, one day, serve as their only lifeline.

On the back of the innocuous letter Aster scribbled her tender feelings, confessing to Gudu things that she wouldn't dare say to him in person. She told him of the tortured love that burned like a fire between her legs. She told him of a very revealing dream she had had, butterflies seemed to spring out of her skin. Leaving the cocoon of her body, the tiny creatures hovered over her bed before turning into a baby in her arms. She left out, however, how she had shot out of bed in a cold sweat when she realized that the baby's face was blank, with no eyes, ears, mouth, or any other human feature. Enclosing a few orange fruits, Aster sealed the package.

* * *

Soon, the two lovers were trading not just love letters but escape plans as well. Gudu had come across men of the Amma faith at the warfront. He had been impressed by their candid and friendly demeanor. Many afternoons, after the merchants had peddled their supplies of milk and grains to the besieging army, they sat down under a tree to have their meal and invited Gudu to join them. Initially he was taken aback by the offer, suspecting that the Ammas were unaware of his social standing. When he found out that slavery had no more meaning to the nomads than a camel with wings, he was driven to tears. He eased into their warmth; he shared with them his deepest feelings for Aster and their intentions to elope. He received not only warm words of encouragement, but also the promise of support should he ever need help.

The growing power and influence of Ammas in the region heartened Gudu. Even Count Ashenafi seemed to acknowledge their mounting influence when he speculated that the besieged enemy could not have held out for so long—over three months—without a secret supply of food and armaments from the nomads. The days were gone when a feudal lord could enforce his wishes on the Ammas with impunity. But just as Gudu dreamed of returning home alive and putting his romantic plans into effect, the Siege of Harar took an unexpected turn.

After four arduous weeks of tunneling, the besiegers had completed a three-hundred-foot-long underground passage. If the besieged enemy had learned of the scheme, it hadn't let on. As the final fifty feet were being dug, the anticipation of success was so unbearable to Count Ashenafi that he refused to sleep. Then came the last few shovelfuls of dirt. The final wall of earth came down, and from their cramped hole, the diggers lay staring not at an open courtyard where the enemy blissfully sauntered—as everyone had expected—but at the existing ring of a defensive tunnel.

Unbeknownst to the miners, the walls of the ancient hamlet had been girded by a tunnel, leading away from the fort. In times past, a flood of water had been diverted from a nearby river to drown another mining enemy. Today, a wall of smoke greeted the would-be intruders. A pile of firewood doused in kerosene had been lit the moment the miners stumbled into the trap. The smoke grew deep and heavy, competing with the retreating army for the narrow exit. Few managed to drag themselves to safety. Over twenty of the vanguard perished, their remains entombed in blankets of soot.

For two days, Count Ashenafi broke no bread. He didn't sleep either. He paced up and down the woods, muttering to himself. He did everything he could to avoid human company, and, when that proved impossible, he refused to look anyone in the eye. The shame of failure weighed on him so heavily that he couldn't stand up straight anymore. He seemed to have aged more quickly during those couple of days than he had in the past five years. After three days, when friends and relations were wondering if he would ever snap out of his trance, Count Ashenafi called a meeting. Eyes glazed by the crackling bonfire, he admitted failure—something that no one had ever expected to hear coming from his lips—and that he needed outside help.

Many a warlord engages a spiritualist to influence the outcome of a war he is involved in. A priest may consecrate a campaign, and may even join the soldiers on the battlefield in a total effort to shore up their fighting spirit; a spell-caster is hired to curse the wretched enemy. But as the war drags on and divine intervention proves hopelessly distant, an Abettor is sought.

A self-appointed admiral, the Abettor is versed in the art of modern warfare, developments in armaments, the strengths and weaknesses of warring parties in his domain, and, above all, is the deciding factor in the most prickly situations. Driven by his passion for a fair fight more than any personal reward or gratification, a good Abettor thinks nothing of abetting both belligerents in a given engagement.

A celebrated Abettor came to the rescue of Count Ashenafi. A slight man with wooden dentures, the war broker had spent many of his ninety-three years crisscrossing territories, often with little regard for political borders, in search of a war to sponsor. He was a living archive: at his fingertips were all the battles that had been fought in his vast domain for the past six centuries and the strategies and tactics that had endured through generations. He was well acquainted with the armaments and able-bodied men within reach of not just princes and kings but also the lesser war-makers—feudal lords.

A quick study of human nature, the Abettor realized that men may endure without bread and water but not without war, and so he made it his calling to afford them a fair and refreshing combat. He spent his days and nights sniffing for gunpowder, carrying on his back his worldly possessions of an old rifle, the Holy Scriptures, an extra copy of the Book of Hymns, and a small sacrifice for the road. He slept while walking. Having adjusted his needs to the ever-shifting clime, he could go without food or water for up to six months. Only in times of abundant harvest did he answer the call of nature.

Though many brave men had sought him out in times of pressing need, the war patriarch had failed to earn their affection. A few of the people he had so diligently served had conspired to put him out of service in the most hideous ways. In an ordinary year, he could expect to be stabbed to death twice. Once, an army of retreating archers shot him with ninety-five arrows. On three different occasions, he was carved into palm-sized pieces and his remains served to hawks and storks; he was also known to have been buried alive. But, each time, the old man resurfaced in some remote corner of the kingdom in one piece, invigorated by his ordeal, ready to influence the outcome of another raging war.

His fortunes changed for the better one memorable summer when a young prince, who was engaged in a pitched battle with his older sibling over the family inheritance, invited him to intercede. When the Abettor arrived four weeks later, the young heirs had already settled their differences through intermediaries and were celebrating the occasion in grand style. In a fit of drunken frenzy, the brothers seized the Abettor, tied him to a stout post, and set him alight. They watched, jeering, as his tottering silhouette changed form, becoming a two-legged zebra. Then, in quick succession, he turned into an impala, a young okapi, a red duiker, a dik-dik, and finally a crowned hornbill before fluttering out of the ashes, clucking *kok, kok* at his wide-eyed tormentors. The banqueting crowd quieted down at once. They prostrated themselves before the charred remains of the post and prayed in unison, asking the forgiveness of the Almighty, swearing never again to cast a bad eye on the war merchant. And so the Abettor, though still despised, was never molested again.

What you need is a catapult," the Abettor pronounced, his contempt for Count Ashenafi's lack of resourcefulness clearly written on his face.

"What is a catapult?" Count Ashenafi queried.

"It is a stone-throwing engine."

"Who can craft such a device?"

"An Englishman."

A small army of volunteers was dispatched in search of an Englishman—it was thought that one might be roaming the region renaming rivers and mountains. Four days and twenty leagues later, the party came across three merchants leading a caravan of camels. At gunpoint, the merchants were led to the army camp. Count Ashenafi, not wanting to waste time on niceties, barked at the captives what he expected of them as wandering Englishmen.

"But we are Arabs," they protested.

"The same thing," he snapped at them, rattling off his tactical requirements. Not to appear entirely insensitive, however, he promised the merchants exclusive access to the markets of Kersa and Harar if and when they succeeded in their endeavor. He also promised to lend them his name when they crossed the open savanna, lest an outlaw ambush them. In the unfortunate event that they failed to live up to his expectations, Count Ashenafi promised not to break up their party. "You will hang from the same tree," he assured them.

The merchants spent two days and two nights under the watchful eyes of their captors, knocking their heads together. Daylight hours were spent under the shade of a eucalyptus tree, drafting stone-throwing engines, and the night, camped around a crackling bonfire, building a miniature machine that they tested and improved. On the third day, they announced success.

"But to build the siege engine, we need two stout posts, a sturdy beam, and a bundle of human hair," they declared.

"Why the human hair?" Count Ashenafi queried, suspicious.

"To weave a rope."

"Why not use sisal fiber?"

"Plant fiber is not elastic enough," was their authoritative reply.

Sensing a hidden plot in the unusual request, yet determined not to be outwitted by nameless merchants, Count Ashenafi dispatched a group of armed men to raid a nearby village for tufts of human hair. The soldiers rounded up every woman with a head of hair measuring one foot in length or more. They led each woman to a nearby shrine, where she was briefed about the war effort and her patriotic duty before a monk was instructed to shave her over her thunderous protest. Before long the bundled hair, along with three logs of wood, was delivered to the ingenious merchants.

The merchants plaited yards of ropes from the imported hair. Erecting the twin posts side by side, they ran two ropes between them. The beam was then placed between the ropes and twisted. Once an adequate torsion was generated, a large rock was placed on one end of the beam and—after muffled prayers—the boulder was launched.

Alas, the boulder landed where no one expected it to go, right behind the gawking crowd, almost killing two of Count Ashenafi's favorite musketeers. All the effort that had gone into building the mangonel—not to mention the long trudge to the village and the struggle that had ensued with a mob of screaming women—seemed lost. Count Ashenafi was about to pronounce his judgment about the fate of the deceitful merchants when a second boulder was hurled, after a small fiddling with the engine, and it landed close to the perimeter wall. A sigh of relief emanated from the crowd.

The third boulder fell right inside the fortified town, where it was greeted by a tortured scream. The musketeers cheered. The merchants winced. Tears of joy welling up in him, Count Ashenafi dabbed his eyes with the end of his *gabbi*. Words failed him when he attempted to thank the men who had so resourcefully rescued his tottering stature. The occasion warranted that he do the most appropriate thing, so Count Ashenafi gave word that all three merchants be tied to the post of their contraption. It would be a pity, he reasoned, if they were secretly to escape and build a countermangonel for the besieged enemy.

* * *

And so, with a newfangled weapon in his arsenal, Count Ashenafi embarked on a renewed and energetic assault. In three short days, a small mountain of rocks was delivered over the perimeter fortification. A pile of shrubs was lit and tossed across the wall. And, as their creative genius flourished, the besiegers employed more diversified weapons to shower on the besieged. Finally, the day arrived when someone advanced an idea that marked the turning point of the lengthy battle.

Hyenas and wild dogs were hunted, and their remains were left under the blazing sun until the rancid smell became unbearable. The rotting carcasses were then mounted at the tips of the launching beam and hurled over the wall. Germ warfare was born. A mere four days later, the besieged sued for peace, sending an emissary over the wall with the conditions of their surrender. Count Ashenafi beamed with the rare satisfaction of someone who has ripped out of the beast that once swallowed him alive. He snatched the piece of paper from the messenger, and with only a swift glance decided that it was not to his liking. To emphasize his displeasure, he fastened the messenger to the end of the launching beam, with a reply note pinned to the man's chest, and hurled him over the wall.

Dawn broke over a quiet horizon. For the first time since the rowdy invaders had begun to rain weapons on the peaceful town, over a hundred days before, the inhabitants refused to answer fire. No matter what the invaders hurled at the community, no response came over the walls, not even the din of terrified mothers. It was as though the townspeople had drifted into a collective sleep. Wondering what the enemy was up to, Count Ashenafi dispatched a scout of four men to investigate.

Stealing into town, the men stood gawking at deserted streets. Not even a street dog was to be seen. All four gates of the perimeter walls were locked and fortified from inside. The walls themselves were intact. The besiegers broke into homes, shops, barns, and the temple for any sign of the former tenants, but only the stench of human refuse greeted them. The residents had somehow slipped out undetected. When Count Ashenafi was about to declare the incident the single most mysterious event since the birth of the Third Universe, a young musketeer yelled his finding: a tunnel, concealed under a pile of rubbish, that led out of town and right into the heart of a nearby valley.

Raging like a wounded bull, Count Ashenafi ordered the destruction of Harar. The musketeers ransacked the abandoned homes, shops, barns, and the temple, denuding them of all valuables before setting them ablaze. Pillars of smoke rose all around the enclave. Restrained by the stale air, the smoke clung to the skirts of the buildings, soaking up the breathable air and sunlight. When hours later soot and smoke forced the musketeers to abandon the ravaged town, only the stone walls remained standing.

Count Ashenafi saddled his horse, a full four months after he had taken up arms, little suspecting that the victory he had just celebrated would soon catapult disaster back at him with such vengeance and alacrity that the kingdom would be imperiled, along with everything he held dear to his heart.

A HUSBAND FOR ASTER

A nauseating stench blew through open doors and windows with each shifting wind, calling attention to the acres of skin and hide laid out to dry under the blazing sun. Alcoholic fumes hung in the air as the dark soil bore oceans of spilled drink. The celebration tent had been taken down two days before, but broken wares left behind, tripping even the most agile feet. Duke Ashenafi rocked himself absentmindedly, perched on his front porch with a switch of horsehair in hand, shooing away persistent flies. He seemed to have warmed to his elevated rank, as he no longer blushed self-consciously when passersby shouted their greetings in homage to his new title.

Four weeks had passed since the historic battle had stirred up the valley. In all that time, it had remained the focal point at social events and become the substance of sermons and prayers. Who would have thought that a feudal host, even with Duke Ashenafi's towering stature and combat record, would be able to endure a drawn-out siege let alone come out the uncontested victor? No small warlord had ever before rallied followers in an engagement that lasted for more than a month. Even princes seldom succeeded in protracted warfare. A mercenary army was the deciding factor in an extended battle, but only kings could afford its prohibitive cost.

Nobles crossed mountains and the wilderness to applaud Duke Ashenafi; he had shored up their flagging authority. The siege of Harar was a godsend to many a lord who had been badgered by restless tenants for better living conditions and threatened by the ever-increasing influence of Ammas in his province. It gave pause for sobering reflection to the young emperor, who, unlike his late father, had chosen to turn his back on the nobles who had helped redraw the frontiers of the expanding empire, preferring instead the company of the *nouveaux riches* to whom he doled out titles based not on the purity of their blood but on the fortune they were willing to part with. Awarding the coveted title of duke to the count was, for His Highness, a small appeasement of the threat posed by the hereditary flock.

If her father could be forgiven for basking in his newfound fame, Aster ought to be pitied for feeling resentful about the limelight into which she was suddenly thrust. She had secretly hoped that the days were gone when young men would come knocking at her door with marriage proposals. At the age of eighteen she was considered, by many, an old maid. The tarnishing of her honor at the hands of the emperor had become the subject of public gossip, reinforcing her belief that no man would lay eyes on her again. But, with her father's soaring fame, suitors were soon parading from dusk to dawn, the line extending far beyond the bounds of her immediate homestead and into neighboring kingdoms. Elders flocked in at such impossible numbers that it became necessary to institute a tier system by which each case was handled. A court of four handpicked judges screened possible candidates—based on a closely guarded set of criteria—before referring the most eligible for further expert scrutiny.

Astrologers read the horoscope of a would-be groom; genealogists investigated his genealogy; hematologists looked into his hematology; neuroanatomists studied the soundness of his neuroanatomy; neurophysiologists scrutinized his neurophysiology; and when the young man sighed an audible sigh of relief, believing that he had skipped the last hurdle, he was thrust into a room full of paleoanthropologists, behavioral ecologists, nephrologists, and six extraterrestrialists. If, after all the trials and tribulations, the suitor gained the day, he was led into the inner chambers of the assizes for a heart-stopping moment of decision-making.

Four months and 228 men later, Duke Ashenafi was saddened by the fact that his only daughter, the likes of whom had yet to tread the earth, had still failed to attract a man that he would regard with approbation. He had all but given up hope when, one particularly sunny day, he hit upon an idea that promised a sure way of securing a worthy husband for his daughter and immortality for himself. He decided to settle the matter, once and for all, in a duel among the final candidates.

Dueling was an art of deadly combat that had long since fallen into disfavor with the public for its lack of refinement. But dueling over a bride was a novelty that had yet to make its way into the history books. And that was the lure for Duke Ashenafi in championing the use of the practice—pioneered on the battlefield—for such a mundane task as a marriage arrangement. His courtiers did not laud the idea, initially. They argued that rivalry over a bride didn't constitute the slight of honor that legitimized a duel in the eyes of the law. An Abettor had to be consulted before it was established that men could duel not only over a future bride but also over the direction of the wind. All that was required was two large circles drawn on the ground, each one representing the mother of a combatant; whoever erased the other man's circle (mother, actually) had violated his opponent's honor, justifying a duel.

The dueling parties chose the weapons and mode of combat, while elders decided on the field of engagement. On the appointed day, the final candidates showed up: a man of fifty-eight years and an opponent young enough to be his son. They were followed by a solemn entourage. After sizing up the age difference, the crowd felt that the outcome had been decided long before the rivals saddled their horses. Still, bets were made, secretly. Bookmakers, keen not to be perceived as profiting from the blood of their neighbors, walked up and down an aisle of men whispering coded messages, collecting wager moneys.

A long corridor separated the friends and family members of each contestant. Armed men stood between Duke Ashenafi and the rowdy crowd. The combatants straddled their decorated horses at the far ends of the corridor. Each placed a lion's mane on his head and the skin of a leopard on his shoulders. Consultations passed between the warriors and their military advisers. Using a speaking trumpet, an

Abettor reiterated the rules of engagement, which consisted of three rounds of spear-fighting followed by sword combat. A priest said rites, and a starter warning was sounded.

Holding spears high above their heads, with leather-padded shields dangling from their free arms, the contestants galloped toward each other. The spears, thrown from an inconclusive distance, whizzed by each other, not so much as nicking one of the overflowing manes. The crowd gasped. Horses whinnied. Duke Ashenafi nodded to the Abettor to rearm the combatants.

The warriors had barely reached the end of the corridor when they galloped toward each other with renewed urgency. But the second round proved no more promising than the first. The spears bounced off the raised shields. On failing the third round, the older combatant would be doomed to lose to his younger opponent, as sword-fighting favored a stronger arm.

The contestants lingered somewhat longer at the end of the run as they reflected on the preceding encounters. Each seemed to have turned to the same leaf in the book of combat, for, as they raced toward each other, both men braced their spears on their distended chests. The distances closed in, and when it looked as if the men were about to pass each other in an act of tacit conspiracy, the younger one thrust his weapon forward. The patriarch must have been waiting for just such a move; he pushed aside the thrusting spear with a swift movement of his shield, and when his opponent lost balance, he impelled a spear into the youth's vulnerable side.

The corridor, once vacant and somber, filled with a sea of excited faces. The blood-soaked body of the young man disappeared beneath a swirl of mourning relatives, while the victor rode home, cheered by an adulating crowd but feeling no more elated for his victory than he would have been if he had killed his own son. Duke Ashenafi found in the old warrior not only a man he could toast as a worthy son-in-law, but also someone who had unwittingly helped him forge his place in history yet again.

Arrangements for the wedding began immediately. Normally, a marriage ceremony lasts three days. But there is nothing normal about the lone daughter of a duke taking a husband; weeklong festivities would be needed to marry off Aster. First, there would be an engagement party that lasted three days, followed by the actual wedding six months later.

Aster was never consulted about her part in the affair, of course, because she would have no real role in the wedding until she was actually wed; likewise with the engagement. She would have remained ignorant for the full two months leading up to the engagement had tripping tongues not betrayed the secret. Headstrong as always, her first reaction was to confront her father. But Duke Ashenafi was not in a compromising mood. The days were gone when Aster could cry her way out of tight corners.

Duke Ashenafi might have reminded his daughter that not every girl is privileged enough to have her family choose a husband for her. In fact, in much of the country, the family of a young woman is no more master of her destiny than she herself is. The mother of a peasant girl lives like a hen with a day-old brood, in constant fear of a predator lurking in the shadows to snatch up her young, because marriage by abduction is the norm for the toiling majority.

But Aster didn't feel exceptionally privileged. Soon after realizing that the nets were dropping, she redoubled her effort to elope. Small hurdles had been thrust in her way over the intervening months. For one thing, Gudu had been replaced by two new guards, who took turns watching her every move. With so many visitors coming and going, Gudu's court performance had been in constant demand. He didn't visit her even when he had some free time on his hands, since it would require some explanation to the wary guards. Messages were passed between the two lovers in the form of rolled notes, tucked away in places only the two of them would look.

Reestablishing his contact with the Amma nomads, who not long ago had promised to lend him a hand if he decided to elope, was not an easy matter for Gudu now that he seldom ventured outside the valley. The one consolation the two lovers had was the six-month respite that Duke Ashenafi had unwittingly given them before the marriage.

Aster's residence, once distant and frosty, became a hive of excited relatives who had made the long journey from yonder to kiss her cheek with unabashed bliss or to donate their views on how to handle a man. Men are like dogs, they would say, giggling; if they can't eat it, lick it, or screw it, then they piss on it. Some brought to her tidings that kept her awake for many, many nights, such as when she learned that the bridegroom had been married five times before, and that all but one of his wives had died under suspicious circumstances. Two had drowned in a half-filled tub, one had succumbed after eating a poisoned mushroom, and the other had been garroted by a masked assailant for refusing to eat her mushrooms. The husband was the sole inheritor of all his wives' assets.

Tailors were dispatched to outfit Aster; jewelers sneaked in to size her up for trinkets. She never felt violated, though, until early one morning when a midwife walked in and asked to peer under her skirt. Utterly shocked, she broke down in tears. Not for the first time, she felt like a slave at an auctioneer's lot. The old maid must have been used to such outbursts of emotion, for she patted the bride-to-be on her back, assuring her that she was only doing to her what she had done to hundreds of others. A midwife was called upon in situations where the virginity of the bride was in question, or, more pertinently in Aster's case, if there was a lingering suspicion that the young lady might be in the family way. Long before hearts were broken and fortunes were spent on dowries and revels—even if the occasion was betrothal and not a wedding, as in Aster's case—the midwife settled the prickly issue in the most discreet way.

The night before the ominous day, a lady's maid was dispatched to scrub Aster as clean as a newborn infant. She groomed and coached the bride-to-be in the finer details of betrothal. Whatever you do, don't appear anxious to get married or look your fiancé in the eyes, she said; and, when Aster broke down in tears for being so utterly misunderstood, the maid clapped her hands, elated. She advised Aster to reproduce that outburst at the exact moment when she stepped up to the altar. Nothing was more rewarding to a parent, and nothing a more proven stop-plug to gossips, than a well-shed tear at the altar, she assured her mistress. Rumor had been rife in the valley that Aster, as an old maid, was so desperate for a husband that she was willing to sell her soul. The lady's maid was only doing her part as a good publicist to counter the gossip.

* * *

With her gown overflowing and eyes burning from lack of sleep, Aster was led to the altar escorted by her loving parents and cheered by an affectionate crowd. The words of the lady's maid were still ringing in her ears when she spied the man standing next to her. Tears coursed down her face at the sight of the heaving decrepit. For once in her life, she felt venom well up inside her, but when she glanced at her dad to register her anger, Duke Ashenafi merely beamed a relieved smile, for now he knew that no one would suspect that his daughter, fashioned from the same clay as many an uncrowned king, was achingly desperate for a husband.

Standing on the sideline as he ushered in the luncheon guests, Gudu could read the agony written so clearly on Aster's face. He could see her dabbing her eyes with the end of her veil, seldom responding to the banter of her fiancé. Twice he passed by her table, appearing to be refreshing the groom's drink, and pinched her on the arm consolingly. He ached to whisper in her ears what she already knew of—his raging love—but above all, he wanted to reassure her that betrothal was a tired sideshow that meant little; at the end of the day, she would go back to her bed, no worse for the experience. But far too many eyes were riveted on Aster for Gudu to speak unnoticed.

As the day mellowed and the guests lost themselves in raucous merriment, Aster found comfort from trading a subtle smile with Gudu. The slight abandon that would normally have gone unnoticed by a leery pastor caught the attention of Beza, mother of the Areru twins. Sitting behind the inebriated crowd, she gauged every twitch of their muscles, every twinkle in their eyes. She was like a huntsman, watching an elusive beast lumber toward his trap, hoping and praying for a misstep.

The next morning Beza left her bed with a tin of water in hand and wandered into the woods for a ritual Outing when she caught sight of Gudu standing outside Aster's bedroom window. If the night before Beza had felt that she might have been dreaming when she saw her master's daughter flirting with the family slave, the morning after put her doubts to rest. Cautiously, she crept closer for a better view. What her eyes beheld was something Beza had never thought she would live to witness. Leaning over the windowsill, and dressed only in her nightgown, was Aster, her hand locked with Gudu's, her passionate eyes caressing him, her whispered words slipping into his mouth. The tin she carried had long been spilling water on her feet when Beza realized that her heart had stopped beating.

For the next day and many days to follow, Beza lay in wait for more dramatic events to unfold. She shadowed Gudu every spare moment she got; she monitored the comings and goings of Aster, the moments Aster spent unattended. Beza wondered if the new guards were privy to this scandal. Her mind raced so fast, Beza thought of so many conflicting things that she seemed to be on the verge of losing her sanity. It was not the honor of her master, or that of his daughter, that engrossed Beza, mind you, but an ancient score that she longed to settle.

Beza couldn't bring herself to report her suspicions to her master, because given the choice he would have to make between her word and that of his daughter, Duke Ashenafi was bound to place faith in the candor of his own blood. What is more, the gravity of the accusation might even force him to make an example of Beza, for she would have denied him a well-earned respite. After all, he had just been through the most trying time of his life, both at home and on the battlefield. Beza needed hard evidence, a crime in progress that she could point her finger at, before claiming credit for saving the family's honor.

If Beza was consumed by unspent vengeance, spewing fire of hate and anger, the young lovers betrayed no sign of awakening to the imminent dangers. They saw less of each other in public, but, secretly, they kept up their effort to elope. Messages were passed between them through rolled notes left behind in secret places, and they often met at Aster's window in the small hours of the morning to hash out finer details and enjoy a shared breath.

Fortune, finally, smiled on Beza on a lazy afternoon; she discovered one of those notes. No sooner had Aster tucked away the piece of paper in a crevice than Beza ran away with it. Unable to read, she took the note to a monk she could trust. Her heart leaping to her mouth, she sat watching as the old savant savored the message himself, his visage changing color and tone with each passing sentence. Beza interrupted the monk nine times for a tidbit, but in vain. She had to douse him with a pitcher of cold water before the holy man deemed fit to share his findings with her. Never before had he come across such a universal prayer, he admitted, with four levels of interpretation forming a single reality. Did Beza know who might have written it?

Unable to make out whether the old goon had gone off the deep end, or if he were playing games with her, Beza sat waiting for an answer that didn't come. She took her leave not knowing that the young lovers had anticipated the small chance of the notes falling into the wrong hands, and had, therefore, kept up the time-proven method of communicating their intimate feelings in invisible ink, while leaving the diversion of a well-written verse for prying eyes.

THE LAST LAUGH

Her new guards couldn't have been more accommodating to Aster if she had picked them herself. Having tired of their routine, they gave up shadowing her except for unusual circumstances—an event in the compound attracting guests and visitors, for example, or if she was venturing outside the small perimeter drawn around her. At night, an intruder would have had to come in through the front door to know that there was a guard on duty. With the old diviner long removed from her life, Aster felt safe enough to resume her clandestine affair in the sacred barn.

Nightfall brought to the valley not just the habitual hyenas, but also wild dogs, foxes, and jackals emboldened by the relentless drought. Homes were doubly fortified; livestock, kept out of sight. Aster would listen for the chorus of the guard dogs, her cue that the prowling beasts were around, before jumping out of her bedroom window and darting across the open yard into the old barn. Waiting for her in the shadows was Gudu, in whose embrace she whiled away the balance of the night. Just before dawn, she returned to her own bed, undetected.

The two lovers reveled in their trysts, emboldened by each passing day. They fashioned a functional berth out of discarded planks and rags, and fetched a candle to add warmth and romance. Food and drink were brought in, and the little corner, once desolate in its naked neglect, was transformed, each night, into a kernel of love. It was not actual sexual intercourse that drew the two young lovers out of their warm beds, mind you; they had renounced carnal knowledge until the day they could wed. What brought them together was a primeval love, love that is sown in isles of the blessed and harvested in hearts of the innocent. It is the sort of love that scholars are trained to denounce, wars are waged to stamp out.

And there had been constant reminders, both real and imagined, of the risk accompanying their forbidden love. There were moments, for instance, when they felt a presence in their midst: approaching footsteps, a knock at the door. Each time, they leapt out of the bunk, hearts pounding so loudly that they couldn't muffle the sound in each other's embrace as they waited for the inevitable. Such moments usually passed uneventfully, and the threat was forgotten. Except for one evening, when the gate of the old barn was thrown wide open, and there facing them stood Duke Ashenafi, accompanied by Beza and the two guards.

The moon fell out of the sky. The stars burrowed behind the thin crest of darkness. Beasts prowling the alleys took cover. Duke Ashenafi underwent a visible change: he gained height, ascending higher and higher, like an ominous vine. His distending shoulders brushed up against the crumbling rafters, his stretching arms stuck out of the paneless windows, his ballooning belly squeezed the condemned pair into a small corner. Then, as if in a nightmare, he threw his head back and roared, before deflating to his original self. As the quiet was settling, he set the sights of his rifle on Gudu and shattered the stillness with rapid gunfire.

Aster shrieked. Gudu collapsed on the ground. Crawling through the debris, he found his way out of the barn and into the chilly night. With the howl of hunting dogs trailing him, and the guards on his heels, Gudu melted into the darkness.

The lovers had been in denial of such a disastrous outcome, and Gudu hadn't planned an escape route. Following an ancient instinct, he ran down the expansive valley and out of his master's province. He realized that a posse would be dispatched by daybreak, with a bounty on his head. If he were to elude a band of horses, he would have to get across a deep ravine, over a murky river infested with crocodiles and hippos, and into Amma territories. At sunset, he was well out of range. He set up camp for the night in a heaving bat cave. His blistering bare feet ached; blood oozed out of his tired body, nicked by thorns and shrubs. Nevertheless, he pained not over his physical ordeal but over the uncertainties that lay ahead. Sitting in a dark corner, he agonized over the fate of Aster and the course of their unrelenting love. What is the meaning of escape, he asked himself, if it means to live in guilt and remorse, if there is no tomorrow to look forward to. His mind raced so fast, his thoughts tripped over each other so recklessly, that Gudu blacked out where he sat.

When he came to, the darkness had lifted. Passing by his cave was a caravan of camels: Amma merchants returning home from distant markets. His ghostly apparition emerging from the unsightly cavern sent a shudder through the nomads. They made supplications; some tossed *markesha* at him. Gudu had to reassure the merchants in their own language before they knew the phantom they beheld was not otherworldly, but an embattled young man.

Four days and fifteen leagues later, Gudu came to a place that felt more like home. The merchants who had nursed him through the long journey, carrying him on the back of their camels, sharing with him what little food supplies they had, handed him over to the tribal chief of the village before resuming their even longer journey.

Gudu achieved instant martyrdom in the eyes of the Ammas who adopted him. His treatment was further proof, to the nomads, of their neighbors' distorted sense of righteousness, one more reason why they should carry on their fight. Invitations were extended to him to make cause with Amma crusaders, who were waging a campaign to spread their true faith, but he declined at first, believing that his battle was not with his ancestors' religion but with those who perverted the Scriptures by way of sacrilegious applications. Gradually, however, he came to see his rescuers' ways.

Two months had passed since Gudu fled; just three and a half months stood between Aster and her wedding date. If there was ever a chance for the two lovers to be one, this was the time. Once Aster had gone through the formality of holy matrimony, however much against her wishes, the moral issue of abducting someone's wife would come into the picture. Then, even the most liberal-minded Ammas couldn't be counted on to back up Gudu's scheme. Gudu needed armed support to wrest Aster from the clutches of her father, before it was too late. And though his new cohorts were ready to lend reinforcements, he thought it more fitting to seek backing in Harar.

The tenants of the walled town had long since returned home. They had rebuilt their houses, shrines, schools, and shops—all destroyed by the duke's besieging army. Like any good warriors, they remembered the lessons of the last battle, but they remembered even more the assistance they had received from the Amma warriors. They welcomed Gudu with open arms, not least because he was an Amma recruit; his mission was a godsend. What better way was there to get revenge on their old master than by depriving him of his only heir? The rescue preparations began at once.

Duke Ashenafi did invoke a posse, as Gudu had anticipated. A reward of one hundred *birr* was placed on the fugitive's head. Over two hundred men saddled their horses to join in the manhunt. And though many of them were puzzled at the incongruity of the mathematics—why one would pay the price of six slaves to locate one of his own—none vocalized their bafflement. The posse left home with the conviction that a runaway slave, barefoot and without supplies, wouldn't last another day in the parched savanna. Not for the first time, they were proven wrong.

Duke Ashenafi doubled and tripled the reward money, with no success. Finally, he decided to move the wedding day ahead two months. With Aster safely in the hands of another man, he figured, the responsibility of keeping her in line would be taken away from him. She would no longer be a liability to him, a stain on his good reputation. He even believed that, in the unlikely event of her resuming her scandalous affair with Gudu, or, God forbid, running away with another man, he might be considered the actual victim.

Duke Ashenafi was, in many ways, like a condemned man, viewing his daughter's wedding not just as a discharge from his fatherly duties, but also the conclusion of his purpose in life. Dispensing his fortune with great abandon, he slated some two hundred of his choice cattle for slaughter, in addition to the one hundred and fifty head of goats, sheep, cows, and bulls donated for the occasion by friends and relations. He ordered tables and chairs from a carpenter's lot, when he could have borrowed them from neighbors; he purchased utensils, plates, and glasses when they lay in abundance at the shrine warehouse for use in religious festivities. In a monumental act of extravagance, the fences of the compound were removed, making way for multiple tents.

With the start of the wedding preparations, Duke Ashenafi began getting up early to renew his pact with his Creator, reiterating the promise he had made—a new and glorious temple—in exchange for a successful conclusion of the ceremony. Shrines within a day's ride of Deder were urged to concentrate on the same petition, setting aside such mundane supplications as urgent prayers for a lost sheep or goat. He had even surpassed himself when he pledged financial compensation for such small losses, thus clearing the way for the one plea that mattered. Life must have taken its toll on the old warrior, for he concluded his daily prayers with sobs of repentance.

There were many more clues that his daughter's wedding had mellowed Duke Ashenafi. When his feudal tenants in Kersa complained that they were unable to provide gifts for the occasion, he simply waved his hand and assured them not to overly concern themselves; they could make up for what they lacked in wealth with their hands and hearts. When word reached him that the tenants of Harar had vowed to dice him into mincemeat if he ever set foot near their enclave, he simply sighed out loud and offered the messengers cold refreshments.

Aster had not mellowed with the passage of time. In fact, from the moment she was closeted in her room following the raid on the barn, she had grown more and more bitter with each passing day. She promised her father that she would rather go to her grave in a banana leaf than marry the man of his choice in a silk gown. She professed her love for Gudu so loudly that, some days, her father was forced to gag her with cotton balls, thus preventing the scandal from reaching the wrong ears. But, when Aster refused to eat her meals and remained bedridden, even Duke Ashenafi couldn't feign indifference.

Soothsayers were hired to determine what was ailing Aster. They were undivided in their findings that she was under the spell of the treacherous slave. How else could one explain the fact that a woman of her standing would throw away everything for someone who was not entirely human? Securing the remedy, however, proved to be extremely knotty. Roosters were sacrificed at her doorstep; her backyard was combed for signs of buried fetish; she was force-fed sundry concoctions; and attempts were made at exorcising the evil spirits that might have been planted in her, using the fumes of mixed herbs on a hot burner. Alas, the key to her affliction lay in the hands of the runaway slave; with the blessing of the holy men, the reward money was raised to a sum of five hundred *birr*!

With the wedding date fast approaching, and the whereabouts of Gudu a baffling mystery, Duke Ashenafi's desperation heightened daily. And, when it seemed to many that the old warrior had become the proverbial mouse that had lived long enough to deliver her young's body but not its tail, he prevailed once again. Thinking not like a wronged father but an embattled admiral, Duke Ashenafi marched into his daughter's chamber and made her an offer of armistice: either she would do as he said and pledge herself in marriage, in which case he would remove the bounty from Gudu's head, or she could do as she pleased and he would hunt down the man who had dragged his proud name through the dirt and feed him to vultures. He allowed her a mere twenty-four hours to make up her mind.

As one might expect, those twenty-four hours were Aster's most trying moments. She spent the night huddled up in a dark corner, considering and reconsidering options that she felt she had in her arsenal. Taking her life was a serious temptation but she had the presence of mind to realize that she wouldn't be casting away her life alone; surely Duke Ashenafi wouldn't rest until he had made certain that Gudu joined her in the hereafter. She thought of feigning a mysterious illness; she longed for something as drastic as bleached skin that would confound the experts. But, once again, she was canny enough to realize that her fiancé was not marrying her for her looks, health, or youth, but for her family name and the vast wealth that she stood to inherit. Escaping from her prisonlike mansion had never been an option, but she could escape from her honeymoon bungalow. All she needed was a powerful sedative to throw the old decrepit into a sound sleep, then dart out of her bedroom window and into freedom. What a brilliant thought!

Aster gave her consent to the wedding, but something important was forever lost between father and daughter. An eternity would pass before they could even exchange a civil word. The days were gone when the two would linger around the family dining table, or the fireside, arguing about issues ranging from the morality of slavery to the divinity of the throne. For a man who surrounded himself with an army of sycophants, Duke Ashenafi had always shown a remarkable tolerance toward his daughter when she accused him of viciousness of conduct—defending the rights of his vassals one day, and that of the tribesmen he had helped conquer, the next. When, as a count, Ashenafi had saddled his horse, answering the calls of the throne to bring, yet again, another outlying region into the folds of the expanding empire, Aster had often been the only soul in the valley who refused to wish his entourage good luck. She had even told her father once that this might be the day that someone broke his leg, as he richly deserved. Her curse triggered a roar of laughter among his men; Countess Fikre felt that her daughter's denunciation might come true, and she urged Aster to go back inside and wash her mouth with black soap. Count Ashenafi teased his daughter that without his legs, she would be the one who would have to carry him around.

Throughout the three weeks leading up to the wedding, Aster communicated the few words she had to say to her father through an intermediary. Duke Ashenafi attempted to make light of her pout, believing that once she had settled into the marriage, she would grow out of it.

The wedding ceremony was a spectacle to behold. Some three thousand guests and dignitaries put in an appearance. The high point of the event was when the royal carriage pulled in and the emperor disembarked, flanked by princes and princesses. If Mawu-Lisa had come down to earth, the effect wouldn't have been more impressive. It took the entourage a good hour to walk the hundred paces to the shrine hall, weaving their way through a shrieking crowd, a crowd that fought to kiss the feet, the hands, and even the carpet the emperor walked on.

The bride emerged accompanied by a select band of bridesmaids, chosen not only for their ravishing good looks and youthful grace, but also for their social standing. As he walked with poise and grace, holding his daughter's arm, Duke Ashenafi looked like a child who had finally secured the toy of his dreams. Even his nemeses couldn't help but share his happiness. The veiled silhouette of the bride making her entrance was greeted with rapturous applause. Glancing at the special pew, Duke Ashenafi was moved by the sight of the emperor standing on his feet, like an ordinary mortal. If there had been any lingering enmity between the two, it existed no more.

The groom was late in making an appearance, which was not entirely unexpected given the tens of leagues that he had to travel across treacherous terrain. A select choir was on hand for just such an eventuality. The band played choice melodies, helping the guests while away the tense moments. As the delay continued, however, the crowd began to conduct itself like a troupe of gods waiting on the birth of a new universe: jaded and increasingly anxious. Two hours would pass before Duke Ashenafi became visibly angered. Keeping an ordinary crowd languishing might be thought of as bad taste; making a royal entourage linger bordered on a crime. Duke Ashenafi was about to make a special trip to the pew at the back to express his apologies to the royal guests when a signal was heard and the best men burst in through the front door.

Looking entirely disheveled and unkempt, the best men marched toward the front pew, not once glancing sideways. They rattled off the reasons for their lateness in Duke Ashenafi's ear, as the bride, sitting next to him, registered attentively. The rapt silence that weighed on the crowd was suddenly shattered when Aster tossed her veil up in the air and burst out laughing. Gesticulating toward her father, she staggered from pew to pew with each bone-cracking guffaw. The crowd followed her mad spectacle with an uncertain grin, but didn't find out the underlying cause until the bride was hastily shuffled into an adjoining room. The carriage bringing the groom and his entourage had been accosted by Amma warriors that morning. The rebels had demanded to see the prospective groom, whom they addressed by name. Not wishing to hold the entourage longer than necessary, the Ammas didn't spend another moment explaining themselves; no other words passed their lips before they made away with the severed head of the groom in their saddle bag.

BOOK FOUR:

REVELATIONS

INQUISITORS

❋ ❋ ❋ ❋ ❋ ❋

"Answer the door," Dad commanded as he puffed on his corncob pipe from the comfort of his habitual platform.

"It is the wind," Mam repeated, mending my shorts by the dim light of a candle.

The gale had been raging with unprecedented vengeance, intent, it seemed to me, on ferrying us to the Third Universe. Flying debris pelted the door and windows. The rafters creaked. Dirt and grit seeped through the wet rags that Mam had placed under the door and in each crevice. The knocking sound was soon augmented by the unmistakable call of someone wanting to be let in. Mam dropped her bundle of rags on our bamboo table and hurried to greet the unexpected caller.

Holding the door ajar, Mam regarded the outer world with uncertainty. Grudgingly, she stepped aside. There entered not one but a multitude of ragged men, each carrying some form of armament and a bulky woolen sack on his back. I recognized one of them: it was the hunchback monk, Reverend Yimam, who had not long ago graced us with a fiery sermon.

Dad was more welcoming to the visitors than Mam. He sprang out of his languor to help them unload their gear. He ushered them graciously into the crowded room, but soon even Dad seemed to be baffled by the crowd. The tiny hut was brimming with foul-smelling men, and still there was a large throng outside waiting to be let in. Mam had to protest out loud about the blinding draft before they reluctantly allowed her to close the door, leaving some of them outside.

Reverend Yimam was still on his feet when he announced the onset of the Crusade that he had talked about with such passion on his last visit. The ragged crowd was made up of volunteers, not least among them convicts from the nation's brimming penitentiaries who had been promised by the Supreme Pontiff salvation in a holy war as opposed to an ignoble death on the prison gallows. Some four hundred men had joined the hunchback monk, bearing a collection of arms as colorful as their owners' peculiar scent: machetes, nail-studded clubs, iron-tipped spears, but also muskets and many breech-loading rifles.

While still standing, the monk primed himself on the events surrounding the much-talked-about failed wedding. He inquired as to the authenticity of the bounty that Duke Ashenafi had placed on the runaway slave, gathered tidbits about the mysterious slave—when and how he had made contact with the Amma infidels—and asked if there were any other suspects in the neighborhood, to Dad's knowledge, who might at any moment reveal themselves as stooges of the heretics. Reverend Yimam then headed out for the big house, leaving behind his ragged crowd of men.

Not minding their hosts, the men deposited themselves on the dirt floor, shoulder to shoulder, until there was no room to swing a cat; then they sat on the family bed and on just about any other piece of furniture they could find, breaking our only table and a laundry basket in the process. And just when there seemed to be no room left to blink an eye, let alone ruminate in peace, two of them nestled beside Dad on his personal platform, further abusing the hospitality extended to them.

The men raised a deafening racket. They coughed and roared, baring mouthfuls of rotting or missing teeth; they scooped their spit with their fingers, and tossed it on the walls. Some pulled out pouches of tobacco that smelled like a sick weasel, tore pages from the Holy Book—never noticing how the defilement horrified Dad—and rolled themselves cigarettes. Some produced needles and began in earnest to remove jiggers from their shoeless feet, peering in between their toes and sniffing at their soiled fingers. There were also those who were heard from only when they belched or farted.

Mam stood frozen at the far end of the room, holding me tightly at her side, never once offering our visitors a drink or water to wash with, as one would normally do. The longer the strangers lingered about, the more irritated Mam seemed to become. Dad smiled weakly at her and me. He seemed to have realized the shift of power in the valley, the extent of the monk's supremacy, for he raised no objections. Half the walls would be covered with a sickly coat of spit before Reverend Yimam showed himself again, announcing he had found a shelter for his spirited entourage at the Shrine Hall and at the decrepit barn. The men left as suddenly as they had appeared.

Daybreak brought to light a side of the ragged band of men that the darkness had mercifully kept veiled. The men grabbed at the skirts of women, both young and old, single and married, with feverish abandon. They stole into homes and made away with valuables; some carried off pots of stew that had been left to simmer on the kitchen fires. Duke Ashenafi must have been crippled by fear of crossing the clergy, the uncrowned emperors of the kingdom. When a tattooed beast of a man marched into his study and ransacked his bookcase for toilet paper, for instance, the lord of the manor, who would ordinarily have dispatched the insolent invader across the bourn with one quick blow to the head, merely reported the incident to the hunchback monk.

Soon it was evident where the real power lay, not just within the bounded valley but also in the kingdom at large. Reverend Yimam made it known, in his first public address, that the monarchy had lost its sight of reality; that, left in the hands of the reckless emperor, the nation was bound to race down the slippery slope that it found itself on, and into the waiting hands of the infidels. The kingdom had been besieged by false deities on all sides; the emperor not only failed to see the threat posed to the true faith, but had conspired with the enemy when he issued grazing rights to the infidels' herd in return for taxes. The Mawusa clergy had stepped in at the eleventh hour to rescue not just the spiritual lives of the mortals and the tattered image of the kingdom, but also to stitch the country back together.

A feast day was announced, on which residents of the valley, together with their children and slaves, would have to attend high mass and hear Reverend Yimam read an edict. The mass was conducted by the resident priest, who afterward turned the podium over to the guest of honor. The hunchback monk demanded the townspeople line up before him, place their right hands on the Holy Book, and repeat after him a solemn oath to support the Inquisition that had just been launched and its ministers.

Reverend Yimam was most convincing when he declared the first four weeks an "edict of grace," during which those parishioners who had strayed away from the right course could freely come forward and relieve their consciences with no fear of reprisal. The edict of grace would be succeeded immediately by an "edict of faith"; whosoever had failed to come forward and denounce himself during the period of grace would in the days that followed be subjected to the full effects of the precept.

Twenty-eight men and six women came forward to accuse themselves, or their neighbors. Over half of the men had committed the sacrilegious act of claiming, in a conversation with their wives, that fornication was no sin; one man said to his opponent during a game of cards, "Even with Mawu-Lisa's help you won't win this game"; there was also a woman who had been heard to say, in a moment of heated argument, that there was no heaven or hell; and there was a boy of fourteen who had been seen smiling when he heard mention of Mawu-Lisa before an annual cockfight. None had strayed so far as worshiping the icons of Amma, or conspiring, in any tangible way, with the Amma infidels who were making war against the true faith.

The minor nature of the infractions wasn't lost on Reverend Yimam, who gave the repentant a penance of a mere ten *birr* a head. And twenty lashes each. He took into account the fact that they had come forward within the said edict of grace. Others hadn't been so fortunate. A man who was heard saying that there was salvation outside the Temple of Mawu-Lisa and a young man who was denounced by a neighbor for urinating against the walls of a shrine were both sentenced to a hundred strokes of the lash before being banished from the valley for the duration of six years. Their confiscated goods were divided up into three equal parts; one part each was then given to the person who denounced the heretics, to the court that convicted them, and to the prison building in the county where they were taken. The houses where they lived were burned to the ground by order of Reverend Yimam, legate of the Supreme Pontiff.

Dad was summoned before an Inquisition tribunal consisting of the supreme legate and two local priests. He was confronted by the hunchback monk for a heresy committed not very long ago in the reverend's hearing. Father had questioned the justness of the Holy Scriptures when they excluded the vast number of men and women of bondage from a normal life. He had even gone so far as to collude with the teachings of the Ammas by advocating marriage among slaves. As Dad hadn't come forward to denounce himself, the tribunal held, there was no telling how deep the poison of his perfidy had spread, and so the ministers felt duty-bound to place him behind bars.

Clerks were dispatched to draw inventories of our meager belongings, before taking possession of them. Every item in our house, including pots and pans, woven baskets, rags, and old clothes, was carefully jotted down in the presence of a notary. The value of the items in *birr* was assessed, as it might become necessary to auction the goods, piece by piece, to pay for the upkeep of Dad, and to meet the expenses of the prosecutors and our living allowance. Mam was assured that anything left over from the sequestered property would be returned to us upon the release of Dad two years later. Advising us to look for a place we would call home, the authorities sealed the hut.

Slaves couldn't make accusations against a freeman or bear witness in a case involving one, but they were encouraged to come forward with damning evidence against one of their kind. Beza was promised a speedy entry into the Heaven of the Underling when she revealed that Enquan, Gudu's mother, had fed her boy a meal of mutton and onions on a Wednesday, after the manner of the infidel Ammas. Enquan was unaware of the charges brought against her because of the secrecy involving the identity of informants, but was permitted the privilege of proving her innocence; when she denied having ever committed a heresy, the authorities punished her severely. She was stripped to the waist, smeared with honey, and made to lie on ground visited by fire ants. Not only had Enquan committed the unspeakable crime of heresy, but she had lied under oath.

Reverend Yimam was a man of considerable learning and theological depth who had rounded out his education traveling across high seas. He had an intimate knowledge of the Inquisitions that had endured through the centuries across the Mediterranean. Much of his travels had left an indelible mark on him. He vowed, for instance, never to permit relapsed or unrepentant heretics to be left unmarked. He ordered Enquan to wear a penitential garment—a black cloth with a large sword painted in white both on its back and front. She was condemned to wear the mark of infamy for three long years, whenever she went outdoors.

Mam and I made Duke Ashenafi's family kitchen our home. Mam wasn't placated by the fact that we were only one of numerous families who had been forced to relinquish their homes on the orders of the supreme legate. Most had been evicted to make room for high-ranking clerks, without ever being indicted of a crime. Aster gave up her residence and moved in with her parents, because Reverend Yimam had set his eyes on her quarters for his personal dwelling and field office.

As more and more rowdy pilgrims flocked in, answering the call of the true faith, the original wave of crusaders began to look like nuns on a spring picnic. Those hamlets that had the misfortune of being on the newcomers' route were the first to experience the brunt of their disruptiveness. Homes were ransacked so thoroughly that some of them were left standing with missing doors, windows, gutters, and flooring. The items were put up for sale in the next village. People bought pots and pans, doorjambs and lace curtains at an affordable price, but soon realized their mistake as the crusaders walked from door to door collecting the items sold—and much more—for the market on their next stop. Those who went complaining to Reverend Yimam were castigated for lacking adequate zeal and religious fervor.

Strange men walked in and out of our home (Duke Ashenafi's kitchen, actually) at all times of day. The crusaders waited on the kitchen doorstep and made away with the stew and *injera* right out of the stove. Duke Ashenafi was not particularly pleased when his meal disappeared long before it could find its way to his table. When the townspeople wised up and cooked their meals in the dead of night, the crusaders decided to raid their homes during the lunch hour and swept the dining tables clean.

Reverend Yimam couldn't ignore this wave of human locusts when it descended on the Holy Shrine, stripping the temple clean of all ornaments, decor, incense burners, and candleholders, as fodder to trade for gourds of wine. The straw that broke the monk's already well-bent back was the occasion on which the men removed pews and the pulpit with the intention of breaking them up and selling them as firewood. He decided to harness the unspent energy of his army, while spreading out the losses among his diocese, by taking the crusaders out to look for heretics rather than waiting for the guilty to be brought before him. An itinerant tribunal was born.

The Inquisitors left a thoroughly enlightened parish in their wake. Some nine towns and rural communities took the oath of the general Inquisition in a period of three months. Edicts of faith were read and testimonies taken. Minor offenses were dealt with on the spot; graver ones were brought back to Deder for consultations and purgatories. Heretics were sequestered in the burgeoning prisons. Fines were raised, to pay for the expenses of the Inquisitors.

As the crusaders traveled from one village to another maintaining this Inquisition, life in their absence began to assume a normal course in Deder. Like a leopard in a tall tree besieged by a pride of lions, the merchants gauged the distance of the retreating beasts before descending from their sanctuary. They brought to market items not seen for some time: bottled fragrance, cooking oil, salt, herbs, milk, and butter.

The crusaders' presence in the valley had limited my range of movement plus that of the merchants. Not that they bothered me personally; it was merely because Mam felt that I shouldn't stray too far, if only to stay out of their way. With the pilgrims out of town, however, I resumed my wandering. I visited the home we had lost to Reverend Yimam, and gazed, in sullenness, at the damage done to the walls and thatched roof by the rowdy pilgrims. I passed by Aster's bungalow, which was now the field office and residence of the hunchback monk, and reminisced about the good times that I had witnessed behind those fortified doors. One afternoon, as I was roaming the market, a woman verified my name and then pressed into my palm a piece of paper for me to hand to Aster, and five silver *birr* for Mam, with the compliments of Gudu.

Though her personal guards had long been removed from her life, along with her private residence and backyard garden, Aster was seldom seen outdoors. To meet her, I had to slip past Duke Ashenafi's study, the sleeping bulk of Duchess Fikre in the living-room love seat, and two housemaids laboring a few steps past her. The little note that I brought to her seemed to have sapped the last energy out of Aster; as I watched horrified, she passed out on the tiled floor.

When she came to, Aster lit a candle with shaking hands and warmed the piece of paper on its dim light. Before long, she was sitting on the edge of her bed savoring the message. She read and reread the note, until her last tear had coursed down her face and over her makeup, giving her the look of an amateur clown. Only when she got up to freshen herself did she seem to notice my continued presence in the room.

For the next few weeks Aster, like my mother, waited anxiously for messages from Gudu. On the market day, Tuesday, I would roam the crowded stalls until I was accosted by a messenger, a woman, who handed me a rolled package that I took home. I was never to meet the same courier twice. Gudu must have been aware of the zealots lurking in the shadows looking for Amma instigators. The day came, though, when I returned from the market empty-handed. Only Aster didn't seem to be overly concerned.

The crusaders had arrived back in town. They paced up and down the narrow streets in small groups, dirty bandannas on their heads, weapons on their shoulders, and lit cigarettes in their mouths. The townspeople kept out of the soldiers' way, as much as the soldiers looked over the townspeople's heads. Unless they noticed someone carrying something of value, the crusaders seldom bothered to stop anyone. I was, therefore, thoroughly taken aback when one of them called me by name.

It was Gudu, dressed like one of the pilgrims and accompanied by two armed men. I was about to cry out his name in my excitement when he muffled my mouth with his hand. I recalled the warnings of Mam and Aster, never to mention his name in public for fear of endangering not only Gudu's mother but our own safety. The anonymity of the outfit and the wild beard that he sported had left few clues to the young man that I remembered. I was able to recognize him only because of the unmistakable song of his voice.

Rocking herself on her father's chair, Aster was studying the ragged band of men ambling past her patio. Some of the men directed lurid remarks at her, others snickered. Aster ignored their waywardness. She was like a concerned mother waiting for her belated child when, in the anonymous crowd, she discerned Gudu's unmistakable grin and darted out of her seat. Her eyes smarting, hands shaking, she stood gazing at him. Aster would have given the world for his embrace, the stars and the moon for a passionate kiss. But the dangers were real, the threats imminent. All the two lovers could do was trade smiles and heartache over the heads of the crowd.

With his two companions facing him as a protective shield, Gudu exchanged his unspoken love with Aster until the number of men on the streets dwindled and the pretense of small talk that had passed between him and his two friends faded. Nervous about the attention they were drawing, his companions shifted at their post, but Gudu remained oblivious to the dangers. No one had given more weight to this strange spectacle than the ever-vigilant Beza, to whom it all seemed like recurring dream. Wasn't it only a few months before that she had witnessed a young bride-to-be flirting with her family's slave? Passing closer for a better look, Beza confirmed her suspicions, for there was no mistaking the eyes of the bearded young man.

For once in her life, Beza was torn by the decision that she had to make. Not that she had any lingering goodwill toward the upstart slave, mind you, nor a trace of sympathy for the spoiled young mistress. What Beza had to decide was whether or not to place financial security ahead of ancient and deserved revenge. Duke Ashenafi might not shell out the full two-thousand-*birr* bounty to one of his slaves, but even one-tenth of the sum would be riches for someone who had seldom been paid for her efforts.

On the other hand, what were money and fortune if Beza had to live out her life not knowing what had happened to one of her twins—who had been so vengefully sold over her motherly tears—and when her remaining boy had been rewarded for his services to his master with a permanent leg iron. Beza might not be permitted to testify officially against her master, but the opportunity that had presented itself would allow her to fare better than if she had pointed a finger in open court. After all, her testimony was safe with the hunchback monk; Duke Ashenafi would never know what had hit him.

With her legs tripping over each other, Beza stole into Reverend Yimam's office. Soon the monk's retreat, once serene in its setting, became a hive of excited soldiers. An army of fifty men rushing toward them alerted Gudu's two companions to the dangers, and they received the company with a volley of gunfire. Before long, bullets and arrows were flying in all directions. With the combatants indistinguishable one from the other, the town of Deder seemed to have slid into undeclared civil war. Hours later, when peace finally reigned, eighteen blood-soaked bodies lay on the ground. Among the wounded was an ill-fated rebel.

HOLY SMOKE

The barren cornfield, which had once seemed awesome in its expanse, became a hive of curious faces. Spectators had traveled from far and wide to witness the unexpected trial of the season, that of a rebel soldier and their master's daughter.

Reverend Yimam cherished every passing moment, his carefully rehearsed speech lasting five long hours. He dispensed the seven meanings of the term "heretic," and the identifying traits of one, in a language that the crowd could easily fathom. In his own words a heretic was someone who had willfully perverted the sacraments of the true faith or separated himself from the unity of the Holy Temple; someone who had been excommunicated, whether by reason of sexual excesses or trading with the enemy; someone who had erred in the exposition of Sacred Scripture; a person who had invented or followed a new sect; one who understood the articles of faith differently from the True Temple of Mawu-Lisa; or someone who thought ill of the sacraments of the Holy Temple. Aster fit the expanded interpretation of the seventh and last meaning of the term heretic in that she had willfully harbored a known Amma, Gudu. The captured rebel, one of Gudu's two cohorts, fit all seven identifying traits of a heretic.

Reverend Yimam personified tolerance and charity when he noted that salvation was a matter of individual virtue. There was, however, no salvation outside the Temple of Mawu-Lisa, and no legitimate society that was not Mawusa. Dissenting belief and action threatened not only to corrupt the blameless, but was also bound to bring the wrath of the Creator upon the guilty and innocent alike. The effort to root out heretics was aimed, therefore, not at punishing the guilty per se, but at protecting the innocent. Reverend Yimam ascended the pinnacle of reason and understanding when he advised that even when the most severe punishment is visited on the guilty, it ought not to be meted out with the zeal of righteous vengeance, but out of love for correcting an erring brother. He concluded the session by reading out loud the verdict against Gudu's fellow soldier: "Burn him at the stake."

Ever appreciative of the ways of those distant countries that he had visited in his youth, Reverend Yimam held that the most effective way of stamping out heresy was by the power of the flame. In fact, the monk's admiration of those foreign lands extended far beyond the ecclesiastical realm. If he had his way, the secular courts would reform their practice so that arsonists would also be burned to death; perjurers would be flung off a high cliff; composers of scurrilous songs would be clubbed to death; crop thieves would be hanged or decapitated; and those who killed a close relative would be confined in a sack with an ape, a dog, or a serpent and thrown into the sea—all in accordance with the ancient laws of Rome.

The convicted rebel was led to the far corner of the cornfield, where a large pyre awaited him. He was chained to the stake, over his tearful plea for mercy. Reverend Yimam offered the heretic a last chance to redeem himself by renouncing the infidel Ammas and adopting his ancestors' faith, which he had so willfully rejected when he joined the rebel movement. A pregnant pause settled on the crowd as the young man carefully weighed his options. Then, in a voice barely audible to the executioner standing next to him, the dissenter pronounced his conversion to the faith of Mawu-Lisa.

The anxiety hanging over the crowd like an ominous cloud broke, infusing the spectators with enchantment. Those standing nearby rushed forward to embrace the convict; they gave thanks to the Creator for opening the door to his conversion. The executioner knelt before the rebel and apologized for insulting him before, acknowledging that they were now brothers in one faith. When quiet had finally settled, Reverend Yimam asked the damned in what faith he would die, and the reformed rebel repeated in a voice so unmistakable in its clarity and conviction that few doubted his sincerity: in Mawu-Lisa. The hunchback monk, who was kneeling down, rose and, in a rare display of emotion and tenderness, embraced the convict. And to assist the soul of this troubled young man the supreme legate gave the order that he be strangled without delay; the lifeless body was then set alight.

Aster's sentence was delayed by order of the supreme legate.

Beginning the day his daughter was carted off to jail by a ragged band of men, Duke Ashenafi hadn't slept in the same bed twice as he galloped from town to town, village to village, crossing national borders to rally support for his cause. He would ride to death six horses, four mules, a donkey, and a three-legged zebra before it finally dawned on him how difficult it was to fight off a crusade, but he hadn't lost hope until a two-hundred-year-old Abettor advised him that no one had ever waged a successful campaign against the clergy. If Duke Ashenafi was intent on pioneering such a battle, however, the war patriarch was willing and ready to lend a hand. "On one condition, though," the Abettor hastily added. "Before we can slit open the monk's throat, you must steal his habit."

"What does a monk's habit have to do with winning a battle?" Duke Ashenafi retorted.

"Perhaps nothing, but I wouldn't want to be the first to find out that it does," came the answer.

In desperation Duke Ashenafi sought the help of the emperor, only to learn that His Highness now had his own worries—he was in imminent danger of being branded a heretic. His sexual excesses had finally caught up with the young ruler. The Supreme Pontiff saw to it, well before the onset of the Inquisition, that if the emperor could not be bought over, he could at least be carried off in a bag as a latent enemy and threatened with excommunication. For Duke Ashenafi to be of any use to his daughter, therefore, the only course available to him was to find a middle ground with the hunchback monk.

Reverend Yimam could be an astute diplomat as well as deal-maker. He agreed to be lenient toward Aster if her father would make common cause with the crusaders, assist them in exterminating heretics in his domain, and surrender his main mansion as a pledge of his intentions. Aster would be permitted to make amends and reparation for the wrongs she had committed and earn suspension by walking around the Holy Shrine on her knees, chanting a select prayer—a mere slap on the wrist.

Duke Ashenafi believed that he had purchased his daughter's absolution but he would soon find out the true meaning of all those fine words. Aster's case was merely suspended, meaning, in the parlance of the Inquisition, that she could be retried for her crime at any time, under any provocation, and subjected to the full effects of the edict. Duke Ashenafi was ill-advised to dispose anytime soon of his fortunes—his large estate in Kersa and any money he might have stashed in his backyard—for he might be required to purchase and repurchase his daughter's freedom in the weeks and months to come.

A thoroughly defeated man, Duke Ashenafi wasn't even allowed to pack a saddlebag before he was hastily removed from his mansion. With nowhere to go but a tent, he was forced to tender for one of the hovels in the care of the hunchback monk. An auction was called that soon turned into a minor spectacle as Duke Ashenafi engaged in a bidding war with a man he couldn't see—only the monk knew the identity of the other contestant. The price of the hut escalated to such a dizzy height that many suspected a gold mine had been found under its thatched roof. When the sale was finally closed, with a rap from the monk's gavel, Duke Ashenafi paid the price of a small palace for a room that was barely tidier than a goat shed.

For her part, Beza was rewarded by being nominated as the overseer of the campaign being waged in beds and kitchens—a daring move on the monk's part that left friends and enemies alike scratching their heads in utter bewilderment. Only later the townspeople understood that the hunchback monk was not blind to ethnic and class hierarchies when he appointed Beza; he drew pleasure from snubbing the noblewomen, forcing on them a master they despised, just as the noblemen would feel about taking their orders from him.

Beza proved a quick learner. She grasped that the crusade had been launched to set upright not only the faith of the nation and the ways of the state, but also the moral disposition of each family unit.

A woman might be the central figure of her family, holding the unit together, but it would be folly to leave the grave task of preserving the individuals' morality to her care. A mechanism had to be put in place to monitor and correct such vices as lewd behavior and depravity. Reverend Yimam had conducted himself with adequate zeal and insight when he shored up the faith of his flock and the ways of the state; he expected Beza to do likewise for the family unit.

No longer answerable to her former master, Beza devoted her waking hours to laying out the foundations for a godly system. Like all new converts, she was ardent in her conviction. Believing that the moral decay of society was triggered by female sexuality, she issued directives that would stamp out the breeding grounds of prostitution, adultery, and divorce. Beza introduced a strict dress code for her female charges, requiring each woman to wear her skirt a touch longer than her ankle; a chador that hid her hair from view; a load of bricks that hung from the neck, forcing the woman to look down at her feet and not at a passing man; and, as her creative genius flourished, Beza issued more directives concerning both public intercourse between the sexes and the vocabulary of a virtuous woman. A moral and righteous woman no longer felt "hungry," for instance, which would have been akin to a wild beast or her uncouth half, but "winding down her fast"; she was not "mournful" if she suffered a loss, but "reflective." Beza blacked out a whole array of adjectives from the feminine dictionary, creating burgeoning discord between intention and comprehension.

Public discontent, which had been simmering, came into full view when Beza changed her mind about the chador, demanding, instead, that her charges shave their heads. Women—old and young, single and married—paraded to Reverend Yimam to voice their protest. They argued that Beza was motivated by jealousy when she issued the amendment, since her own head of hair could grow no longer than her eyebrows. Far from being swayed by that rationale, Reverend Yimam hailed Beza's demand as one of the Good Book's missing ordinances. Besides, he added, it would be hygienic if men shaved their heads as well. Reverend Yimam was a bald man.

And so Beza stopped women in the street to check not only the length of their skirts and the outline of their figures, but also the stubble of hair on their heads. She ran the back of her hand up and down their bare skulls, grunting her discontent. She often issued her verdict on the spot, if the penalty was a fine or community service. More serious and recurring problems were referred to the weekly tribunal. Women lined up next to a shackled band of men each Wednesday, defending themselves against charges of heresy, blasphemy, adultery, usury, sodomy, and idolatry.

Beza exceeded herself when she developed a noninvasive mechanism by which the virginity of unwed women could be established. She had noticed how women, unlike men who urinated against a tree or brush, preferred the open field to make water; how the trajectory of a woman's urine and the splash it created as it hit the ground correlated with her age and sexual past. A virgin, for instance, was bound to leave a pointed hole in the dirt, whereas a grandmother sprinkled half a cornfield in one sitting. Beza waited in the shadows before the tracks of her prey had settled, resolving the issue of virginity on the spot. Those suspected of premarital sex were referred to a midwife for further scrutiny. Nine girls were effectively prosecuted for fornication using Beza's technique.

Beza's most daring overture was, perhaps, when she set out to curb alcohol consumption, censor secular melodies, theater performances, and abolish the annual cockfight, arguing that such excesses were bound to stimulate the passions of men, leading, ultimately, to the breakup of the family. An avid fan of the cockfight and a celebrated carouser, Reverend Yimam, for once, didn't warm to the idea. He admitted that abstinence did speed up the penitential purgation that began with one's birth, but not on the same scale as a demonstrative truth at the stake. Only Reverend Yimam understood the full meaning of his argument.

Reverend Yimam's confidence in his unlikely disciple became apparent when he allowed Beza the assistance of her son. Areru the Taller had already proven himself in possession of unique traits and qualities that placed him squarely head and shoulders above the average man. His battlefield exploits had already been known to the crusaders. What impressed Reverend Yimam was the young man's readiness to embrace the most far-reaching edict. When the tribunal judged the entire family of a celebrated lord to be heretics, for instance, condemning two of the family members to the stake and the remaining four to be branded with a hot iron and publicly mutilated, Areru the Taller readily discharged the ruling despite the fact that he had, in the past, benefited from the family's goodwill. When public denunciation of suspects waned and Reverend Yimam despaired over the course of the Inquisition, the young slave offered to go on foot from village to village, across a vast steppe, flushing heretics out by inciting controversial discussions, so that they would be burned at the stake, their house would be razed to the ground, and their children would suffer perpetual deprivation for the sins of their parents—all in the spirit of the Inquisition.

If Areru the Taller hadn't been awarded the distinction that his mother had enjoyed, it was only because his ravenous appetite had got in the way. In the days and weeks following his release from the open-air jail, his hunger steadily deepened despite the mountains of food that he was ostentatiously served. A month hence, he was still eating round the clock when Reverend Yimam ruled that there was not a village but a kingdom of demons residing in the young man's stomach. Careful not to traumatize Beza, who was passionately devoted to her son, the hunchback monk prescribed an antidote, mild in its administration yet potent in its remedy, to the disease that afflicted the young slave but ailed everyone around him. Areru the Taller was served a small helping of date palm that would prove to be his last meal on earth.

Her son must have been the last stay that held Beza anchored to the temporal world, because with his sudden and mysterious death, she became a changed person. No longer concerning herself with the moral status of her charges, she spent her days brooding over her mortality and salvation. She awaited anxiously the arrival of the weekly Inquisition, so that she would receive penance for the crimes she had committed since her last confession. Reverend Yimam suffered the anguish of having to listen to her fabricated sins; compared with his treatment of most of the heretics facing the tribunal, he passed light sentences on her. Beza was "reconciled" after a public flogging; she was "relaxed" after townspeople were made to walk on her prostrate body. But, when she showed up for the third time to confess her sins, Reverend Yimam couldn't help but up the stakes.

And what a stake it was that awaited Beza, a large post doused with seven coats of kerosene and buttressed by a pile of brushwood. To look at the crowd that had gathered to pay its last respects, one would never have suspected that the condemned had once been in disfavor with her neighbors. Many of the spectators had sacrificed their daily needs when they donated a load of firewood and charcoal for the function. Reverend Yimam himself spent an uncommonly generous moment when he solemnized the occasion by reading a carefully chosen passage from the Holy Scripture, before signaling the executioner to set alight the four corners of the pyre.

Her eyes shifting with incomprehension, Beza watched as the fire gathered fury, rising swiftly up the platform and consuming the plank, her clothing, and, finally, her troubled flesh. The crowd had settled into rapt silence by the time the bulk of her body had been reduced to ashes. And, though Reverend Yimam hadn't said so in as many words, a milestone had just been reached, marking the turning point of an Inquisition that had begun, with little fanfare, just over six months before.

THE SAINTLY SLAVE

Good warrior that he had become, Gudu didn't agonize for long over the inattention on his part that had cost one of his cohorts his life and the two women he worshiped, their freedom. He did store away an important lesson, however, vowing never again to place passion ahead of reason and accountability. For his dreams to come to fruition and the world to change, wars would have to be waged, enemies vanquished.

And what a formidable enemy the crusaders had become. In a mere six months, their ranks had swollen to three thousand men, mediocre in armament, perhaps, but self-effacing in their zeal. If they had yet to leave training camp for the real testing ground—Amma territories—it was only because the hunchback monk kept seeing heretics under his bed. Gudu needed to exploit this rare laxity in an army commander, by building up his fortifications and strengthening his army.

Harar had long since been preparing for war. With Gudu as its commander in chief, the ancient enclave had raised a militia of a thousand men, dug extra water holes within its walls, erected two more food storage facilities, and fortified the curtaining walls with battlements. The devastating effects of the mangonel in the last battle were still fresh in the minds of the town elders, who now demanded the erection of gunports. The battlements permitted protective merlons, so that gunmen could fire at the enemy below from the open embrasures in between.

The real testing ground for Gudu's leadership lay not in battle-hardened Harar but in friendly Kersa. The sleepy village hadn't been the subject of a major military expedition since it fell into the arms of the expanding empire two generations before, subsequent to which Duke Ashenafi's father, now deceased, had acquired dominion over the tenants by grants of fief from the late emperor. Duke Ashenafi had maintained the unique relationship forged between his father and the vassals through judicious stratagems and deal-making, never once resorting to an exchange of blows. Now that the serfs were openly rebelling, however, refusing to pay the homage owed to their master, that relationship was being reevaluated.

Behind the insurgency of Kersa lay a thinly veiled band of Amma radicals who found in the plight of the serfs not only a platform for their lofty ideals, but a test of their leadership skills in the face of the looming Crusade as well. Indeed, land was to the nomads what a deity is to the initiated: one may draw on its might, but not lay claim to it. Amma herdsmen roamed the vast steppe at will in search of a green pasture and watering hole, with little regard for man-made boundaries. They questioned why a settled society should behave any differently, why one man should toil in the service of another merely because the stronger had staked out something that had never belonged to him in the first place.

Amma elders flocked to Kersa intent on molding the vassal-turned-landowners in their time-proven cast. Communes were set up to look after the welfare of the tenderfeet. A governor of Kersa was elected from the ranks of the commune leaders, replacing Duke Ashenafi. Amma patriarchs set the rules governing the newly established communes, grafting their egalitarian practices. If, for instance, one man suffered at the hand of another, he no longer resorted to a vendetta, as was usually the case in settled societies, but sought mediation. Elders levied compensations in the form of cattle, blocks of salt, silver and gold ingots for infractions ranging from a slight of honor to spilled blood.

Spilled blood was on their minds when a troop of Abettors came to join the uprising. Long after they had been forced into early retirement by the predictability of an ordinary combat, the war patriarchs were being nudged to life by the mutiny in Kersa. Since vassal rebellion came with the rarity of a four-legged rooster, commanding positions were most sought after. The Abettors had to submit to both oral and written examinations before they could formally appeal for the admiral's chair. Bids flew in the sultry air, bringing to a halt all activities in seven villages, as hundreds of war veterans dug up their secret backyard deposits, raising the stakes of partaking in war to a new high. A week later, when the auctioneer's gavel sounded closure of the bidding, only three Abettors would come out as uncontested winners, each paying a king's ransom of five hundred *birr* for the coveted title.

Gudu welcomed the war patriarchs not so much for their illustrious battlefield exploits but for the caches of weapons they had garnered during careers that spanned six generations. The Abettors donated muskets, sabers, crossbows, and a wide range of pole arms designed for thrusting, hacking, and hooking. Five hundred young men were drafted in the first wave of recruitment; by the time the Abettors itched for combat, six months later, the ranks of armed men would have swollen to two thousand. The militiamen were divided into groups of foot soldiers and mounted men. Each was then immersed in a repertoire of war tactics befitting his talents, beginning with hit-and-run methods, then focusing on siege-and-field warfare. The war patriarchs were unanimously against adopting a policy in siege warfare where a defending army would attempt to stick out an onslaught and see if something positive turned out—as in the case of Harar. Instead, emphasis was placed on sallying out to defeat the besieging enemy.

Unlike Harar, Kersa was not a walled town, and when Gudu pointed out this oversight on the Abettors' part, the war patriarchs submitted a ready solution: make it one. The windy community was already huddled between a mountain fastness on its eastern front and the ominous Death Valley along its western length. Only a small run of open field along the north and south frontiers needed to be looked after. Trenches would be dug and spiked-wood fences erected along the vulnerable runs, with the cavalry as well as the foot soldiers' protection in mind.

The stroke of genius that immortalized the Abettors was when they unleashed an undisclosed number of secret agents on the crusaders. Soon, Gudu, the commander in chief, was privy not only to news of enemy size and armaments, but also to the tactics and strategies that were discussed behind closed doors. The Abettors salivated when they thought of taking the enemy by surprise, but Gudu, never a man given to precipitous haste, resisted all temptations. Even when the Abettors submitted a lucid and symmetrical justification for poisoning the enemy's water hole—an action that would help eliminate hundreds, perhaps thousands, of enemy soldiers, while ensuring an acceptable level of civilian loss and, above all, no friendly casualty—Gudu refused to budge. In his own words, Gudu's intention was to establish peace and accord, not to invoke mayhem; he would resist an enemy invasion, not initiate one. The Abettors' frustration heightened when Gudu redirected the unspent energy of the militiamen toward projects for peaceful times.

The devastation of the perennial drought was carved onto the vast landscape. Both cattle and humans had become so emaciated that they tripped over their shadows; children with bloated stomachs remained immobile where they sat, weighed down by overfed houseflies. After another year of the relentless drought, the crisis would be beyond human control. Gudu needed to come up with a revolutionary idea before the landscape was littered with the skeletons of his unfinished project.

And what a revolutionary idea it seemed when passing Arab merchants proposed that the villagers tap the water coursing the Death Valley below for irrigation purposes. The Arabs had witnessed a similar project in the land that had been called Mesopotamia, where the peasants had, in a single year, transformed their situation from poverty to wealth. Only the wealth in their case was a curse, for all able-bodied men had quickly succumbed to corruption and excesses, surrendering the green-felted landscape back to the ravages of a dust bowl.

Siphoning water uphill was considered so preposterous at the time that Gudu felt the Arabs could only have been right. He summoned elders and scholars to a meeting to ponder the thought, but the wise men found the idea so ridiculous that they concluded the Arabs were under the influence when they stopped by their village. Not a man given to easy frustrations, Gudu unfurled the proposal, once more, before his most trusted strategists, and this time one of the Abettors recollected in vivid detail having come across a similar project across the seas some ninety-five years before. The Abettor had been so overwhelmed by the formidable power of people redirecting water from its natural course to do wonders at command that he had razed the project to the ground, so that others wouldn't emulate it. He had hoped to patent the technology and live off the royalties, but war always got in the way.

Though the Abettor lauded Gudu's initiative to introduce irrigation and stave off famine, he was reluctant to take part in the scheme for fear of being labeled a sissy by his peers and losing his fighting license. It took a bit of persuasion on Gudu's part before the war patriarch finally relented. "On one condition, though," the Abettor stressed; "under no circumstances should you divulge the fact that I have taken part in farming." Gudu agreed.

And so, with the most unexpected counsel whispering in his ear, Gudu crafted an irrigation system consisting of a fifteen-foot-diameter undershot wheel with sturdy spokes, a shaft running through the radius hub and anchored on either side of the open gorge, holding the wheel in place, and a water trough—all fashioned out of timber ferried from distant highlands. Buckets were mounted at each spoke location, and the wheel was carefully lowered. No sooner had the wheel touched the raging water than it began spinning, filling up each successive bucket with clear, though steaming, water. The bucket emptied its contents into a trough laid a whisker away from the rotating pail, which, in turn, channeled the water to the fields on either side of the valley.

Soon the stretch of valley, once shunned for its ominousness, became life-giving as dozens of undershot wheels sprang up along its exacting course, their precious cargo reshaping the vast landscape. Seedlings pressed out of the ground a mere twenty-four hours after the first drop of water had settled the dirt. Birds returned from a distant refuge to celebrate the dawning of each day. No one was, however, more enraptured by the miraculous transformations than the people of Kersa. Their adulation for Gudu turned mythical; priests offered to put him at the top of the list for an upcoming wave of sainthoods, but Gudu, ever unassuming, politely declined. Anyway, by this time he had already been canonized as the Patron Saint of Salt Miners by six other villages.

A mere four months would elapse, after construction of the ingenious wheels, before the tenants of Kersa celebrated the first harvest—which yielded cabbages, tomatoes, red beets, and sweet potatoes. Children were mystified at how the scorched earth, so hostile and suffocating a short while ago, could have become so forgiving, producing things that they had never imagined—many of the youngsters had never before known a drop of rain or a breathing cornfield.

Merchants made Kersa their destination, instead of a stopover during a long journey. Caravans of camels showed up after each harvest—three times the first year—scooping up edible stuff for markets far away. Soon, auctions were held for produce that had yet to be grown. Prices doubled and tripled after each successive harvest until, by the end of the first year, an ear of corn could fetch the price of a prized dagger; a sack of sorghum, a rifle; a bag of potatoes, ammunition of equal weight.

THE THREE ABETTORS

The villagers of Kersa traded their bows and arrows for exotic weapons. Shots rang out at all times of the day; the nights were no more serene. Casualties ensued as the novices ignored all safety precautions in their rush to hone their skills. One man lost an arm when a musket exploded in his grip; another shot his wife through the heart as he fiddled with his new toy at the dining table. There was also a young man who inadvertently set his hut ablaze when he left his ammunition by the fireside, unattended.

The new weapons elevated the community's longing for safety to a dizzying height. No one appreciated the fact more than the three Abettors, who ecstatically declared that, with such an array of armaments in hand, one would be willfully criminal or ridiculously timid not to initiate war. Any war.

The opportune moment seemed to have presented itself when Duke Ashenafi dispatched a small army of scouts to investigate the prosperity that everyone talked about. Though news of the abundant harvest had duly reached him, information about his enemies' lethal firepower had escaped the former master.

The Abettors hankered to take the messengers prisoner, igniting the long-awaited battle, but Gudu rejected the idea. He reminded the war patriarchs that it ran against the grain of a fair fight to detain messengers, even if those messengers were armed and cocky, as were these ones. Gudu opted to be the ideal host to the guests, instead. He wined and dined them, gave each decent sleeping quarters for the night, and when morning broke, handed each envoy a heaving sack of assorted produce for his family. Tears of shame welled up in them, and many of the messengers looked away, embarrassed. Some offered to stay behind and help in the uprising; Gudu had to remind them of the consequences that awaited their families if they opted to desert.

While the fortuitous harvest and exotic weapons cushioned the harsh reality of the uprising for the former vassals, ingrained prejudices that had lain dormant in the confusion of the revolt resurfaced. At the heart of the problem lay the position of slaves and the Amma faith in the new order. Priests of the traditional shrine had shown remarkable restraint toward Gudu, since he was at the center of the uprising and to oppose his leadership would be viewed by their parish as treason. The priests had become increasingly restless as the ranks of runaway slaves joining the uprising swelled, and the most prominent positions in the local militia were assumed by the newcomers. The clergy didn't take lightly the fact that Amma pagans would compete with them for the ears of the mortals as well as the Almighty. An everyday mass became a forum for a disaffected priest to air his prejudice from the holy pulpit, stirring up a revolt within the revolt.

Life for an ordinary vassal had never been much better than that of a man in bondage, but somehow the vassal drew comfort from the belief that he fared better socially than not only a bondsman, but also a potter, a blacksmith, a trader, and a herdsman—those who eke out a living from nonfarming occupations. Even when one of these handymen was from his own ethnic group, a self-respecting vassal was seldom seen with him in public. Under no circumstances would a vassal break bread with an outcast. The clergy as well as his feudal master encouraged his prejudice. Unfortunately, such bigotry didn't sit well with the spirit of the uprising.

Gudu proved himself, once more, an astute diplomat as well as a visionary when he arranged a public debate with opinion-makers of the community on the issues that concerned them most. With the entire village as witness, he called into question the role played by the clergy in the deposed system. He pointed out that the ecclesiastics, and the Shrine of Mawu-Lisa they represented, were not just passive accomplices of the feudal system, but an integral part of it. He reminded the villagers that when the expanding empire annexed Kersa and confiscated all land, one-third of the farmland had gone to the clergy, one-third to the loathed feudal lords, and only the remaining one third to the state. Gudu questioned: Wasn't the clergy one of the largest vassal owners in the region? Didn't the monks and nuns constitute one of the biggest slave runners around? When the vassals suffered at the hands of greedy feudal masters, had any of the clergy intervened on behalf of the oppressed? Gudu brought to rest some lingering suspicions about the motives of Amma warriors in the uprising when he posed the questions: What had the Amma warriors gained from the revolt but the satisfaction of witnessing the vassals' freedom? Had any of the Amma clergy ever forced his faith on the villagers? Had Amma warriors demolished the villagers' shrines, poisoned their water holes, or raped their wives and daughters as their clergymen had confidently predicted?

The scowling visage of the crowd gave way to a chorus of tributes to Gudu. It was not latent hatred for their ancestors' faith that rallied the crowd against their clergy, mind you, but resentment at having been deceived for so long.

If the clergy were taken aback by the spread of perfidy in their parish, they were jolted out of their seats when the three Abettors marched toward them, with extra swords in hand, and invited the holy men to a duel. Gudu had to remind the war patriarchs that differences of opinion didn't necessarily entail war. The Abettors submitted unassailable justification as to why they should nip off the ears of the priests—it would allow for easy identification at a later time—but Gudu held his ground.

Gudu lobbied for reinstatement of the clergy in the community and resumption of payments toward their sustenance—not on the basis of a vassal-landlord relationship, but a connection like that of an aging father and caring child. The move would prove to be one of his rare and costly mistakes. Many of the disaffected Mawusa clergy would make use of the absolution to serve the crusaders, sending out information not only on the status of the militia but also the spiritual alignment of each villager. Not until the long-awaited battle was at its apex, some eight months later, would Gudu find out the extent of damage inflicted by the enemy within, but by then the course of history would have been irredeemably altered.

Though the villagers had transferred their trust from the clergy to their commander in chief, there were times when they were torn by the decisions Gudu had made. When, for instance, Gudu declared it legal for bondsmen to marry not just one of their own kind but also a free woman, if the woman so chose, even the most ardent supporters of the rebel leader voiced their concern. Fear of the Almighty, who, in wrathful vengeance, might send them back to their days of hunger and destitution, made them doubt Gudu's wisdom. Two harvests would be safely hauled from the fields, without any sign of avenging locusts, before the villagers realized that they had earned the Creator's absolution.

Neither was Gudu's proposal for a slave and freeman to pray under the same roof welcomed with open arms, at first. Many villagers were edgy, fearing that their pleas would remain unanswered, as those of bondsmen; worse yet, that they would be mistaken for members of a lower caste and bestowed the wrong largesse. One full year would elapse before the amendments were accepted, but by then many prayers had been answered, whether it was a new addition to the family; the delivery of twin calves; the recovery of the bedridden; or the death of a loathed neighbor, through the intervention of the Almighty.

The clergy felt vindicated when, in the week Gudu commemorated the first integrated school—school to be attended by children of both bondsmen and freemen—pillars of dust devils descended on the village, raising the thatched roofs of nine huts, including the newly finished school. The twister leveled half the cornfield, defeathered a flock of chickens, and emptied ponds of water before its anger was spent. At the villagers' insistence, Gudu abandoned the scheme. Not until many years had passed would the issue of integrated schools be brought up again, but by then Gudu would have already passed the torch to a new hand.

The most gratifying moment arrived for Gudu when the first child of a bondsman and a free woman was, finally, due to be born. Though many had known or had suspicions about a master fathering a child by one of the women in his servitude, there had never been a proven case of a freeborn woman giving birth to a mixed-blood child. Priests, however, cited cases from the missing pages of the Scriptures when they told of instances when women who transgressed had given birth to deformed babies: a child with a small tail between its legs, a baby girl with a third arm sticking out of her chest, an infant of indeterminate sex, and a baboon with a jackal's head.

Aside from the free-spirited nomads, Gudu was, perhaps, the only other person who dismissed such fears. He welcomed the occasion to lay to rest, once and for all, the last vestiges of prejudice that pervaded his people. On the night of the expected delivery, he stood guard at the door of the soon-to-be mother, while most of the villagers congregated outside the locked gates of the Holy Shrine, burning bags of incense and petitioning for the Almighty's forgiveness. The priests stayed home, having given timely warnings against such transgressions; they didn't wish to be the lightning rod of the wrath of the Redeemer.

The night folded in on itself, tucking away the last twinkle of the stars. Birds sang songs of awakening. The villagers realized that another day had passed without any relief from their anxiety. Gudu was about to pronounce the beginning of the new workday and head for the wheat fields when wails of the newborn were heard emanating from the hut. It took a small army of men to restrain the villagers from marching inside. What seemed like an eternity would pass before the midwife allowed visitors in.

Five elders were chosen, and with Gudu leading the way, they walked into the dark recesses of the hut to check on the condition of the infant while the crowd outside held its breath in suspense. The elders turned the baby boy from side to side, making sure that the midwife hadn't removed a suspicious part in her zeal to aid the new mother, before they proceeded to verify that all parts were in their appropriate place: eyes not on top of the head; nose not fashioned after a pig's; ears not the size of a rabbit's; and body not covered with hair like a baboon. Beaming with relief, the elders declared to the throng outside not only the health of the newborn but also the exceptional size of the boy's penis, which would make it utterly unnecessary for him to search for a donkey in heat later in life in order to nurture and grow his member.

Tolerance of the Amma faith hadn't evolved at the same pace as the integration of slaves. In fact, with the erection of the first shrine, a civil war was almost ignited. It all began when some zealots burned down the prayer house, under the cover of darkness, long before it opened its doors. Ever careful not to antagonize the people they set out to help, Amma elders decided not to pursue the matter, preferring, instead, to relocate their shrine up the hill and away from all homegrown temples.

The villagers didn't need their priests to tell them that prayers made from higher altitudes and under clear skies reached the Almighty a lot faster than prayers made under the canopy of a tree and raging wind, wind that dissipated every spoken word long before they ascended where they could be answered. If the homegrown shrines hadn't made it up the rocky mountains, it was only because no one knew how to erect a building on a solid rock foundation. Amma priests had hired Arab architects to fashion their shrine.

Though it had been the policy of Amma elders not to force their faith on others, as many of the thriving religions had done, and though they had, so far, shown preference to compromise as opposed to blind confrontations, the decision to keep the new shrine in its place was unanimous. The elders were, however, willing to share their much-talked-about brass horn and tom-tom drums, imported from the Orient, with the temple of the establishment. It had long been proven that these devices, if expertly operated, not only resonated high in the heavens from any location on earth, but also elicited responses from long-deceased relations. No one came forward to accept the offer.

Rumors abounded that Amma priests sacrificed babies at their altar, that they sprinkled menstrual blood on their icons. The most insidious of all indictments was, however, the accusation that an Amma priest could change shape, assuming the skin of a leopard, wild dog, bat-eared fox, or, more frequently, a hyena. When a neighborhood was visited by a pack of hyenas, people ceased to chase after the beast and rescue their property; instead, they watched from the safety of their windows and doorways for identifying marks that they could later trace back to a known Amma skin-changer.

The problem compounded as more and more villagers came forward with their individual experiences and suspicions. A boy who had lost packaged meat to a black kite on the way home from the butcher's shop, for instance, told a gawking audience how he had shot the bird with a sling and a well-aimed stone; on hitting the ground, the bird transformed itself into an Amma deacon that the boy immediately recognized; then, into a puddle of water. There was no trace of the water when villagers went to investigate minutes later—further proof of the mysterious ways in which the newcomers operated.

Judges were asked to levy penalties for properties lost, and petitions were initiated by overzealous neighbors who demanded that Amma priests be chained to the pillars of their huts after sunset and that guards be placed at their doors to deter further damage. When children were sent out on errands it became the norm to remind them to steer clear of wandering spirits, known to frequent damp sites and cactus bush, and that Amma priests were to be avoided. Wandering spirits might snatch away unwary children to make them their own, but at least there would be a fair chance of finding a missing child; a child lost in the stomach of a ravenous Amma skin-changer was lost for good.

As tensions escalated, Gudu decided to intervene. He arranged his customary meeting with the opinion-makers of the community: elders, clerks of both temples, diviners, and soothsayers. In the presence of the entire village, Gudu voiced all that had been said behind closed doors and in alehouses. If a man claimed to have stories of skin-changing Ammas, he was asked to come forward and spit on a black slate so that the experts could determine from his bubbling saliva if he was telling the truth. Twenty-eight cases were thrown out this way; an additional nine charges were ruled inconclusive by a board of learned men whose integrity no one questioned.

Gudu placed reconciliation ahead of retribution when he proposed that priests of both shrines get together once a week and go over upcoming sermons, thus avoiding accusations of tampering with each other's prayers, and encouraging each of them to make an effort to learn something about his neighbor's faith. Amma elders embraced the proposal wholeheartedly. They lured children to their classes, by handing out free sweets and toys, and taught them of their faith. They offered financial aid to reluctant parents. Years later, when Amma shrines outnumbered the homegrown ones, disgruntled elders would look back at those early days—the free sweets and toys—and shake their heads in disgust for not having caught on to the plot long before it was fully in effect.

Though the uprising had freed the vassals from any obligations they might have had to their former masters, it had yet to profit them. In fact, as the villagers had to man their new borders, build their own prisons, police their markets, and look after the judges they appointed, the amount of money that went to communal use steadily increased. Many ended up paying out more this way than they ever had under the deposed system. But the uprising was never undertaken for riches; it was about basic human dignity. Nor was it for revenge, but self-determination; not for shedding blood, but ending bloodshed. Above all, it was about realizing fair access to natural resources.

Two years after discarding the old shackles, as they kissed their wives and children good-bye and headed for the trenches, many of the village men would look back at the distances they had traveled and shake their heads in disbelief. Indeed, what an exhilarating feeling it must have been for someone who had never made a decision for himself to have, finally, his destiny firmly in his grasp: to grow the crop of his choice, to paint his home the color he fancied, to marry his daughter to the man he favored, and to be able to send his children to school, all without fear of repercussions from a feudal master. What is more, the peasant no longer needed to submit himself to the humility of waiting on his master's guests while his wife and daughter labored in the kitchen, preparing food they were not allowed to sample. The peasant might die fighting to hold on to his newly gained freedom; in the past he had always been dying fighting for someone else's cause. This was a feeling many outsiders, Duke Ashenafi and Reverend Yimam, above all, would never understand.

BOOK FIVE:

UPRISING

THE FEARED ONE

It was a day that I would be able to recall vividly half a century later. Dad was allowed to walk away from jail, having served the full two-year sentence brought down on him by the Inquisition. He seemed to have got off lightly for his crime; the type of heresy he had been convicted of carried a certain death sentence these days, now that the slaves he had sympathized with—Gudu and his cohorts—had colluded with Amma infidels and declared war on the true faith.

Dad's homecoming should have been celebrated on more than one account: because he had gained his freedom, and above all because he was getting away with his life. No friends came to drink a toast with us, however. Fears lingered that associating with a convicted heretic might draw the wrath of the Inquisition. Dad was out of work, and he would remain that way: there were no more vassals for him to oversee. Kersa was in the rebels' hands, and Harar had long since fortified its gates against unwanted visitors.

After two years without my father's wages, we were impoverished. Whatever money the hunchback monk had gathered through the sale of our hut and its contents had unaccountably vanished during the two years. There were no longer usurers in the valley of Deder to approach; usury, like idolatry and blasphemy, now carried a death sentence. We had no collateral to go looking for a loan anyway.

Feeding his family came to mean that Dad had to spend interminable hours away from home, as he searched for game or wild fruit. Each passing day took him farther and farther away, until one night he failed to return at all. Mam's desperation heightened when the next day passed with no word of his whereabouts. There were no friends or relations we could ask for help, so Mam and I set out to look for him.

Three days of intensive searching passed, and Mam and I were convinced that Dad had fallen prey to an *ergum,* that he had survived Reverend Yimam's wrath only to end his days in obscurity. His disappearance didn't rally his former friends to our side any more than his release from detention had.

Preparations were already under way to lay Dad's spirit to rest when, two weeks after his mysterious disappearance, the door of Duke Ashenafi's kitchen was kicked open and Dad stumbled inside, clothed in a new outfit and carrying a heaving sack of produce on his back. When the odds of survival in the barren valley had seemed unlikely to him, Dad had gone to more familiar ground, Kersa. The vassals there were pleased to see their former overseer. They extended to him hospitality they hadn't afforded him before and were leading him to the gallows with his hands firmly secured behind him when Gudu intervened.

Gudu felt ambivalent toward Dad. Even as a young boy growing up in the valley of Deder, he had thought of my father as an enigma, the one riddle that Gudu would never be able to solve. Gudu still remembered the day Dad had made history, saving the life of a bondsman who stood accused of making unwanted advances toward a freeborn woman. The accuser, an aging divorcee, suffered from an affliction: a constant craving for sex. There were rumors that she took up to six different men to bed each night. Dad won the accused the right to continue his life when he exposed the fact that it was the young man, not the accuser, who had snubbed unwanted advances. His successful defense earned Dad an equal number of friends and foes.

Gudu had been baffled that Dad, champion of a slave's rights, would nevertheless go out of his way to undermine the rights of vassals. "Why won't your father be like other overseers and treat the tenants with some degree of fairness?" Gudu used to ask me when we were growing up. I understood his meaning when I joined Dad on a trip to Kersa and witnessed the extortion he visited on the serfs. The Siege of Harar had revealed to Gudu yet another side of Dad, one that would remain hidden from me until I grew older.

Gudu embodied the finer traits of a true warrior and astute pacifier when he dissuaded the vassals from lynching their former tormentor. Cajoling them into sharing their windfall with their loathed enemy, however, proved more difficult. Gudu had to escort Dad out of the watchful sight of the vassals before handing him a bag of assorted produce for his family.

Over the next two months Dad would slip into Kersa three more times and return home with bags brimming with healthful produce—fresh roots of red beets and carrots, as well as beans, lentils, wheat, and barley. But if Mam and I were meant to be the actual beneficiaries of Gudu's largesse, we had yet to find out; Dad disposed of the goods in the proliferating underground market. The money didn't make it home either. Instead, the local alehouses celebrated Kersa's windfall.

Dad stayed out late more and more frequently, often returning home only to sleep. At first Mam was angered by his unseemly change of character, but soon her anger gave way to concern. She feared the wrath of the hunchback monk. She warned Dad that if the supreme legate caught on to his flirtation with the heretics of Kersa, it was not Dad alone who would pay for his crime this time around, but his entire family. Dad scoffed at her worries. Months would go by before we found out the reason.

Behind the scenes, Dad had reached an agreement with the men responsible for his prolonged imprisonment. He had forged a friendship with the crusaders, one that would embarrass his family more than the destitution we had suffered, the hunger and want we had endured. Mam could no longer go to the market by herself for fear of being jeered at by her lifelong neighbors. She couldn't go out to collect firewood or water, lest she was ambushed by the new enemies we made. Dad may not have shared his newfound spoils with us, but we inherited his dues.

Strange men frequented our home. Whispered conversations took place between Dad and the crusaders outside our door. Gudu's name was a touchstone of their conversations. I pricked up my ears, hoping to find out the kernel of their secret: Dad and his newfound friends had been plotting to wage a surprise attack on Kersa to kidnap the rebels at the core of the uprising, including Gudu, and bring a swift end to the revolt. Dad had become a spy!

"I want a divorce," Mam told Dad when she learned of his scheme. "How dare you betray the boy we raised?" she cried. But Dad simply brushed her off. He knew as well as anyone else in the valley of Deder that, though Beza had gone up in smoke, her legacy had endured. Avoiding divorce and family disputes was no longer a matter of saving face, but an article of the true faith.

Despite my passionate feelings for Gudu's cause, I might not have left the valley of my childhood to join the rebellion had it not been for my father's alliance with the crusaders. Many a life was at stake, above all that of the young man I considered a brother. My reputation was in tatters. I was being taunted by boys I had grown up with for the mistakes of my dad.

Though I was thirteen, and considered grown-up, my knowledge of the world outside the valley was severely limited. I had been to Kersa only once. I had never participated in an expedition before, much less an armed conflict. When I decided to slip out of Deder, all I had in my possession was the dim memory of a seven-year-old boy in the wilderness and a hastily gathered bag of provisions.

The mount I chose was a robust one. The horse belonged to Reverend Yimam's first lieutenant, and that I appropriated it without detection gave me a measure of satisfaction. The weapon I slung over my shoulder belonged to Dad. The rifle had been given to him by the hunchback monk for the planned raid. I had never fired a gun before, but that was one skill I could easily learn on the long journey to Kersa.

I was aware of the consequences of my decision. I worried about Mam's plight in the face of my desertion. Who could say what the hunchback monk would do to her to seek his vengeance? But I hoped—and I was proven right later—that the monk would think, like my father, that I had simply run away as boys in search of a destiny were known to do. By the time the truth became known, I figured,

Mam would have a safe haven—in Kersa, perhaps, or the walled town of Harar.

Lost in the wilderness, my provisions almost gone, I blew into an extended savanna where the only landmark was a pair of giant baobab trees. Memories of a childhood journey came back to me in a rush. Above all, I remembered a certain pilgrim—Reverend Yimam—who had come to share the warmth of campfire with us below these same trees. I wished that Dad had had the foresight to pack a crystal ball in which to see the future instead of a bag of *markesha* with which to banish a phantom. We would have been spared our predicament.

My ghostly appearance at the gates of Kersa drew a great deal of attention. A lone rider coming to town might not be news elsewhere, but this was a village geared up for war. Each passing caravan of traders, every drifting pilgrim was carefully screened to ensure the safety of the fortress. I was treated like a decoy sent by an invading army. A thirteen-year-old boy, five days and leagues away from home, on a noble mission sounded fabulous even in the eyes of an open-minded captor. I was spared interrogation (torture) only after a passing soldier remembered my name from the confidences he had shared with Gudu.

Before I got to see Gudu, another sun would burn itself up. I was made to wait for him in a half-finished bungalow that bore an eerie resemblance to Aster's residence in Deder. Even the asymmetrical posts holding up the patio were carefully duplicated from the original structure. Later, I would learn that the project was one of Gudu's efforts to make Aster's transfer to her new home and new life less traumatic.

I caught a glimpse of genuine deference to their leader when the villagers flocked to welcome me as Gudu's childhood friend. They brought me steaming pots of stew and baskets of fruits. I had barely finished answering the amused queries of one group when another one showed up repeating the same refrain: "Where is the young boy who defied the wilderness?" I drifted to sleep with my stomach painfully bulging and the room full of chattering strangers.

When I opened my eyes again, in the dead of night, it was as though the crowd hadn't left at all. This time, though, it was a ragged band of men who stood towering over me, grinning. I detected Gudu in the middle and darted up from my bed to hug him. The merriment died down the moment I told the soldiers the reason for my unexpected visit.

In the following days Gudu, the three Abettors, and a select band of men held conferences that sent militiamen scuttling around. Scouts were dispatched to observe the arrival of the anticipated raiders. A week and a half later, when it seemed as though I must have imagined the whole plot and people began openly doubting me, a cavalry of men was sighted five leagues away from Kersa.

"Blood must not be shed," announced Gudu, as they prepared a welcoming party for the invaders. Even at such an early stage in his career as commander in chief, he realized that the key for a bloodless victory lay in persuading the enemy of the hopelessness of his position. Gudu decided to outnumber the invaders by a ratio of a hundred to one. Barely had Dad's cavalry wound its way down an open plain than it was greeted by the defenders from behind the surrounding mountains. As Gudu had hoped, the enemy lay its weapons down without thinking twice about using them.

Dad was separated from his troop and, under the protection of a few armed men, led toward the village hall, past a stone-throwing crowd. The remaining twenty-odd prisoners were marched toward an open court to hear the verdict that had been passed on them in absentia: they were to remain in Kersa, working the fields and living like vassals. In return, they would be fed and sheltered. Should any one of them attempt to escape, they were told, he wouldn't go very far: he would be weighed down with bullets. Gudu chose to speak to Dad alone.

Facing each other across a small table, their sweaty faces glinting under the flickering light of a lantern, Gudu and Dad were, to all appearances, old friends caught in an awkward situation. No hostilities were visible in the room. Dad was permitted to light up his corncob pipe and draw a few long puffs before answering the crucial question on Gudu's mind: Why had Dad betrayed them?

Dad explained how the hunchback monk had discovered his association with the rebels of Kersa and forced him to make the painful choice of either saving his family and himself from a blazing end at the stake, or serving the Inquisition. Dad attempted to explain, in vain, that though he had agreed to raid Kersa and take a few prisoners to satisfy the monk, Gudu was never on his list.

"What do you think will happen to you if I send you back home while your friends are detained here?" Gudu asked, without bothering to say whether he believed Dad's story.

The relief on Dad's face was visible, even from my view through a crack in the door. "I never thought of that," was all Dad had to say.

Gudu got up. In utter silence, he paced up and down the small room, gazing at his feet. A young soldier, half-hiding behind the shadow of the lamp in the corner, walked up to the commander in chief and whispered something in his ear; Gudu shook his head in disagreement. Dad's eyes shifted from the man responsible for his fate to the young soldier, hoping perhaps that Gudu wouldn't change his mind about granting him his freedom.

Keeping Dad as a citizen of Kersa was unthinkable, but there were places in the province that were still outside the reach of the hunchback monk. Gudu gave Dad a pouch of money and escorts. He told the escorts to give the captive his weapon once he was out of range. Having promised Dad to send Mam to keep him company at the opportune moment, Gudu bade him farewell.

Tears coursed down Dad's face. He looked as though he was about to give Gudu a grateful hug, but the commander in chief took a scornful step backwards. Just before Gudu marched out of the room with his guards in tow, Dad asked the one question that had been eating at him since he had been held prisoner: How had Gudu found out about the raid? Gudu was still deciding whether to answer when I burst into the room.

Dad was crestfallen. When he finally spoke, it was not to reprove me. "I am not angry with you for the decision you have made," he said. "At least one of us has done the honorable thing." Dad and I hugged, shed more tears, and separated.

Before the door came between us, I saw a strange look on Dad's face. It was the same look I would see on his face when our paths crossed again some thirty-six years later. I had just concluded a six-year war against a troublesome prince and was imperiously dictating the conditions of the prince's surrender when one of my lieutenants walked inside the army tent and whispered in my ear that there was a man outside claiming to be my father. A wry smile crossed the soldier's face. The young man, like many of the soldiers under my command, knew of my mother, who moved with me from place to place to stay by my side. As I had never spoken of my father, however, everyone had assumed that Dad had died in the most dishonorable of circumstances, an ending that was too painful for me to divulge.

The look on Dad's face during that reunion was unforgettably awkward. "I wasn't mistaken in naming you Teferi, after all," was what he said as we were greeting each other after the long separation. I told him that my faith in the stars had long been restored. For by then I had seen far too many good men fail, despite their lofty ideas and laudable efforts, merely because they were born with their stars askew.

This reunion led to my finally understanding my father. The very next day, a warlord I defeated in battle shook my family tree to see who else might fall out, and discovered that Dad had been born to a woman in bondage. My father had left his hometown at the age of eleven—upon being granted his freedom by a dying master. Wistfully, I came to appreciate his strange attitude toward the vassals, and his equally baffling goodwill toward bondsmen. It was simply an ancient grudge. Nothing irks a bondsman more than being looked down upon by a vassal—a man who fares socially no better than himself. Unbeknownst to Gudu and me, Dad had been waging a war of his own—with himself.

TAKING CARE OF ASTER

Even before the botched attempt to kidnap Gudu, Reverend Yimam had never lost track of the developments in Kersa, but he chose to keep his army on a short leash, convinced that a disorderly uprising of slaves and serfs was bound to fail. It was his belief that a bondsman lacked not only the capacity for self-government but also for the higher pursuit of civic virtues and culture, that a slave might hold a true belief but was unable to know the truth of his belief.

Since the start of the revolt, Reverend Yimam hadn't let a single sermon pass without touching upon the divine laws that governed the relation of master and slave, of sovereign and subjects, of body and soul. He often sought inspiration from the cosmos to explain away the hierarchical patterns and contradictions that pervaded society. The universe, he noted, is beset by a dualism consisting of good and evil—drought and flood, famine and gluttony, wildfire and rebirth, to name only a few—so one can seldom eliminate evil without destroying the beauty and balance of the whole. To the hunchback monk, the vassal might have grievances—which in his rustic innocence he could well interpret as rectifiable inequities—but any attempt to redress the wrong constituted a breach of the higher unity of good and evil.

The vassals of Kersa would harness the Death Valley, tame their hunger and insecurities; they would raise a militia of two thousand men, arm and train them; they would even go on to integrate the slaves and Ammas with the freeborn and devoted, in direct violation of the spirit of the Inquisition, and Reverend Yimam would still be waiting for the uprising to implode. When he finally stirred out of his lethargy, two years later, the risks of waging war loomed higher than the rewards of winning one. Kersa might be brought to its knees, if at all, but at a cost of hundreds, perhaps thousands, of lives and months of pitched battle; if there was one man who stood to benefit most from the vassals' defeat, it was not the hunchback monk.

Reverend Yimam set out to draw small concessions from Duke Ashenafi for rescuing his property in Kersa. When logic and reason failed, he resorted to discreet pressure. Duke Ashenafi, for once of late, held his ground, for unlike Harar, where he had exercised dominion only recently, Kersa had been in the family far too long for him to part with easily. The hunchback monk, who would rather have brandished his avenging pitchfork, bit his lip at the rejection; the sun hadn't yet set since he had received an admonition from the Supreme Pontiff for alienating the aristocracy, for inciting war on one too many fronts. Reverend Yimam issued a secret directive to his aides, instructing them to keep a watchful eye on Aster. Perhaps the young lady's suspended sentence was due for reconsideration.

Aster was seldom seen outdoors. In fact, she rarely left her bed. Ever since the family had moved to its new quarters, following the celebrated trial, she hadn't been the same person. She ate little, and often was force-fed. When she went without a meal for a day too long, a company of nurses was summoned. Four pairs of hands held her firmly in bed while a midwife forced a spoonful of soup or gruel down her throat.

No one would hazard a guess as to whether Aster would be able to overcome her afflictions, not even the most omniscient Hermit of Hermits. Four months would go by before Duke Ashenafi decided to take his daughter to a holy fountain. Though the trip was no more arduous than many others he had taken in his days, the condition of his daughter and the time of year he chose made it exceptionally dangerous.

The winding basin that lay ahead was the migratory route of the wildebeest. Twice each year, the herd swarmed the dried-up waterbed in a mad attempt to break the stranglehold of drought, stampeding all that got in its way. Predators followed the herd to rescue the dead and wounded. This was one of the rare moments when the least aggressive of beasts would think nothing of pouncing on a passerby without reason.

A journey that was usually over in two weeks took father and daughter a full month, not because of any four-legged beast that got in their way, but because of bandits that waylaid pilgrims. The name Ashenafi, which had once carried tremendous weight in the region, sending shivers down the spines of many a brave man, meant little to the outlaws who stripped father and daughter of all valuables, including their horses and carriage, prayer books and sacrifices for the road. It was a small miracle that the two were spared their lives. Even more miraculous was the fact that Aster made it to the holy fountain on foot.

With only three springs in the kingdom recognized for their curative powers, and access to all three free to the public, the ragtag line of pilgrim patients extended willy-nilly to the far side of the moon. Bulky men paced up and down, peering into the faces of the desperate, and offering access through a side entrance for the nominal fee of a king's ransom. These self-appointed ushers readily stepped in to help when a patient resisted taking the curative showers. Only too late would relatives of the patient find out the price of such goodwill.

Having lost his fortune en route, Duke Ashenafi resigned himself to standing in line for eternity. After three days, however, two of the self-appointed ushers came to see him. Addressing the duke deferentially, the men offered to take him and the patient through the side door and therefore ahead of the slouching crowd. His surprise at being recognized by these thugs was eclipsed only by their indifference to his inability to raise the ransom.

A further surprise awaited him when Duke Ashenafi turned the corner. Ahead were the horses, carriage, suitcases, weapons, in fact all the valuables that he had lost to the bandits. While he stammered with incomprehension, one of the ushers grabbed a heaving sack from the carriage and snatched out the severed head of the bandit leader.

"We have been instructed to make your stay comfortable; let us know if there is anything we can do," the men concluded, before bowing away.

"Who should I thank for this?" Duke Ashenafi sputtered, when he finally found his voice.

"Gudu," came the answer.

Duke Ashenafi remained rooted to the ground where he stood.

The duke did not suspect further help from Gudu when, after only a day under the falling waters, his daughter sat down with him for dinner. The day after that, she sang in her shower. Before a full week had elapsed, Aster asked to be taken home, having thoroughly recovered her health and vigor. With paternal farsightedness, Duke Ashenafi arranged to carry barrels of the curative water on their return journey, over his daughter's disapproval.

Aster's condition had been known to Gudu all along, but, to avoid imperiling her safety any further, he chose not to communicate with her. He had been working on a plan to rescue her and his mother, Enquan, when news of the ambushed father and daughter reached him. No sooner had the bandits involved sat down to divide the loot amongst themselves than their loosely stitched friendship had come undone. Driven by personal revenge, one of the disgruntled robbers decided to bring the news to Gudu, not because he felt the rebel leader had any personal stake in the individual victims but because he suspected that banditry ran against the spirits of the uprising. Gudu dispatched a small army headed by one of the Abettors.

With the renegade bandit leading the way, the Abettor closed in on the brigands camped in a cave high up a rocky mountain. Assured in the safety of their hideout and the infallibility of their exploits, the robbers were blissfully drunk. The Abettor dispatched all five of them before they could blink twice, and for good measure he decided to let the converted thief join his cronies in the hereafter. Reeling with excitement, the war patriarch ached to go the distance and wrestle Aster from her father's grip; it took Gudu's iron clutch to restrain him. Though he had ceased to live by the rules of his old master, Gudu appreciated that nothing could be more humiliating to the duke than seeing his daughter snatched from his very fingers.

Gudu bided his time. He wanted to make Kersa a safe place for his future wife. But, above all, he wished to make sure that Aster lacked nothing in her new home. Building a manor fashioned after the residence she had known proved more difficult than anyone had anticipated. The decor, the garden, and every piece of furniture in every room had to be identical to what she would leave behind. Locating the necessary items in the markets wasn't easy. If he had only accepted how little Aster valued the trappings of her old life, if he had only believed that she really did want to soil her hands building their new home together, Gudu wouldn't have sacrificed the resources that he could hardly afford.

The seasons would roll by and the granaries of life would overflow with unbounded optimism before Gudu, finally, put his plan to reunite with Aster to work. Six men were chosen for the assignment. For two long months the men marched into Deder, leading caravans of camels that carried firewood, charcoal, and sacks of sorghum and corn, to earn the trust of suspicious guards. Careful not to betray their association with Kersa, the men left town at dusk; they never took the same trail twice.

While the rescue team trained in the dark, secret agents communicated with Aster and Enquan, coaching them for the imminent journey. Aster trained herself by taking long walks, while Enquan marched to and from distant markets with her small load of produce strapped on her back, instead of fetching a mule or a donkey. Though she had been promised safe conduct, and her trust in Gudu was unwavering, Aster spent many sleepless nights speculating about the unknown. Stories of beasts that sprang out of thin air, and of *ergums* that ferried entire expeditions into realms where they could never be found, came back to her. She shuddered at the thought of becoming one of those young women in the fables who fell prey to lustful monkeys and gave birth to anything from a half baboon to a chimpanzee. But such fears subsided quickly and were replaced by sheer giddiness at the prospect of being reunited with her love and living out her life in peace and contentment.

During her last days at home, Aster was assailed by emotions of which she had never thought she was capable. The idea of leaving everything she had known behind, perhaps never to see it again, brought tears to her eyes. She ate little, prayed a great deal. She refused to look her father in the eye, lest her legs give out on her. Duke Ashenafi was troubled by his daughter's mood swings and hoped they were not the first signs of an affliction that might, yet again, send him on a quest for a remedy. If he had only looked under her bed, he would have found the clues to his daughter's affliction wrapped in a tight roll—items Aster intended for a trip of her own.

The expansive valley was deserted after sunset, when the townspeople took their unfinished business of the day behind closed doors, whether it was sifting through a bale of legumes, mending a piece of furniture, or catching up with the latest scandal. The aroma of cooking lingered in doorways, the scent marking the owner's status. A whiff of clarified butter and roasting meat wriggled out of the kitchen of the rich, while a waft of bean soup or roasting chickpeas seeped through the chimneys of the have-nots. After dinner, the last of the day's three coffees were brewed, and neighbors joined in to celebrate. Since the arrival of the Inquisition, it had become the norm to attend a nightly mass; after coffee, doors opened, and the townspeople—huddled in their identical *gabbi*—came out and shuffled through the pitch-dark streets toward the Shrine Hall. The service lasted well into the night. The highly regimented life in the valley left few windows open through which Aster could make her escape.

Tossing and turning in bed, Aster monitored the rhythmic breathing of her parents lying in a bunk next to her. She gauged the downfall of her family by the cracks in the thatched roof, door, and windows. The most hideous crack was, however, the one she chose not to see. It was the fissure that broke apart her household permanently: her elopement.

At the slightest shuffle outside her door, Aster pricked up her ears, hoping for a coded message and the arrival of her escorts. Just before dawn, she heard the high-pitched wail of a jackal, repeated three times; she slid out of her bed, wended her way through the clutter, pausing every so often to see if her parents had been alerted, before she slid the latch on the door and slipped out of the room and into the morning breeze, undetected.

No words passed between Aster and her company until the band was safely out of the valley and beyond the draping mountains. The horses settled into a gentle gait, and the rebels snatched a breath of relief. Overcome by an indescribable sensation, Aster felt nauseated and threw up on herself. The rebels must have appreciated her agony; they drew up under the shade of an acacia tree for an early break. The patient was treated with a medication of mixed herbs and was soon back on her horse. They didn't stop again until the thin air around them had fused into an oceanic mirage under the midday sun. Aster spent her first night of freedom in the open, tucked away between overgrown bushes and a steep cliff.

Duke Ashenafi was about to go to the outhouse when he discovered that the door he had securely latched from the inside the night before was now locked from outside. Lighting the bedside lamp, he was contemplating the mystery when his eyes caught sight of the empty bed beside him. Aster never left her bed before sunrise, and when she did she always alerted someone. His heart leaping to his mouth, Duke Ashenafi called out for help. A moment later, a guard opened the door, and a small crowd gathered to investigate.

The valley buzzed louder than a beehive on a kindling tree. A search team was called and every possible hideout was combed, twice. By noon it was evident that, unless the young lady had been kidnapped by a beast from her dreams, she had eloped. There was only one place where someone who doesn't wish to be found could go, and that was Kersa. The face of the hunchback monk lit up with rancor. He readily rounded up two hundred able men and galloped into the hinterlands.

Anticipating the posse, the rebels didn't lounge around while the sun was up. Each night they located a campsite off the beaten trail and rested their backs and their horses. By the third day they felt assured of victory, as there were no pursuers in sight and they were so close to home. Come the following night they would all be sleeping in their own beds. Reaching this milestone called for a celebration. A husky impala was hunted down, and they feasted on the barbecue. The fatigue of the past three days must have taken its toll; when they opened their eyes, it was not because of the rising sun, but because of hundreds of smiles blinding them. The crusaders had caught up with them.

Five of the six rebels were disposed of where they lay, by order of Reverend Yimam, who figured that it took only one of them to tell him what he wanted to know about the uprising in Kersa. With Aster and Enquan on one mule, and the remaining rebel following on foot, both his hands tied to a leash, the crusaders sang their way back home. The time was ripe for Duke Ashenafi to sign over his remaining property to the cause, for Gudu to make concessions to save his mother from the stake, and for the crusaders finally to stamp out the plague of faithlessness that infected the people of Kersa.

DUNG BEETLE

Midday loomed, and there were still no townspeople in sight. Doors and windows were locked. The chimneys were still. Anticipating a more raucous departure of the crusaders than the one visited on the valley two years before, the townspeople were wisely staying indoors. The night before, many of them had witnessed a dress rehearsal for the performance in Kersa, as drunken men pillaged the shrine, yet again; raped women, young and old; set ablaze three barns; and laid waste a newly built school—all in full view of the supreme legate and his curates.

And that was not for lack of adequate support from the locals. In fact, the week before, the townspeople had devoted much more of their time to the crusaders than to their own families. The women had labored through the night preparing food, which they packed in woven baskets; the men had unstrung lines and lines of beef and mutton that had been hanging out to dry, and seasoned and pressed it into hundreds of rolls. Their children would have to go hungry for a while, but they reasoned that this was one sacrifice worth making. With the eye of the storm shifting to the rebellious village of Kersa, many hoped this would be the last time they would see the crusaders.

As they saddled their horses, the crusaders couldn't help but suspect that their departure was being celebrated by the townspeople. It was, perhaps, this pent-up anxiety that prompted some of the pilgrims to poison the town's water hole before they decamped.

With over half of his men trudging along on foot and a quarter more on the backs of donkeys, Reverend Yimam looked like a dung beetle rolling a ball of elephant droppings up a treacherous precipice. He attempted to rectify the situation by raiding villages and monasteries along the way, and appropriating horses and mules. He promised the gullible a reward in the hereafter; the quarrelsome, the gibbet. Merchants lost their loads to the cause; salt miners, their axes and shovels.

The ranks of the crusaders had diminished over the years. Many volunteers had slipped back to their provinces when the riches they had anticipated began to prove more elusive than an afternoon mirage; some of the vassals had to be let go, however reluctantly, because they were obligated, through the service of their fiefs, to campaign for no more than three months each year. The hunchback monk was forced to top up his army along the way. Though there were always men who joined the Crusade hoping to expiate the vices and crimes of a whole life with a single good deed to the Almighty, there were also those who were bought over with a more earthly reward.

Reverend Yimam earned the goodwill of new recruits with the promise of plenary absolution of all sins committed from the day of their birth to that of their death, and of any obligations they might have to their landlords, including the payment of interest on their loans. Above all, he abandoned to them all the confiscated household properties of the heretics they had slain, and a share of the bountiful harvest that everyone talked about—he made sure, however, that no one got the wrong idea about the land and possessions due Duke Ashenafi, which he intended for higher purposes.

His real plans for Kersa became apparent when he gave a fiery sermon the day before the army stormed the rebellious village. As much for the enemy's ears as for his own army, he pronounced that there would be no leniency for the heretics; that if the infidels were not crushed and their race exterminated, there would ultimately be a conflagration throughout the civilized world that would be beyond human control to stop. He advised that no converts be admitted once the avenging sword was unsheathed, no prisoners be taken.

If the hunchback monk had a well-thought-out strategy, it was not apparent on the first day of engagement. As soon as a verdant cornfield came into view, his army of men ran apart, like a ripple in a still pond of water, leaving behind their mounts and their guard. For most of the pilgrims, the sight of a green-felted landscape was a spiritual rebirth; the taste of a fresh ear of corn, baptism. None had anticipated any evil or danger lurking in the serene overgrowth when, suddenly, men started dropping right and left, caught up in a whizzing dance of arrows. More ominously, none of the men on the outside realized what had befallen their comrades.

The traps had been set long before the crusaders left Deder. Anticipating such an interlude, Gudu had ordered that holes be dug in the cornfield. The holes were covered over by innocuous-looking weeds and stalks. Men lay waiting in the dugout while the invaders sated their hunger, jumping up and down the field like a bunch of baboons, tearing ears of corn, taking one bite and discarding the rest.

The defenders waited until many more of the pilgrims had walked inside the expanding trap and settled into their intoxicated merriment before springing on them. Arrows and spears were chosen, instead of guns, for greater effect. One hundred and seventy-two unsuspecting soldiers would breathe their last and seventy-five more would lie mortally wounded before Reverend Yimam sensed something was awry, but he didn't realize what it was until a man with seven arrows in his back and one arm missing staggered out of the field and fell dead at his feet.

The alarm was raised. The field reverberated with the echoes of war drums and trumpets. Frantic men dashed up and down a clearing, firing blindly at any shuffle within the crop, unwittingly killing or wounding many of their own. The hunchback monk despaired of restoring even a semblance of order, but power had long since slipped out of his arthritic fingers. Many of the pilgrims would exhaust their meager supply of cartridges before they settled down. When the casualties were tallied at the end of the day, over three hundred soldiers were unaccounted for. What was more disheartening to the wounded was, perhaps, that no one dared walk into the deadly field to rescue them.

Reverend Yimam ordered the destruction of the verdant tapestry, and soon smoke and soot rose high above the surrounding mountains, eclipsing the dying sun and bringing an early closure to the day. The fire was, however, far too inadequate to consume the entire crop. For the following three days, men would toil from dawn to dusk, cutting down plants, burying the dead, and attending to the wounded.

On the fourth day, Kersa came into full view. The crusaders stood gawking at the menacing fortress that awaited them, and the notorious Death Valley that lay hidden just behind the flattened cornfield.

If Reverend Yimam had expected the campaign to be a stroll in the park, he was jolted out of his saddle when he discovered the park entirely missing, for there was nothing but an eerie skeleton of a village ahead of him. There were no enemies in sight, no watchtowers to aim his guns at. He reached deep inside the small recesses of his brain for a parable passed down by a farsighted ancestor, but nowhere in the dark caves of human history had a note been scribbled, much less a sketch, of a battle comparable in its ingenuity and caliber. Wars were routinely waged and settled each year, but almost all of them took place in open fields with the combatants bravely facing each other. The weapons of choice were limited, so no one would attribute success or failure in a battlefield to anything other than sheer bravery, or the lack of it. Until a generation ago, men would not have been found in trenches unless they were dead and rotting, for a brave man was expected to remain on his feet when facing a whizzing arrow. An enemy hiding behind high walls, like the tenants of Harar, or one materializing out of a cornfield, like a regular bandit, was something for the storybooks.

Disregarding all the warnings he had heard about the powers of the foreboding valley, the supreme legate decided to send a handpicked band of men into Kersa under the cover of darkness. With the setting sun, the demonic fumes that were emitted from the gorge had already begun to rise higher than the valley walls. From the far end, one could make out a bird or two dropping down to sip from pristine waters, but they were never seen flying again. A fish eagle carved a circle high above the crusaders' heads before deciding to pick off victims of the valley.

Though his soldiers had drawn his attention to the small spectacle unfolding before him, the retribution of Death Valley, Reverend Yimam maintained that their fear was due more to lack of adequate zeal for the cause than to the presumed powers of the ravine. Anyway, he would never dispatch a scout on an assignment, however remote the threat of danger, without giving them a touch of Holy Ash for their foreheads, and six rounds of prayers.

Having been ordered not to light campfires or torches, which might give away their location, the crusaders relied on the dimly lit sky as they charted their way. Twinkling eyes sprang up all around them, causing a shuffle in the herd and restlessness among the men, but the still night betrayed no more of Kersa's secrets than the daylight hours had done. No fires crackled from the rickety kitchens dotting the corridors, no shafts of light leaked through doorways and windows, no women emerged to observe their customary Outing, no one bothered to attend to cattle in the barn. Three long days later the only evidence of the existence of the enemy was their ghostly sallies that had deprived the pilgrims of their heads.

If he had been mystified by the way his enemies operated, Reverend Yimam had also found his inspiration from their success. He reasoned that, if the infidels could march across the ominous valley at will, inflicting scandalous casualties, the crusaders, with the true faith behind them, could only fare better. Not once did he consider the power wielded by the three Abettors working with Gudu.

The three Abettors had participated in over two hundred pitched battles, three hundred hit-and-run sorties, cases of arson, and ride-by shootings, as well as one blind ambush, but what had immortalized them was that they had fought on opposing sides, shifting their allegiance during the course of a raging conflict, not out of malice or sublime disregard to the known rules of engagement, but out of concern for the flagging spirit and waning energy of the losing side.

It was because of the three Abettors that the militia of Kersa had quickly matured into the seasoned and formidable army it had become; the three patriarchs were also responsible for the celebrated sally. They trained a group of men to creep across the valley hanging from the shaft of the undershot wheels as if it were a bridge (the wheels had been rolled into a shed). The demonic fumes were less dangerous at the top, but, even then, the Abettors took few chances. They made the men breathe through bamboo stalks, not unlike a man under water, while covering their faces with moist sheepskin. Timing each successive sortie carefully, the Abettors were able to reduce the time it took for a soldier to make it across the valley, and to safety, to under ten minutes. During the conflict, the shafts were removed before sunrise, lest the crusaders caught on to the ruse.

Reverend Yimam fell into the hands of the Abettors when he dispatched his men along the beaten trail. No sooner had the scouts disappeared behind the towering walls of the valley than their distressed calls surged through the darkness. The dead were carried on the backs of the few survivors to the other side of the divide. Not all were accounted for. Over twenty men lay at the bottom of the ravine.

No sooner had the few survivors finished laying the wounded and dying on the ground than the earth under their feet opened up and they were showered with well-aimed arrows. Many of the men were too distracted to know what had befallen them. There were also those who breathed their last, firm in their belief that the ghosts of their victims from the past had come back to haunt them. So sudden was the ambush, so complete was the surprise, that if the witnesses on the other side of the ravine had turned their heads only once, they would have missed the entire debacle.

Dawn broke over a somber horizon. The ragged crowd of pilgrims had visibly dwindled. Aside from the war casualties, there were also those who had slipped back home, undetected. Even the neutral earth seemed to have betrayed Reverend Yimam. In the middle of the calm morning, tiny columns of whirlwinds bubbled out of the ground, linked up arms, and grew into a towering dust devil. As it headed toward the pilgrims, the dust devil gathered such force that it laid waste the few standing trees, tents, carriages, and the crusaders' only portable altar. Pebbles and tumbleweed pelted the men as they huddled together, heads pressed against one another. Some lost the cloth on their backs, while others were shaven clean by flying debris.

When it seemed to many that this was further proof of the wrath of the Redeemer, and they wondered who amongst them might be the reprobate, the wind died down at once. If the pilgrims were surprised by the suddenness of the whirlwind, they were stunned with incomprehension when they found no trace of the retreating twister.

A further surprise awaited them when they set out to assess the damage, for standing in the midst of the rubble were three strangers. A slow befuddlement gave way to palpable panic. Guns and bows were drawn, and the crusaders retreated for cover. In a rare display of leadership and accountability, the hunchback monk ordered his men to hold fire. Something about the demeanor of the visitors, their unearthly grace and stoic indifference, made the monk take notice. Upon closer inspection his suspicion proved justified, for there was no mistaking the birthmarks on the eyelids of the strangers.

The three Abettors had hitched a ride on the back of the dust devil when they realized that the battle they had dreamed about for two long years had quickly degenerated into slaughter. Nothing is more maddening to a self-respecting warrior than partaking in easy butchery. To many a brave man, soldiering is not all about killing; soldiering is about proving one's valor in the face of mounting danger. It is the stale breath of Death on his open and vulnerable neck that immortalizes the hero, that lends a fireside story its luster.

The Abettors had been compelled by the vows they had made as impartial warriors to come to the aid of the crusaders. They chose to ride the dust devil, instead of their conspicuous mounts, lest the rebels suspect, in their rustic innocence, that they were being sold out.

And so, pressed by time and their obligations on two fronts, the Abettors immediately disclosed the weak positions of the crusaders in the preceding two engagements. The crusaders' lack of field sketches and a fallback plan surprised them, but what troubled the Abettors most was the rigidly structured nature of the army.

In a campaign where the opponents had to face each other across an open field, it was crucial to relegate all power into the hands of one man. Standing well behind the firing range, the commander could observe the entire spectacle from the height of his saddle and make an informed decision. In guerrilla warfare, such as the kind facing the crusaders, the patriarchs favored relegating some decision-making into the hands of the field officer. If the men crossing the valley had been allowed to decide on the conduct of the engagement, the Abettors argued, they would most likely have sent a man or two to gauge the level of danger before jumping in as a team.

Throughout the afternoon, a vast number of scenarios were discussed, but nothing was singled out as the next maneuver, on the insistence of the Abettors, who didn't wish to be blamed for any possible failure.

Though they refused to say anything about the size and armaments commanded by Gudu, the patriarchs didn't shy away from answering a question or two about tactical matters. When asked how the rebels were able to march across the valley without imperiling themselves, for instance, the Abettors readily replied that it was because of the portable bridge in their possession. Since the sparse acacia field behind the crusaders was hardly a good place to harbor a bridge, there was little danger that the crusaders could exploit this volunteered piece of intelligence.

When someone wanted to know how the rebels managed to stay out of sight even when they were not underground, the Abettors answered that the villagers were actually in full view of the crusaders, even as they spoke, only they had mastered the subtle technique of walking without shadows.

Reverend Yimam congratulated himself for staying the hands of his overeager men, for the cost of firing at the Abettors could have been monumental indeed. Not only were the war patriarchs immune to random attacks, but they were bound to answer fire with multiple fire, resulting in a colossal loss of life. Only two proven ways existed to cause premature death of an Abettor: by lightning, or by burning his hidden amulet.

As the rains keep to no man's schedule and since holding an army of Abettors behind bars would tax the resources of even the most affluent emperor, preference was often given to finding the hidden amulets. A dedicated tribe of men would shadow an Abettor from sun to sun, in the hope of coming upon him as he sat down to offer sacrifices to his concealed soul. For the successful tribesmen the rewards of the find could be a small fortune indeed. The tribesmen would conduct the auction, and the Abettor's powerful antagonists engaged in the bidding.

Reverend Yimam had tried his hand at obtaining the amulet of a celebrated Abettor years before. On finding out there was a price on his soul, the war patriarch rode for seventy-five days, nonstop, running to death seven horses in the process, to meet his opponent head-on. His overgrown beard brushing against his knees, and his body reeking like a territorial civet, the Abettor made his way into the monk's hut through the chimney. Dragging his enemy out of bed, the war patriarch made an example of him by tying him up to the center post of the hovel with his worldly possessions balanced on top of his head; he gagged the monk's mouth with his soiled underwear, removed his testicles and the tip of his nose before slipping out of the room the way he had come in.

Days would go by before neighbors suspected that the monk might still be in his room, but they were not assured of their suspicions until the unmistakable waft of human waste greeted them in the hall passage. When the monk was finally rescued, eleven days later, his back was irretrievably buckled, his manhood utterly compromised, his face disfigured, and he had begun to stutter. Never again would he malign an Abettor, much less aim his gun at one on purpose.

LETTING DOWN THE GUARD

For the first time in weeks, we, the inhabitants of Kersa, woke to the sound of songbirds. The enemy across the valley had mysteriously disappeared. Suspecting a ruse, we didn't let down our guard for another seven days. Then we began adapting to a normal life. The sentries relaxed, and the children resumed school. A full two weeks went by, and by then the crusaders had faded far into the back of our minds.

I began pressing Gudu to assign me to one of the army divisions—the cavaliers or, preferably, the guerrilla units. He refused, citing the promise he had made Mam to keep me out of all danger. Mam had remained in the valley of her birth, refusing to join either Dad or me. If the Almighty meant for her to die, she reasoned, there was no place safe enough for her. Indeed, her time must not have been up, for there was no other way to account for the fact that she remained one of the few individuals spared the Inquisitors' wrath.

Gudu assigned me the roles of bookkeeper and archivist. I kept ledgers on the activities of the new government and the enemy we fought. Information gathered by infiltrators on the conduct of the crusaders was directed to me to enter into one ledger, alongside the progress made by Amma warriors on the various fronts. I kept a separate record on the economic activities of the village, the agricultural produce, and how it was divided up. There was also the most confidential file, one only Gudu consulted, regarding the spiritual alignment of the inhabitants of Kersa. Gudu had dreamed of the day when the entire village would convert to the new faith, Amma.

Many a night, when Gudu and I tired of poring over the files, we reminisced about our times with Aster. We speculated on what Aster might be doing at the moment we were thinking of her, what her prayers might be. Examining the half-finished bungalow in detail, we wondered how Aster might react to her new home and surroundings. "You will live with us until you get old enough to set up your own home," Gudu would assure me. Before going to bed, we said prayers for Aster.

But prayers were not enough to stay the onslaught of the hunchback monk and draw peace closer. Only a few weeks elapsed before we heard from the crusaders again. Having made his way around the curtain of mountains, Reverend Yimam covertly advanced his army on to the northern end of the settlement. The garrisons were quickly overpowered, without a single bullet being fired. The hunchback monk had proved himself a quick learner by refusing to overrun the sleepy village and opting instead for guerrilla tactics.

He dispatched a scouting party of fifty men, accompanied by dog charmers and spell-casters. The village dogs had barely begun to growl when the dog charmers bribed them into silence with a morsel from a fresh kill dosed generously with henbane. Following the dog charmers were the spell-casters, who cleared the alleys of unwanted spirits for those directly behind. Torchbearers set ablaze homes, shops, barns, shrines (of either faith), prison cells, and playgrounds—in fact, just about everything that stood in their way. If a sheep or goat wandered in their direction in its mad search for refuge, the torchbearers set a match to its wool. When the cows broke out of the kindled pens, they were met by rings of fire along the escape route. In a matter of hours, the stretched-out village, once serene and confident in its fortress, had been transformed into a bed of flames.

Doors opened and men and women poured out, clad only in bedsheets or *gabbi.* With fuzzy eyes they stood gawking at the fires, wondering if they were witnessing the Final Judgment or experiencing a collective dream. Men began dropping left and right, saluted by flying bullets. Children perished under frantic feet. Nowhere was safe for the villagers to hide. Not even the skies were impartial, for arrows rained from the dimly lit heavens.

The trio of Abettors knelt on the searing ground and said grace; their prayers had been answered—they had finally found a worthy opponent.

The ravages of the night stunned the villagers at dawn. People couldn't fetch water, since the windlasses had been burned down; they couldn't cook, because their firewood and piles of charcoal had been reduced to ashes. Only a quarter of the escaped herd would be gathered up by the end of the day. Some perished in the fire; most were seized by the crusaders. Perhaps the most disheartening loss for Gudu was that of the horses and mules, severely compromising his yet-untested cavaliers. If there was one consolation to the villagers, it was the fact that their granaries had survived the raid.

The immediate shock of the ambush began to wear off by noon, and was soon replaced by the sheer determination to prevail. Since surrender meant a certain death at the stake, men and women, young and old, labored equally to fortify their defenses. The village of Kersa was made up of eight communities spread out over an area four leagues in length and two leagues in width; it would take an army much superior in number and arms than the ragtag crusaders to invade a considerable section of the stretch of land. After a weeklong battle, all Reverend Yimam would command was the northern tip of the settlement, comprising three communities with a combined population of only five thousand.

If the villagers had any lingering hopes about the intentions of the crusaders, the days and weeks that followed laid those hopes to rest. No sooner had the hunchback monk dismounted his horse than he set out to uproot faithlessness. First to be consigned to flames were the few remaining Ammas who had been too young or too infirm to join the refugees; next went their place of worship and homes. Then followed those Mawusas who had sought asylum in the Mawusas shrines. Ninety-five men, women, and children were dragged out of the temple and beheaded by order of the supreme legate, who reasoned that if they had been innocent of crimes, they wouldn't have sought shelter behind the altar.

The purge was expanded when local priests submitted to the hunchback monk a previously prepared list of apostates, blasphemers, usurers, traitors, sodomites, and idolaters. One hundred and twenty-two men and women were rounded up and placed behind bars.

When one of the local priests whispered in his ear not to show any mercy to the heretics, Reverend Yimam, a man who had never been known for his human emotions, burst out laughing. He had been reminded of another man of God, the Bishop of Saintes, who was immortalized when he pleaded with the son of the king of France, Louis, to make an example of the captives in his hands. "Sir," the bishop is believed to have said, "my advice to you is to immediately kill and burn all these people as heretics and apostates, and then you do neither more nor less to those of the city." But Louis couldn't bring himself to put to the sword prisoners of war.

Reverend Yimam was no Louis. He made the prisoners file into his chamber one by one, and praying for their redemption, he proceeded to gouge out their eyes and cut off their noses and ears. Under the guidance of a one-eyed man, he sent the mutilated prisoners to the garrison across the newly drawn border so that his enemies would take note of the fate that awaited them if they didn't lay down their arms at once.

"That was the most original chastisement, sire," a curate couldn't help but proclaim.

"Not at all," replied the hunchback monk. "The credit goes to Simon de Montfort, count of Leicester. I only added the ears."

Reverend Yimam passed the torch to his followers, and they in turn tortured, raped, and killed both young and old, men and women; broke into homes and made away with what few valuables they found; they set alight what they couldn't carry. When some of the villagers raised moneys to save their homes from the flames, the crusaders took the ransom but set the houses ablaze anyway. Drunk, they staggered into the only convent of Mawu-Lisa in the region and ravished the nuns, defecated on the icons, cleaned themselves with pages torn from the Good Book, and set the monastery's centuries-old library ablaze—all in full view of the hunchback monk, who swaggered by sipping sweet wine from a silver decanter.

* * *

If he had thought that blind terror would conquer the rebels, the monk must have been confounded when the resistance intensified. A few hundred rebels set out to surround the annexed corner and flush the pilgrims out. It was simple and daring, but a well-thought-out plan. A variation on the guerrilla ambush, it adopted some of the finest aspects of field warfare as well. The success or failure of the campaign depended on complete secrecy and swift action.

As it happened, the plan had been relayed to the hunchback monk by informers inside the enemy camp. The crusaders dug themselves in; they waited until the rebels were well out of range of their base, and, therefore, cut off from reinforcements, before springing their trap. All of a sudden, it was a repeat performance of the cornfield drama—without the cornfield. It was the rebels' turn to run blindly all over the barren mountains in a desperate attempt to save their lives from an enemy they couldn't see.

The carnage continued throughout the night and well into the dawning day. By sundown, a small group of rebels had dug in at the mountaintop and refused to surrender. Reverend Yimam sent emissaries with a promise of reconciliation, but the rebels refused to budge, having perhaps heard what had happened to others who had taken the monk at his word. On the third day, when they realized that no help was forthcoming, all fifty-five men jumped off the cliff, and to their deaths.

Though he had won a few good battles, earning himself a name as a warrior—including commendations from the Abettors' guild—three months later, the hunchback monk was no closer to conquering Kersa than he had been the day he set foot in the region. His diminished manpower might have been a handicap, but his refusal to admit converts into his army was a severe oversight. If the monk had not yet lost the war and his head to the stronger enemy, it was mainly because of the human shield at his disposal. Women and children were often used as a screen by the pilgrims when they suspected sallies.

Desperate for reinforcements, Reverend Yimam sent emissaries to monasteries, conservatories, parochial schools, and concerned citizens at large. Swallowing his pride, he even approached his fellow legates—who had successfully concluded the Inquisition in their provinces—all in vain. Finally, he raised the rewards of taking part in the Crusade to a new high.

Six sainthood positions were made available to all new recruits, to be awarded on a lottery basis, one each month. Bandits abandoned the bushes for they could now plunder to their hearts' content, receiving in return an income-tax credit and recognition in the world beyond. Beggars gave up begging. Serial killers and arsonists joined the group, realizing that their hobbies could now become profitable.

Reverend Yimam celebrated the resurrection of his army, which by the end of the recruitment campaign would outnumber his civilian subjects by a margin of a thousand heads. Admittedly, not all recruits were up to par; nor did they all adapt wholeheartedly to the life of a crusader. Some of the bandits went back to their old ways when they discovered that doing stickups with a permit had stolen the thrill out of their trade. Some of the serial killers had also found killing under command was little fun. Though the arsonists had remained true to their profession, their disposition to set a match to both enemy and friendly property did not go down well with the hunchback monk, who, after a thorough examination of his conscience, ruled that the therapy to their affliction lay in the flame and consigned them to the stake.

One major obstacle faced the fast-growing army: the shortage of nourishment. There had never been enough food to go around, but now the crisis had reached epic proportions. Six foraging expeditions were dispatched in a single week; traps were dug along the migratory routes of wild game, and a variety of traps were laid for the fowl of the savanna, but with little luck. All that was edible was in the enemy's hands: the granaries were protected like the tomb of a revered god, and the enemy's cattle never roamed within easy reach.

Reverend Yimam began to despair when his cavaliers began missing parts of their saddle: leather straps, skirts, saddle strings, and even leather boots were boiled and consumed by ravenous pilgrims. If the horses and mules were spared their lives, it was only because the cavaliers slept next to their mounts. The final blow came when the road sacrifices that the monk had kept hidden under his pillow mysteriously disappeared. As no man of God would begin his day without giving a token gratuity to his Creator, the situation was grievous indeed.

An ever-passionate student of history, the hunchback monk found the perfect parable for the crisis in the plight of the Knights Templar. Not unlike him, Peter the Hermit had reigned over an army of brigands who pillaged, raped, and killed, sparing not even their own churches. But, when faced with a superior enemy in the east, and easy pickings became a thing of the past, the pilgrims couldn't feed themselves. That was when the ever-resourceful Peter the Hermit uttered the much-celebrated words: "Are there not corpses of Turks [the enemy] in plenty? Cooked and salted, they will be good to eat." Reverend Yimam repeated those words, suitably tailored to the local situation.

And so the hunchback monk conducted his battle with a full stomach. Gudu was caught completely off guard, having left only a nominal army at the place of combat while he siphoned his resources into rebuilding the ravaged village. He was not alone in his conviction that the enemy would be starved into submission if denied access to food supplies. The Abettors had begun lobbying to transfer their war efforts to a worthier opponent elsewhere.

When he decided to rebuild his home base, Gudu also set out to solve the crisis he had left unattended back in Deder. His mother, Enquan, had been a condemned woman since the botched escape attempt. She had been placed in a dugout prison. Her exact whereabouts remained a complete mystery, as she was relocated each night. Though she slept in her own bed, Aster was not much freer; she was seldom seen outdoors.

Gudu purchased his mother a temporary reprieve when he sent bags of grain and money to the hunchback monk in Deder; and, since the start of the conflict, he had been sending a maintenance fee of ten *birr* a week across the border. All this was unbeknownst to his closest friends.

There had been an unspoken agreement between the hunchback monk and the rebel leader that the captives would be left out of the war for as long as the ransom was paid on time. But when Gudu decided to take the conflict to the next stage, putting the monk's life in clear danger, there was no telling what the supreme legate would do to retaliate. Gudu didn't want to find out that the women he protected would be the bait that lost him the war. Over the Abettors' thunderous protest, he dispatched a company of the ablest men to Deder; he concentrated the remaining army on the northern front.

This rift between the commander in chief and his admirals would divide the community even further. Rank-and-file soldiers would be torn between their love for their young leader and their trust in the instincts of the unconquerable Abettors. Long after the battle had been relegated to the frayed pages of history, the strategy would be debated in academic circles and military colleges across the continent; the Abettors' guild would remain divided over the tactics that won the war.

The incident that was to captivate the scholars began to take shape when the hunchback monk dispatched a small expedition force to the southern end of the settlement, with the intention of boxing in the villagers. A bold tactic, not least because the invading army had a sketchy knowledge of the rebels' movements. But, as luck would have it, Gudu, having overruled his admirals, had set his sights on the enemy across the divide only. The commander in chief chose to trust his instincts rather than the counsel of the trio of Abettors, for, unlike the war patriarchs, who fought to sate an ancient hunger for battle and mayhem, he had a more personal stake in the conflict.

The expedition force quickly overpowered all three garrisons along the southern front. They set alight the fortifications, watchtowers, sentry boxes, and ammunition depot; razed to the ground the field hospital, dispensaries, mess halls, the command center, and the only brothel that had catered to the rebel force. Women and men scrambled out of bed undressed and naked with fear. Mothers dragged their children to the safety of the shrines.

The alleys and market stalls became littered with weapons of all descriptions as terrified rebels unburdened themselves of their load while dashing toward the mountains and the safety beyond. By midday, when the rebels had finally regrouped under the command of the three Abettors, the crusaders had command over all strategic points. If they hadn't overrun the entire length of the settlement, bringing an early conclusion to the war, it was only because the invaders had overextended themselves.

With the crusaders creeping from north and south, and the eastern and western fronts remaining unassailable to all but the strongest of men because of the precipitous mountains and the Death Valley, the civilians didn't need a commander in chief to remind them of the fate that awaited them. Panic swept the settlement. Gudu's command center was besieged by desperate mothers, pleading to be released from the ever-tightening noose.

As the days gave way to weeks and the crusaders proved unrelenting, it became evident that any hope of breaking out of the siege hinged on outside help. Gudu wondered what had become of the men he had sent to Deder; did his comrades in Harar and beyond know what had befallen him? It became clear to him that he would have to search inside himself for help.

Gudu counted safe passage of the civilian population to neutral ground among his top priorities. But the Abettors were set against the idea, on the grounds that negotiating with the hunchback monk at such a late stage would only give away the weakness of their position.

Once again, Gudu brushed aside his admirals' counsel and dispatched four Mawusa priests across the divide. Because of their shared faith and convictions, he had hoped his emissaries would be assured of an audience. His humility would be complete when the hunchback monk ruled that such negotiations were above and beyond his powers; that if the rebel leader wished to obtain any mitigation of the measures adopted against him, he must address himself to the Supreme Pontiff, who at that very moment was busy planning to extend the reach of the Crusade.

Gudu's sense of doom became evident to me soon afterward. He had come home from an extended meeting with his lieutenants looking unusually disheveled. He sat me up on a stool, facing him. "I am going to smuggle you out of here; I will send you to Harar," he told me.

"I don't want to leave you," I cried.

"No use arguing with me. You are going not because I want to save your life but to get us reinforcements," he told me.

As he packed the ledgers and important documents for me to take along, Gudu betrayed further clues to the fate that he anticipated. "You might see Aster before I do; tell her that I have led the uprising for her. Assure her that we will meet again—if not here, in the hereafter." He dabbed his eyes with his shirtsleeve, averting his eyes from me. I cried and begged to stay, but to no avail. Two burly men armed with muskets and machetes quickly bundled me out of the room.

The mountain chain was to be our crossing point. Donning a cover of tumbleweed, we dragged ourselves toward the foot of the peak. My escorts didn't want to risk being discovered by a possible infiltrator. Once out of sight of any villagers who might spy on us, we dashed toward the escape route. A rope dangling from atop was to be our means of scaling the cliff. One of the men slung me over his shoulder while the other carried our possessions as we labored to get to safety.

The journey to Harar, I found out, would take a week on a fast horse. Walking, it took us well over a fortnight. I knew then that Gudu had lied to me; he hadn't smuggled me out to get him reinforcements, which would have been too late to be of any help, but to save my life. I was not elated by his gesture; I felt cheated instead. I wanted to steal a horse and return to Kersa, as I had done some four months before when I ran away from Deder, but getting past the sentries proved most difficult. One needed written permission from the town elders to go in or out of Harar.

Though Gudu didn't get reinforcements from Harar, he did get company. The emperor intervened. Of all the enemies and friends that he could recite with the utmost ease, Gudu couldn't have placed the young emperor in either camp with any degree of conviction. At no time had he imagined himself becoming the subject of interest to His Highness. But what extraordinary interest he would generate in the upper echelons of the government! The emperor seldom bothered himself with vassal–feudal lord conflict, much less runaway slaves, for such crises came and went with predictable regularity. What was so captivating about Kersa, so alluring to His Highness, was the fact that a village, which, not so long ago, few people could locate on the map, was proving an entire school of scholars wrong on aspects pertaining to agriculture. In fact, had it not been for the fresh produce that graced his dining table, the emperor would have remained skeptical that a river could be taught to climb uphill and perform miracles on command.

More than ever before, the emperor was desperate to preserve the wonders of that distant land, the one singular achievement of his pubescent reign. He sent emissaries to the Supreme Pontiff and his hunchback legate. He proposed a settlement whereby innocent civilians would be spared their lives; homes and shrines would be saved from the flames; and the irrigation mechanisms would be left intact. In return, the hunchback monk would have his booty delivered in the form of the rebel leader and his cohorts, the Amma warriors. By reinforcing the crusaders, the emperor would see to it that the conflict reached an early conclusion.

In what may have been his most brilliant and impenetrable of moves, Reverend Yimam extended an armistice not to the villagers, as the emperor had wished, but to the rebel leader, his friends, and allies. He offered them safe passage through his stronghold, and, if necessary, would escort them across the mountains and onto neutral ground. He advised the remaining villagers to defend themselves as best they could for he would show them no mercy. Unlike the Amma nomads who were delivered pagans, or the rebel slaves who were condemned by the baseness of their servile origins, the Mawusas of Kersa had made a willfully erroneous choice in the matter of doctrine and contumacy, which the supreme legate couldn't easily forgive. The faithlessness that annihilated their souls could be purged by the powers of the flame alone.

If any one of the rebels had had faith in the timeworn adage that "he who defends himself finds mercy at last," it would have evaporated into a morning mist. There was only one way for the villagers to prevail, and that was by vanquishing the crusaders. Every man and woman capable of standing on two feet was instructed to dig a private trench and greet the invaders with whatever weapon there was time to fashion. The monk's resolve and haughtiness was a boon to Gudu in many ways, above all in patching up the fissures that appeared in his command, between himself and his admirals. Though success or failure in the battlefield meant life or death to the rebels, to the war patriarchs it had a significance that could not easily be measured by any mortal scale.

The final battle of Kersa was fought not only with guns and weapons, but with bare hands as well; many of the defenders died with enemy throats in their grasp. When the final tally was made, the dead and the dying littered the alleys and market stalls, shrines and school buildings, kitchens and bedrooms, ditches and wells. And when the winners finally emerged from the carnage, tattered and bloodied, and staggered through the debris toward the podium, it was not Gudu who stood to celebrate victory, but Reverend Yimam, legate of the Supreme Pontiff.

As the hunchback monk stood over the wounded body of his mortal enemy, a feeling that he couldn't place swept over him. For once in his violent career he made a judgment that left his men gasping: he decided to spare Gudu's life. What was the rebel slave worth to him dead, he argued, when he could collect a reward of two thousand *birr* for handing him alive to his owner, Duke Ashenafi? He instructed his men to bandage up the prisoner and place him on his personal carriage.

Over a thousand survivors were rounded up and herded into an open field. Unable to tell the faithful from the heretic, a curate approached the hunchback monk for help. Reverend Yimam's eyes lit up. For, long ago and far away another man of God, Arnold Amlaric, abbot of Citeaux, had been approached by his men, seeking judgment on the fate of the people they had just conquered, the citizens of Beziers. Reverend Yimam was struck by the parallels of the two incidents, but above all, by the pertinence of the abbot's reply: "Kill them all; the Lord knows his own."

DELIRIUM

His tiny hovel resembled the nest of a minute coucal raising a cuckoo's gigantic chick. On one side of the hut slumbered Duchess Fikre, whose heaving weight and ill health had deterred her from straying too far from her bed; tucked away in the remote corner was Aster, whose frail body had long since buckled under the weight of her unrealized dreams. Duke Ashenafi believed he had done for his daughter what no other man would do for his child. Not only had he played the role of both parents in raising her, often at the expense of becoming the jest of his peers, but he had also sacrificed his comfort and self-worth on her behalf. He had spared no money or effort to cure her of her afflictions. He had taken her to all three holy fountains, twice; hired experts from far-off kingdoms to look into her case; kept an army of nurses that he could barely afford—all the while pleading with her to show him mercy.

Gudu's arrival was a godsend to the old master. For the experts were undivided in their conclusion that the only key to Aster's affliction lay in his hands. Gudu, the authorities pronounced, had placed a curse on his mistress's personal effects—hair and nail clippings, among other things—which he had then buried away. Locating the sealed pouch, which might be as small as a man's thumb or as big as a clenched fist, would require plowing the entire valley—and beyond—and sifting through mountains of dirt. Who could say how many years such an undertaking would consume, or if the patient would live through the ordeal. The most expedient move was to locate the treacherous slave.

Capturing Gudu might have taken long, but eliciting information from him could well take longer. The prisoner was in no condition to speak. In delirium, and slipping in and out of different universes, he uttered few coherent sentences. He didn't respond to his name, nor did he appear to recognize his mother. Duke Ashenafi ensured that the vigil kept at the rebel's bedside was as constant as that at his daughter's. The patient was housed in his old home, so that the familiar surroundings could help his wandering soul remain anchored, but custody was taken away from his mother and placed in the hands of a select group of caretakers. After all, his was not just one life but two, mysteriously intertwined; he had to be kept alive until the experts could pry his other half free.

Gudu's arrival was kept secret from Aster on the orders of her father. Two weeks had passed before she dreamed of someone speaking his name. Pricking up her ears, she realized that it was not a dream at all, but whispers. At the doorway stood her father and Gudu's attendants, discussing the patient's progress. As though catapulted by her father's mangonel, she darted out of her bed and the room. To those witnessing the spectacle, it was difficult to say who was more startled, Duke Ashenafi or Aster. Seeing his daughter on her feet, after she had been bedridden for eight months, took the air out of the old man. Aster had to repeat her question four times before she elicited an answer.

Staggering like a midday drunkard, falling and rising, she made her way to Gudu's hut. At the doorway, guards attempted to hold her back, but she proved much too determined. She stumbled through the dark belly of the hovel, past clutters of incense burners, lit candles, and weeping icons, and the moment she made out the bundled figure on the cot, her legs failed her. She crawled on all fours, brushing aside the offer of help from the attendants, and collapsed at his side. None of the attendants moved, or breathed. Tears welled up in them, and the women dabbed their eyes with the ends of their sashes. The men feigned stoicism, but their quivering chins and the blood that rushed to their temples betrayed their emotions. What seemed like a generation passed before Duke Ashenafi stepped in and woke the nurses up from their collective reverie, instructing them to vacate the room. Then he followed them out and closed the door.

However embarrassing his daughter's behavior had become, Duke Ashenafi found solace in the knowledge that this was yet another manifestation of the curse placed on her. But he suffered in his solitude. Though there were documented cases of women who had committed grievous acts after being visited by omens, including eloping with men of inferior stock, there had never been a woman that stood out like Aster. She was simply shattered by the experience, unable to control her urges. None of the experts were able to point to another example in the entire kingdom that could be cited as comparable. Once again the old warrior had made a name for himself, though this time he would have preferred to have gone unnoticed.

Duke Ashenafi allowed Aster unlimited access to the patient on the advice of his council. Though little more harm could be done to his good name, the experts argued, the visit would have a twofold effect: it would help the dying man find reasons to live, while, at the same time, helping Aster to regain her health and vigor. No one would suspect that anything unseemly might be going on behind the closed door. After all, Gudu was too sick even to attend to his basic needs. He required nurses to feed him, wash him, change his clothing and bandages, and help him relieve himself, all without his ever leaving bed.

And so Aster kept vigil at Gudu's bedside from dawn to dusk, and beyond. She slept little, often at the foot of his bed. Sometimes, Duke Ashenafi dragged his daughter back to her bed. Tossing and turning, she would gauge the rhythm of her father's breathing before slipping back to the hovel next door. Soon, Duke Ashenafi abandoned his efforts, not because he had surrendered to her rebelliousness, but because he had found something to celebrate: in three short weeks, his daughter had recovered the luster in her eyes. No longer requiring an army of nurses, she could feed and attend to herself.

* * *

A month later, Gudu was still delirious. The few words he spoke came out in fragments and with predictable recurrence. He often mentioned Aster's name. Untiringly, she answered him, but got no response. He asked for his mother, Enquan, and a few names Aster couldn't place. (Enquan had been forced, by the duke, to share a hovel with another family.) The patient begged for water. Though the medicine men forbade her from giving him too much liquid, Aster couldn't stand the sight of his parched lips. Against her better judgment, she slipped the end of her *gabbi* inside the water pitcher, and, when the attendants were distracted, she squeezed drops from the wet cloth into his mouth; she dabbed his chest and forehead with the damp linen.

The two arrows that had penetrated Gudu's chest, like the bullets that caught him on the shoulder and thigh, had done little harm to his organs, but the blow to his head and the amount of blood he had lost had done considerable damage. With each shift of his head, with each foul-smelling ooze, it was Aster who cried aloud with agony. She pressed herbs on his wound, wrapping them in place with a piece of cloth that she had boiled and cleaned with her own hands; she sanctified the bandage with a kiss. As a child, Aster had admired how scratches she had received mysteriously disappeared without the attention of a medicine man, only because a maid she adored had kissed her wounds. Though much older and wiser, Aster still believed in the mysterious powers of human touch.

During those sultry afternoons when the wounds exuded such an awful smell that the nurses on duty made excuses not to stay indoors, Aster remained behind to look after the patient. She undressed him completely, examined the gashes by candlelight, removed any live parasites she came across, and cleaned the wounds before applying holy oil and fresh herbs. Not content with the prescriptions of her father's soothsayers, she traveled far and wide to gather new medicine, new roots, bruised herbs, animal powder—just about anything that might bring back Gudu's health.

Feeding Gudu wasn't the easiest chore, but Aster had discovered a resourcefulness in herself that put smiles on her maids' faces. Some days, she fed him with a baby's bottle; other times, she cooked him enriched soup, consisting of grain extracts, clarified butter, mixed herbs, and a dash of sweetener. As Aster pushed the food past his lips, she didn't fail to appreciate the irony of force-feeding Gudu back to life. Once a week, a chicken was slaughtered at his bedside, and its blood was sprinkled over his forehead, his bedding, and the walls. It was a sacrifice for the evil spirits hovering over him.

In those dreary moments when nothing seemed to break the monotony of waiting for the patient to respond, Aster read him stories. She told him anecdotes that the two of them had once shared, and updated him on the local gossip. Realizing what the ongoing uprising meant to him, she gathered all the information she could whenever she visited the marketplace; she told him the good news, keeping the bad for later. One day, as she was engrossed in a book, reading him a fable, Aster heard a whisper that made her hair stand on end; her suspicion was confirmed when the question was repeated.

"Where am I?" Gudu asked.

Aster's book took flight, jettisoned in her excitement. She gagged herself with both hands. Realizing where the greater danger lay, she hastened to muzzle Gudu's mouth as well. Her heart racing in her chest, her entire body racked with her stifled emotions, sweat gathering on the small of her back and on her brow, she sat waiting for danger to march through the door. Finally, she regained her composure and whispered her answer, telling him where he was and who was attending to him.

Tears coursed down his face. Whether from happiness at being reunited with his love or grief at the failure of his project, Gudu remained ungovernable. He quivered, coughed, and groaned. And, despite Aster's desperate efforts to calm him, his convulsions worsened, drawing the attention of the attendants outside. Soon, his bedside swarmed with men and women; some called out his name in the hope that he might have come to, while others began attending to his needs.

Standing behind the swirling crowd, Aster felt as if she were drowning in her fears. A slight indication of his recovery, she realized, and an army of men would march in to extract information, which, she knew, he didn't have; they wouldn't be done with him until they found the pouch they were looking for, or he relapsed into his comatose state, or worse. Aster decided early on that she would keep his recovery to herself for as long as it took, which meant either until the valley was claimed by the rebels, or the two of them got away safely. By the time the last of the attendants left the room two hours later, little remained of the old Aster.

The weeks that followed were not kind to her. As Gudu slipped in and out of consciousness, he rambled things that drew attention. Once, not realizing that there were others in the room, he wondered out loud what had become of the army that he had sent for Aster and his mother, Enquan. Another time, he spat out a mouthful of tea, complaining of nausea. But nothing raised the suspicions of the attendants more than his request to be taken outside for fresh air. Despite Aster's efforts to make this sound like one of his delirious pleas, they left the room convinced that there was more to the patient's progress than they had been led to believe.

Aster had entertained the idea of announcing Gudu's recovery before someone else did. If it was a pouch they were looking for, she reasoned, they would find one; what was more, she would convince them that she had got over him. But the more she thought it over, the harder she found it to even convince herself. Gudu had been the cause of her father's downfall; he was the one reason why Duke Ashenafi found himself stooping low in order to save his daughter from an ignoble death at the stake. No, Duke Ashenafi wouldn't rest until the treacherous young man had paid with his life. Though killing a slave in cold blood might be a criminal offense, punishable by law, no one would defend a bondsman who had done so much damage to his owner. Gudu would hang from a tree, and only three people would mourn his death.

Duke Ashenafi relaxed the vigil at the prisoner's bedside two months later. He left all the caregiving to Aster, except the changing of the patient's bedsheet and his twice-weekly wash. As time passed, Aster felt emboldened enough to help the patient exercise his legs, though only behind closed doors. With the exception of those moments when Gudu grew silent, reminiscing over the failed campaign, the two lovers reveled in each other's company.

* * *

But the campaign didn't fail. Amma warriors sweeping from the north had taken over what had remained of the rebellious village barely three weeks after its surrender. Reverend Yimam was thrown back closer to his home base, the valley of Deder.

With permission from the elders of Harar, I had gone back to Kersa to find out Gudu's fate. No two individuals could give me the same account of the last days of the battle, much less the fate of their leader. The survivors were men and women who had waited out the decisive battle in underground burrows. Two months would go by before merchants returning from the valley of Deder sold me news of the commander in chief recovering under the watchful eyes of his old master.

I begged and pleaded with the victorious Amma commanders to send an army to Deder and rescue the captured leader, but my pleas were ignored. The story of Gudu's legendary feats hadn't reached the newcomers; to them, he would remain another casualty of the drawn-out campaign. I watched with mounting agony as the commanders charted the progress of their drive on a bed of dirt, wondering how long it would be before the consequential battle.

Two more months would elapse before I was allowed to join an army assigned to take over the valley. With a sketchy knowledge of the goings-on in Deder, I was no longer sure whether Gudu or my mother had survived the random vengeance of the retreating crusaders. Smuggling emissaries past the last line of defense proved impossible.

It was through captive pilgrims that I found out about Gudu's progress, and my own mother's survival. Amma commanders discouraged molesting captives, not merely on religious grounds but for tactical purposes. If those fighting at the front realized that they could get better treatment from the infidels, the reasoning went, they might surrender easily.

Cocooned in their small world, ignorant of their trusted friends staked out behind Deder's mountains, all Gudu and Aster could do was invent distractions to keep their worries at bay. Aster brought some of the manuscripts that the two had been working on, and they once again composed poems and fables. On Aster's insistence, Gudu began to recount his field adventures, and she put them down on paper. Often, the stories left her teary-eyed, but not dispirited enough to abandon the project. The book was expanded to include their personal trials. This was not going to be a love story, or the adventures of a rebellious slave, but the coming of age of a generation. It was a historic document that they both wanted to leave for posterity.

As the days rolled by and she became accustomed to his quiet company, Aster shared with Gudu things that she wouldn't normally confide to a dying angel. "I want you to sit up and look at me," she told him on a lazy afternoon. "I have been rehearsing this most of my life; I don't want you to interrupt me."

Gudu sat up, expectant.

"I want to have your baby, many babies. When all this is over, we will leave the valley and everything we have known here to make a home for ourselves where no one knows our name."

Gudu was too emotional to respond.

"I will never have servants," Aster continued. "Not even if, by some miracle, we came across sunken treasure. None of our children will ever have a title, whether it is earned in a battlefield or bestowed upon them.

"Promise me," she beseeched, sobbing, "that you will do as I say, and that you will never leave me."

Gudu broke down in tears. His cough grew worse, his body convulsed. Hands firmly wrapped around Aster's waist, he lay weeping. When he finally came to, Gudu clasped her hands and pressed them to his chest. "Until death do us part," he repeated after her.

One afternoon, when the only noise that punctuated the monotonous silence came from a housefly, Aster asked Gudu to tell her a story. He sat up, bright and cheerful. Racking his brains for a fable that she hadn't heard before, he found one:

"There was once a young man by the name of Abebe Balcha," Gudu began. "Because of his continuous mischief, villagers ran him out of town. No sooner had Abebe found a new home, in a nearby hamlet, than he went to borrow kitchen utensils. Ever anxious to help out a newcomer, a neighbor lent him his best pot. Two days later, Abebe returned the pot with a small one inside it.

" 'The small one doesn't belong to me,' the neighbor said.

" 'But it does,' replied Abebe. 'Your pot gave birth to it.'

"Scratching his head in bewilderment, the neighbor took the pots. Not a week had passed when Abebe wanted to borrow the pot yet again, but, this time, he failed to give it back. Three weeks later the owner worked up enough courage to ask for the return of his utensil.

" 'Your pot has died,' Abebe told him.

" 'Ridiculous! Pots never die,' the neighbor retorted.

" 'But it did die, in the course of delivering another pot,' replied Abebe.

"The two of them took the case to the town elder. After hearing the story, the elder ruled thus: " 'All creatures that give birth, die.' "

As Gudu and Aster marveled at the exploits of Abebe Balcha, whose escapades spanned volumes and were told through generations as a lesson in morality, the door of the hut was thrown wide open and in came Duke Ashenafi. His quiet demeanor didn't betray his innermost feelings. His measured words conveyed little about his designs for the treacherous slave. And though the only comment that he made, before taking his leave minutes later, was about the patient's progress, the two lovers found a hidden meaning that kept them on edge. They were confirmed in their suspicions when, hours later, elders began marching into Duke Ashenafi's residence. Medicine men, soothsayers, diviners, monks, and nuns filed in and out of the tiny hovel with extreme urgency. When Aster was called for at dusk, the crowd had spilled beyond the small confines of the hovel and into the front yard.

In his quiet solitude, Gudu could only speculate what was going on outside. For the first time since he had taken to bed, he prayed for a glimpse of one of those caretakers. He would have sold his soul for small tidings, sacrificed the world to take a peek at the gathering. There had never been any doubt in his mind that he was the subject of the growing interest, but what troubled him now was the wailing that seeped through the walls. The din of crying women was soon augmented by a chorus of distressed men. Gudu didn't need to be told who the victim was; he didn't need confirmation that Duke Ashenafi, in a fit of uncontrollable rage, had, inadvertently, snuffed the life out of his daughter.

SHIFTING WINDS

A condemned man who could barely care for himself, Gudu was almost crushed under the weight of his sorrow. Unable to walk, he dragged himself out of bed and toward the exit, only to discover that the door was latched from outside. "What a tragic ending," he sobbed to himself. "What a way to bid farewell to the one person who made my life worthwhile." Indeed, without Aster and her love, there would have been no uprising for Gudu; no entanglement with his master; no reason to suspect his ancestors' faith; above all, no reason for Enquan to wear the garment of infamy.

And where was Enquan now that he needed her most? His mother might not have been permitted to visit as frequently as she would have liked, but she wouldn't have deserted her only son at a time such as this. Enquan had remained the one person close to Gudu who had denounced the love affair for reasons she wouldn't divulge; her vehemence couldn't be pinned to the rationale of an enduring master-slave relationship. But, no matter how strongly she disapproved of her son's indiscretions, Enquan wouldn't abandon him at a time like this—unless something terrible had happened to her.

As he dozed off, all Gudu dreamed about was Aster: her laughter, the twinkle in her eyes, her disarming humor and wit. He saw her at his bedside, pressing a wet towel on his forehead and whispering his name with each breath she took. She fed him with her own fingers, cleaned him when he threw up on himself. Her face was like a sunflower, following the rays of his eyes. Whichever way he turned, all he saw was Aster's smile. Soon, he could feel her skin, touch her overflowing hair, and detect her unmistakable scent. "What a terrible dream!" he cried. "You are not dreaming, Gudu. I am here," he heard her inimitable voice say.

If he had lived to be the king of the empire, if he had waged and won a thousand campaigns, Gudu wouldn't have felt the way he did when he realized that Aster was alive and well. A person had died, it is true, but it was someone whose existence he had long forgotten about: Duchess Fikre.

Duchess Fikre hadn't been gravely ill before she succumbed; she hadn't been bursting with health, either. She might have complained of an ailing knee, irregular heartbeat, shortness of breath, or plain lack of energy, but she had never been sick enough to require medical attention. Hers was an obscured existence, lived in the shadows of her husband and daughter. Those who knew her held that she would be remembered in death, as in life, as a footnote to her husband's grand exploits. None had thought they would ever live to see the day when Duke Ashenafi mourned his wife's death. They were proven wrong.

Whether from guilt, for neglecting her for so many years, or because he was reminded of his mortality, or only because he sensed that a lonely road lay ahead of him, Duke Ashenafi proved inconsolable in his loss. A mourning tent was erected, which he could barely afford. A farewell feast was purchased on money that he borrowed. There were no more vassals to pay homage at times like these, no friends who would cross mountains to pay their last respects, because of the ongoing war; all he had for company were the townspeople, and their goodwill.

This was a disquieting epitaph for the queen of a man who, just a short while ago, wouldn't have given a fig what his neighbors thought or said of his wife. He wouldn't have wanted to break bread with many of the men and women who came to share his sorrows. Their kindness wounded him. Their sympathies hurt him more than their snubs would have. Their willingness to share their meager resources with him heightened his grief. Throughout the three days of official mourning, they not only kept him company, sleeping next to him in the tent, but they also stayed behind, during daylight hours, to care for him.

Father and daughter were united in their sorrows. Aster rediscovered in her father what it was that had made him endearing to her: his tender heart. Seeing him so helpless, and brokenhearted, she came to his aid. She watched over him when he sat alone, cajoled him into breaking his lengthy fast. For the first time in years, Aster noticed how frail and haggard her father looked. His face drooped, his arthritic fingers had gone their separate ways, his thinning hair had turned completely white, and he seemed unsteady on his feet. If there was ever a human example of an aging lion that had just lost his pride and territory to a beast in his prime, she mused, Duke Ashenafi was the one.

Tradition required that the bereaved not stray too far from the mourning tent. The family of the deceased received each visitor by shedding some of their conserved tears. Only at midday and in the late-afternoon hours did the family find some respite from its grief.

During one break, Aster slipped out to look in on Gudu. Duke Ashenafi's last visit had snuffed the merriment out of their reunion. They now focused on how to avoid the imminent danger. The options were depressingly few: Gudu was too infirm to make it away on his own, and there were few signs that his cohorts would be able to rescue him anytime soon. One afternoon, as the two were enveloped in their worries and each other's embrace, Aster thought of a solution that, at first, seemed far-fetched, but the more they mulled over it, the more credible it became.

The plan centered around dugouts that dotted the compound. The holes had kept the family dogs out of sight, helping them hone their guarding instinct. But the dogs had long since fallen victim to drunken pilgrims. There were four empty dugouts within easy reach, and though none was intended for human accommodation, at least two of them were big enough to house a man of Gudu's size with little discomfort. A plank would keep the mouth of the hole out of view. This was by no means a long-term solution, only a temporary one. They both hoped that, in time, the search for the fugitive would be relaxed and Gudu could be whisked out of town and to safety.

The night before the mourning tent was taken down, Aster slipped away from her father's side, in the small hours of the morning, to help Gudu move to his new residence. The compound was deserted, the guards had abandoned their vigil. Half-dragging him and half-carrying him on her tiny shoulders, she staggered through the woods, across her childhood playground, to the remotest dugout in the compound. Sweat broke over her brow; her arms went numb. She took one last look around her before tucking Gudu out of sight. While catching her breath, she gazed upward and mumbled her prayers.

Gudu's absence remained unnoticed throughout the next day. With attention focused on cleaning up the tent ground and helping the widower readjust to a home without a wife, few had time to look after their chores. Only when an attendant came to change the patient's bedsheet two days later, did anyone find out what had happened. But out of fear of angering their master, the attendants kept the news to themselves while scrambling to locate the fugitive. Another day had wound down before Duke Ashenafi discovered his loss.

Aster didn't deny helping the fugitive. Defiantly, she admitted to assisting the men who had come to rescue him. With a two-day head start, she announced, there would be mountains and rivers between the fugitive and any posse that her father might raise. Duke Ashenafi stood regarding his daughter as though he had just discovered an anomaly that had long eluded him. For here was a young woman whose care and affection for her father had been exemplary not so long ago, yet she was doing her best to hurt him the moment he tried to put his hardships behind him.

Duke Ashenafi was in no position to raise a posse. He had lost not only his fortune and authority, but also the influence he had once had over his peers. All he could do was scour homes, shrines, barns, shops—possible hideouts in the valley. By the end of the day he had come to accept defeat. Though Aster did her best to reassure her father that she had got over the young man and his curse, and that she was now willing to do her father's bidding, he remained beyond consolation. With a decision that surprised everyone, including Aster, Duke Ashenafi forbade his daughter from setting foot in his home again. She would share a room with Enquan, who was now back in her old home.

My unit faced the brunt of the crusaders' last stab at breaking the infidels. Our progress was measured not by the leagues of land we conquered, but by the trenches we scaled. Now that my home village was so teasingly close, I could hardly sleep. Once behind the mountain curtain, I knew, I would be celebrated as the boy who had come back to rescue his people, as in some ancient fable. I could see the relief in the eyes of my mother, Aster, and Gudu. Gudu would chuckle at the sight of me proudly dangling my musket. Like my mother, Aster would cry and hold me tightly to her chest. To Mam and Aster, I would always remain an innocent boy.

Reverend Yimam's men dug in, surrounding Deder. The wounded and the dying were brought to town for what little treatment they could get. Aster could no longer wander into the woods without risking her safety. Whether it was for Outing or a feigned stroll, there was always a pilgrim shadowing her. Some of the men made lurid and suggestive remarks to her; others stood by and relished intimidating her. Though Enquan vied to take charge of looking after her son, Aster discouraged her, realizing the price Enquan would have to pay if her master found out.

In visiting Gudu, Aster now found resourcefulness in herself that she had never thought she had. Some days she dressed up in Gudu's outfit and slipped past unsuspecting pilgrims; other times, she donned Enquan's rags and a cowl, and with a basket in hand ventured into the woods on the pretext of collecting firewood, animal dung, or wild mushrooms. The visits were, often, brief. Usually, she had time only to slip provisions into Gudu's hand. In those rare moments when they found an opportunity to exchange a few words, the conversations centered around his possible escape. Gone were the days when the two reminisced about the good times and dreamed of the future.

The crusaders had reached a stage in their campaign where they couldn't feign success on the battlefield any longer. Recruitment was intensified. Boys as young as ten years of age were rounded up and sent to the combat zone; prisoners were herded up to die at the hands of the enemy. Smoke rose from behind the immediate mountains as retreating pilgrims set alight properties they didn't want to fall into enemy hands. Then one evening, Aster and Enquan were kept awake by gunfire drifting closer. They had barely closed their eyes when the two women were aroused by a celebration outside. The moment they had been waiting for had come: the rebels had arrived. The weight was finally lifted from their shoulders; they could now sleep, eat, and talk without the burden of carrying Gudu on their minds. And, as they fumbled through the dim lights of the hovel to dress themselves and join the celebrations outside, the two women shared many of their inner thoughts, but above all the hope of seeing the sun shine on the face of the man who bound them together.

The sun did shine on Gudu's face. He was discovered by the crusaders that very morning. What Aster and Enquan mistook for the rebels' arrival was a throng of unruly pilgrims, driving the fugitive to face his master's wrath. Duke Ashenafi's face lit up. He could scarcely believe his luck. When he thought how the rebel had nearly escaped with his secret intact, that his daughter had become a slave of the infidel's omen, he felt vindicated. If only another day had passed, if the crusaders hadn't been as vigilant, Gudu would have lived to laugh at his master's misfortune.

With much haste, the culprit was tied to a post. Volunteers fought each other to jog his memory. Two beastlike men won out, and, with grins that rivaled the piercing sun, the men took turns whipping Gudu. Aster fought the whip-crackers tooth and nail; she fell at her dad's feet begging for his forgiveness; she clutched the arms of spectators, elders, and priests whom she thought her father would listen to, but she only drew curious stares.

Gudu's bare back sizzled like a slab of meat on an iron grill; his face contorted with each strip of hide he lost. But, through it all, he maintained his silence, not admitting having the omen; not denying it, either. Claiming she was speaking for both of them, Aster declared it was she who had tempted Gudu, not the other way round; if it was an omen they were looking for, she cried out loud, "Look no farther than me." But far from swaying the doubters, far from earning sympathy for the condemned, Aster's uncharacteristic display of emotion heightened the townspeople's doubts and her father's worries. Indeed, why would a well-bred woman conduct herself in such a scandalous way, amongst the people she had grown up with, unless she were consumed by the evil powers of the slave's omen?

If there was one person who looked stoic—not wincing, much less whimpering—it was, strangely enough, Enquan. Perhaps she was numb. Standing at the door of her hovel, arms crossed over her chest, she regarded the goings-on much as she would have a passing storm. Every once in a while Gudu turned her way, and she caught sight of his bloodshot eyes, but her looks betrayed little of her inner feelings.

Duke Ashenafi's alarm grew at the rumble of the advancing rebels. Parts of Deder were now within their rifle sights. Before the day mellowed, he sensibly feared, the hands of governance in the valley would change. Then Gudu would walk away free, his master's daughter in tow. Duke Ashenafi owed it to his daughter, the kingdom he had sworn to protect, its titled subjects, the true faith, and himself to save his highborn daughter from the indignity of having to share a bed with a bondsman. With the urging of the duke, the whip-crackers intensified their fact-finding efforts.

A bag of chili pepper was hastily fetched, and before Gudu's misty and dazed eyes the hot powder was mixed with an equal amount of sea salt in a steaming pot of water. A curate dipped a ladle into the mixture and, as if blessing a newborn, he tossed it on Gudu's exposed skin. Gudu let out a piercing cry that would have sent a shiver through the most insensitive of bones. The voyeurs retreated a pace or two away. Aster tore out of the room she was pinned down in and dashed toward her love, kicking away her shoes, her *gabbi*, her sash, everything but the dress she had on, but despite the weight she unloaded, Aster didn't make it much farther. The men caught up with her. Aster sunk her teeth into the hands attempting to restrain her; her legs stirred up a minor whirlwind in their attempt to break free, but she was no match for her captors. Aster was led back to her room, past spectators who openly shared her sorrows.

Embarrassed by the reaction of their women, the men herded their wives and daughters home. Duke Ashenafi could sense that he had been losing face; he attempted to reason with the infidel on the post.

"Save yourself from being skinned," he urged Gudu. "Tell me where you hid the curse. I promise to let you free."

Gudu stopped responding. No matter how generously the salt-and-pepper solution was rubbed on his skin, how hard the whip came down on him, he remained stock-still. Suspecting the worst, Duke Ashenafi ordered his henchmen to quit, but they were too engulfed in their hard work to pay heed. He had to snatch the bullwhip from their grasp before a semblance of order was restored. Checking the patient's pulse, Duke Ashenafi confirmed his suspicion: Gudu was dead. Whether from guilt at being perceived as a monster, or because he felt cheated of his prize by death, the old man was visibly saddened.

Neighbors shuffled. Enquan looked on. With wry smiles, and their day's work accomplished, the two beasts retreated to a tree shed. The wind shifted. With a serene look in her eyes, Aster raised her *gabbi* high into the breeze. Like a baby girl in a spring meadow, she began dancing to the tune of the flapping cloth, trotting up and down the open yard, smiling at the waking heavens. The strange spectacle riveted the neighbors' attention more than the killing had. In rapt silence, they watched Aster's every move.

Awakened from his reverie, Duke Ashenafi followed his daughter's antics, thinking, perhaps, that she was losing her mind. He didn't realize how lost she was to him until Aster began skipping above the ground. Her feet no longer touched the soil. With each leap, she rose higher and higher, until, finally, with a sudden burst of energy, she shot up into the sky, and out of sight.

A collective gasp sucked the air dry. Nothing moved. No one spoke. What seemed like ages would pass before Duke Ashenafi whimpered. Unable to put his thoughts into words, he gesticulated at the skies as he tugged at the townspeople, but no one paid him heed. The townspeople had fallen to their knees, chanting their prayers. Catching sight of Enquan at the door, Duke Ashenafi went to ask for her help, when something about her eyes stopped him short.

His voice came back to him, and Duke Ashenafi shattered the still morning with his wails. Gazing up at the sky, he beseeched his daughter to come down. "Come back here; come back down. You are all that I have; don't leave me alone," he pleaded. Returning to the chanting neighbors, he begged for their intervention. "Help me! Please, help me; do something," he cried. "What are you praying for? It is only Aster." But the townspeople had their own burden of sins to expiate, and, as they saw it, if Aster didn't help them gain redemption, no one else would.

The sky darkened. Cloud jetted across the distant horizons and blotted out the sun. Five years and four months since the last drop of rain, the heavens opened, and water gushed out with unprecedented vengeance. Drenched, the townspeople abandoned their prayers, half-finished. Enquan stood still. Duke Ashenafi sought shelter. Weighed down by the mass of water, the rafters creaked, the trees swayed. The rain looked like a freshly hung curtain. People had to stick their hands out to know that it was still falling, not holding still. No one had ever seen such a downpour, and no one knew what to make of it.

As abruptly as it had appeared, the rain stopped falling. The townspeople's surprise at the suddenness of the downpour was eclipsed only when they looked at their feet and noticed that the dark soil, gritty and restless, stirred under their touch. Not a single drop of rain had reached the ground!

Retreating pilgrims overran the valley. Tossing aside their arms, badges, and bandannas, they tried desperately to blend in with the terrified civilians. My unit, strengthened by battalions of reinforcements, emerged from behind the mountains encircling the valley. The sheer size of the army encroaching upon the town terrified the bravest of men. The absence of war drums or pipers deepened the mystery of our intentions. The townspeople hastened to lock themselves behind doors, as though flimsy wooden flaps would check what years of pitched battle couldn't.

With a deliberate pace, Amma warriors marched into the open field. Many of them were foot soldiers, but there were cavaliers as well, riding not just horses and mules, but also donkeys and camels. The tightening circle of men grew from a single row to two, three, and, by the time it reached the outlying homes, into four distinct rings. The first two rows of men broke formation and marched down the alleys, flushing out the enemy hiding behind doors. The remaining two rows stood guard, making sure that no one got away.

Men were separated from women and children and herded into an open field; the arduous task of identifying the pilgrims from among the innocent began in earnest. Flanked by a select group of men, I marched into Duke Ashenafi's compound. My eyes fell upon the dead man on the post. My heart raced, my pace quickened. A few steps short of the stake, my legs abandoned me.

Images of my gleeful childhood years with a mischievous Gudu crowded my head. I saw myself passionately coached by the young poet and rebel. I saw Gudu, as a commander in chief, proudly leading an army of devout followers to a battlefield; and as a man deeply in love, building a manor that he had yearned to share with the woman of his dreams. I remembered Gudu and Aster, snatching mere seconds at a time in each other's embrace. I cried for the brother and sister that I would never see again—I shed tears because Gudu had died not knowing that the rebellion he had engineered succeeded at last.

Gudu was taken down and in his place, Duke Ashenafi was tied up, stripped half-naked. The rebels went to put the minds of the villagers at rest; they would relish drawing out his death. I began gathering what few mementos had remained of Gudu and Aster. I took along their incomplete manuscript, all four volumes, lest someone use it as kindling.

The sun retired for the day. A whole afternoon later, not one person had been put to death—by order of the victors. The townspeople began to relax their vigil; they served their saviors what little they had in the form of food and drink. Amma men took up homes vacated by the defeated crusaders. No less than a hundred of them put their feet up in the big mansion.

But there was one last surprise that day. Four women were brought by gunpoint into the compound. Suddenly, it was not only the rebels who were captivated by the identity of the detainees but the townspeople as well; men and women, young and old fought each other for a glimpse of the prisoners. For these were not ordinary prisoners, nor ordinary women.

In fact, they were not women at all, but men. One among them was none other than Reverend Yimam, legate of the Supreme Pontiff. Without an overgrown beard, his face looked shrunken; scars on his cheeks—the result of a hasty shave—made him look like a man who had wrestled with his cat. When one of the rebels knocked the chador off the monk's head, his bare scalp glistened; his nosepiece twinkled. And it was the signature nosepiece that had given away the hunchback monk in the first place. A symbol of tyranny and intolerance, the silver cap was recognized far and wide by people who had yet to set eyes on the legate.

The monk shrank under the gaze of his captors. He had never been known for his towering stature, but on this day he looked like an old man with a child's frame. He shifted from one leg to the other. His pleading eyes rolled in their sockets, following the peals of laughter that sprang up all around him. Whatever the monk did or said seemed to trigger a renewed spate of hilarity. They roared at the sight of his ill-fitting dress, his nosepiece (tapping it with their finger), and his stutter.

The monk attempted to earn a reprieve through the power of persuasion, arguing that, as a soldier, he was a mere victim of circumstance. When the argument triggered a fresh round of laughter, he set out to purchase his freedom. Pulling out a money belt from under his garment, he unfurled a fortune the size of which no one had ever seen before. Silver coins, golden ingots, lumps of jade, sapphire, emerald, ruby, and moonstone littered the ground at his feet. A semblance of order was restored when the rebel leader spoke. He assured the hunchback monk that he was not facing an enemy that would condemn him to the stake. The relief brought tears to the monk's eyes; he knelt to kiss the shoes of his savior, who retracted his feet in time. "But," continued the rebel leader, "we will hang you like a man."

Two burly men grasped the monk's arms. If they had thought this diminished man would be easy prey, they were proven wrong. Reverend Yimam fought his captors with wild abandon. His spittle flying in the air, tears streaming down his face, and his legs dancing waist high, Reverend Yimam was carried off to a nearby tree. A noose was hastily fashioned and slipped over his head. And so the man who had committed a slaughter so prodigious in its extent, terror so profound in its depth, was put to death dressed in a woman's outfit, crying his eyes out. Though he might be facing his Maker without an escort, Reverend Yimam was not alone in his final hours: the open field swarmed with townspeople who sang and danced while he drew his last breath.

Duke Ashenafi watched the spectacle from his post, his contempt for the disgraced monk clearly written on his face. Though stripped of all dignity, the old warrior wasn't crushed in his defeat. He stood defiantly, awaiting his executioners. But, whether out of courtesy for the renowned warrior or because they wanted to give him time to reflect on the wrongs that he had committed over a long life, the rebels postponed his execution for another night.

Duke Ashenafi seemed to have slipped out of the minds of his neighbors, who had left him in his solitude in order to join the singing and dancing inside their homes. Out of the corner of his eyes, he spied a movement. With one hand concealed behind her back, Enquan came at him, like a cat stalking her prey. A pace away from him, she paused, making sure that no one was watching, before she slipped a knife out and with a swift movement of her hand, cut her son's killer loose.

Rubbing his wrist as he restored the flow of blood in his veins, Duke Ashenafi stood regarding Enquan incredulously. Of all the people who might have come to his rescue, the last person he would have counted on was the mother of the man that he had just murdered. Though his gratitude was written all over his face, he couldn't bring himself to say "thank you" to someone in his servitude.

"For all it is worth, you should know that I didn't mean for Gudu to die," he compromised. But he got no response.

"I have always considered Gudu as my son," he continued.

"Gudu *was* your son," Enquan spoke powerfully.

"What are you saying?" Duke Ashenafi said uneasily.

"Gudu *was* your son, my lord, but you were too blind to see it. He was born after my encounter with you that fateful night. He was . . ." The words came out tripping over each other. Enquan had a story to tell, a confession to make. She had kept it secret for two decades, but no more.

"Get a hold on yourself! Are you going mad?" the old warrior roared. He raised a hand, as though to slap her, but was deflated by her defiant looks. As the two of them stood facing each other in unsteady silence, Duke Ashenafi found himself ferried back to the night long ago when he had seduced Enquan.

A fourteen-year-old girl had walked into his study. Duke Ashenafi wasn't so old then, and the alcohol in his veins had washed away some of his good sense. The girl had reached over his table to clean the stains left by his glass when he noticed the cleavage in her chest. He didn't know how he got around the table, but the last he remembered he was buttoning up his fly. In fact, had it not been for the bloodstains on his underwear the morning after, Duke Ashenafi would have brushed the incident off as a dream.

"I was a virgin before that day," Enquan continued, as though reinforcing his thought. "And I haven't known another man since."

For once in his long life, Duke Ashenafi was at a loss for words. His mind raced. His head hurt. Crowding thoughts impaired his vision. He felt giddy. It took Enquan's alert hands to stop him from falling. She reminded him that there were soldiers behind every door.

"You better leave now," she urged him.

"What place do I have to go to? Give me some form of weapon, a knife or an ax; I will die defending my home," he protested.

"That won't help anyone. You will have us both killed," she reasoned with him.

Enquan went back inside and came out with a jacket. "It may not be luxurious, but at least it is clean," she told him. The sight of Gudu's clothing rattled him. But his home had been raided, his belongings ransacked. If he were to avoid the chilly savanna nights and the searing afternoon sun, he would have to take the offer, which he did.

Enquan spared the duke's life not out of any lingering respect or affection for her old master, but because she felt he had bestowed upon himself his own worst punishment by killing his son and bearing the responsibility for his daughter's ascension. The duke was an old man, teetering on the edge of his grave. Enquan wanted her old master to relive his crimes, to spend each waking hour remembering the wrongs he had done.

With his fortune long gone, his friends and family members a distant memory, Duke Ashenafi was destined to spend his last days in utter solitude. Wherever he set up his next home, Enquan knew, her old master would strive to hide his past, a past that carried a nasty stigma.

"Here is something else for your journey," said Enquan, handing him a small leather pouch. It was money that she had earned weaving baskets behind closed doors. "I was saving it to buy Gudu's freedom, but I guess there is no need for it now." Her voice was devoid of emotions.

Not since the day of his birth had Duke Ashenafi yielded to such heartfelt weeping. His tears coursed down the gully of time, unearthing all the wrongs that he had done. He felt entirely humiliated. Discarding all that he had stood for, Duke Ashenafi held Enquan in both arms and asked for her forgiveness. Not only did she forgive him, but she blessed his future as well. Before taking his leave, Duke Ashenafi took one last look at the place he had called home.

As she watched the retreating back of her old master, as her ears registered the hilarity emanating from the mansion and hovels, Enquan couldn't help but think of the dawning day, which would bring her not only a new master and a new set of rules, but also a new God.

HISTORICAL POSTSCRIPT

T*he God Who Begat a Jackal* is set in what is today Ethiopia during a period that would have been between 1750 and the late 1800s, when the country was beset with feuding emperors, feudal masters and vassals, slaves and slave-runners, religious tensions and class hatred. Ancient Ethiopia was an ambitious imperial power—the only black imperial power, in fact—that found its calling to expand its borders in the Holy Scriptures. As self-professed descendants of King Solomon, those who ruled over both the Amhara and their closely related ethnic group, the Tigreans, maintained that they had succeeded the Israelites as the chosen people in the eyes of the Lord.

Small and independent kingdoms of the lowland regions lost their freedom to the more powerful highlanders, the Amharas and Tigreans. The curtain came down on Harar in the 1890s. Though much blood was spilled in the conflict leading to the surrender of Harar, there is no evidence that tenants of the walled emirate were ever subjected to siege warfare as suggested in this book. Hararghe encompasses a much larger territory than originally ruled by the small emirate; it was created after the subsequent capitulation of the surrounding regions.

Seventeenth-century Ethiopia didn't have a central army. It relied for its defense and its expansive ambitions on what the various warlords could rally. Such alliances didn't always come for free. The feudal lords expected and often received the rights to as much as a third of the land they helped conquer. The remaining two-thirds of the appropriated land was divided up between the church, the monarchy, and local aristocrats—noblemen who would help enforce the wishes of the new masters on their own people.

The feudal lords ran their fiefs like small kingdoms, complete with jails and private policemen to enforce their wishes. A feudal lord who felt crossed by rebellious tenants seldom looked to the central government for justice. The vassals were not without rights and recourse, it is true; there were documented cases of open-court tussles between a greedy feudal lord and his tenants. Understandably, the courts often sanctioned the ways of the masters.

The practice of slavery was as old as Ethiopia. The slaves were men and women from low-caste groups, and were sold in open markets and passed from generation to generation as family inheritance. The slave owners were primarily from the Amhara and Tigrean ethnic groups, the chosen people. Emperor Haile Selassie is credited for outlawing slavery. In 1919, the emperor had set out to enroll Ethiopia in the League of Nations (predecessor of the United Nations); his application was unanimously rejected by the civilized world—the European powers—on the grounds that slavery was still in practice in his domain. Slavery was out, colonialism was in; no one had told the king! A mere four years later, slavery was abolished by royal decree, though it would take another half century before the practice faded out entirely.

In the period depicted in this novel, Aster's kind of sequestered life was not uncommon in noble households. The plight of a peasant woman is also accurately depicted in *The God Who Begat a Jackal*. Unfortunately, little has changed in the life of a country woman over the centuries. Wedding by abduction is still in practice. And girls as young as twelve are legally given away in marriage to men old enough to be their fathers.

The marriage of underage women causes measurable problems. Many young women suffer from incontinence as a result of childbearing before their reproductive systems have developed fully. A woman who has lost control of her bodily functions can be divorced on legitimate grounds. The sad fact is that she is shunned by her neighbors as well.

An urban woman today can expect to enjoy the privileges traditionally reserved for men. Many go to school, and when they successfully complete their studies they can expect full employment. There are female medical doctors in today's Ethiopia, and teachers, lawyers, cabinet members, and women in uniform—policewomen, for example, and soldiers. A woman riding a bicycle might raise only a single eyebrow in an urban center, in the countryside, she is considered an aberration.

Religion played a significant role in shaping the Horn of Africa, as it did in the Middle East and parts of Europe. Crusades were waged in Ethiopia involving two of the major religions of today. In the central and northern highlands of the country, families are still divided by the heavenly allegiances their ancestors were forced to make. The crusades of bygone years were responsible for many broken homes and the loss of thousands of lives. There is no evidence, however, that an Inquisition as described in *The God Who Begat a Jackal* ever took place. More important, perhaps, neither Amma nor Mawu-Lisa represent the region's actual religions.

Amma and Mawu-Lisa are two of the countless African deities that sprang up over the centuries, only to wither away before setting down roots. To the best of the author's knowledge, there is no group either within Africa proper or on the outside worshiping any of these deities today.

The God Who Begat a Jackal is a work of fiction. Any similarity between the characters in this book and individuals, past and present, political entities, and regional powers is purely coincidental. The author understands the temptation to draw parallels between invented characters and reality. Even for such an oddball creation as the Abettor, it is not entirely difficult for a fruitful mind to imagine a counterpart in history. The superpowers of the Cold War years, for instance, could have been cited as models, for they were, indeed, known to have performed many of the functions of a self-respecting Abettor. They abetted both belligerents in parts of Africa, switching sides in the middle of a raging conflict; they were defeated in battles and when the victors went home believing that they had seen the last of the Abettors, the victors were confronted with the phoenixlike presence of the war merchants. Such is the power of fiction that it stretches one's imagination.